ALPHA
BOX

ANNIE DALTON

THE
ALPHA
BOX

MAMMOTH

*For Roger with love
and with love and gratitude to Miriam Hodgson,
a treasure among editors,
and to Martha Sylvester who will know why*

First published in Great Britain 1991
by Methuen Children's Books Ltd
Published 1992 by Mammoth
an imprint of Reed Consumer Books Limited
Michelin House, 81 Fulham Road, London SW3 6RB
and Auckland, Melbourne, Singapore and Toronto

Reprinted 1994
Reissued 1995

Text copyright © 1991 Annie Dalton

ISBN 0 7497 1178 7

A CIP catalogue record for this title
is available from the British Library

Printed and bound in Great Britain
by Cox & Wyman Ltd, Reading, Berkshire

Contents

1	Indian Summer	7
2	The Earthworks	16
3	The Dark Arches	22
4	The Ugly Box	30
5	At the Apocalypse Café	38
6	The Awakening	51
7	Joss and the Furies	62
8	Birds of Light	70
9	New Lamps for Old	77
10	Prophecies and Pyramids	89
11	Snake Dance	104
12	Going Home	115
13	Tuning In	122
14	Tribal Wave	132
15	The Last Days	143
16	The Return of the Goddess	148
17	The Song of All Beginnings	155
18	Exodus	166
19	Dancing with the Dark	178

'I am Alpha and Omega, the beginning and the ending, the first and the last.'

From The Book of Revelations

1   *Indian Summer*

Joss never knew whether it was the whirlwind, spiralling in a down draught from the attic room where his father still lay sleeping or unable to sleep; invisible and silent at any rate, or whether Fran caught the propped-up guitar with the hem of her skirt as she lugged the last of their bags through the open front door. Perhaps it had been falling ever since she swept past, toppling so slowly only time-lapse photography could record the catastrophe.

But someone should have noticed. If it hadn't been so early in the morning. If Fran hadn't insisted on leaving so early. There was almost no light. His limbs were still vague with sleep, his stomach churning from the dreams of the night. That was how things went wrong. When you rushed into them. Fran hadn't thought it through. He knew she hadn't.

So when Joss came out of the living-room just in time to see the golden blur flash along the white wall with no one but himself to witness the sickening crash at the bottom of the flight of steps, he knew it was her fault. Hers and Martha's.

She was calling irritably, giving up the pretence of being quiet because of sleeping neighbours. In a minute she'd probably sound the bloody horn. He glanced back into the shadowy room, fixing everything in his mind; soft carpets, dark furniture. Home.

The clock on the video glimmered 5.15. He watched the numerals change; once, twice, hypnotised. If he could only freeze his life like the frame of a video. Never step out of this moment. He had the weirdest dread that when they finally drove away the house would unmake itself behind him, like a house in a nightmare, dissolving into dust. It was only the guitar that had kept him inching forward, these last weeks, keeping him going, his pathetic fantasies projecting their vague warm glow into a vast chaotic future, making it almost human-scale, almost manageable.

Now everything was smashed into pieces at the bottom of the steps.

Face it. Face it, he willed himself savagely. He'd got to step out of that video frame and get on with his empty life like everyone else.

By the time he reached the bottom of the steps he had everything more or less under control. The neutral expression clamped over his face like a freezing mask, the worst of his misery choked down. So long as nothing showed, that was the main thing.

The guitar was completely caved in, strings sticking out in all directions, not connected to anything. Now he saw how fragile it had been all along and this filled him with a surge of rage as if not seeing until this moment made him stupid, criminally stupid.

Joss picked up the smashed guitar, walked over to the car and stood nursing it, not saying anything. Fran was frowning, drumming thin brown fingers on the steering wheel. She didn't seem to notice anything, just started complaining crabbily, putting him in the wrong for keeping her waiting.

'Come on,' she said. 'Before there's too much on the motorway. It's a long journey. The van's got to meet us by lunch-time.'

But Joss went on standing there, unable to say a word, all the unwritten songs aching inside him like a spreading bruise.

Martha appeared from the back of the house, scarlet in the face, heaving a basket full of seething swearing fur. 'That wasn't funny, Joss,' she said, blundering past, trying to keep her more vulnerable parts clear of slashing claws. 'You might have helped. Being pregnant slowed Evie down. But I had to climb into the middle of the gooseberries to get Ludwig and then he turned into *Nightmare on Elm Street*. You sit next to him in the car. I get sick in the back.'

Then she stopped in her bossy tracks, veering round, so horrified Joss found he wanted to laugh.

'Your guitar,' she said. 'Oh, Joss!'

She dumped the basket on the road and when it howled, kicked it savagely. 'Oh shut up, you horrible cat!' she screeched.

To his surprise, for Joss felt almost nothing now, her eyes were full of tears.

Martha never cried, except with temper. She was eleven and since the age of seven she'd been as hard as nails. Just like Fran. Yet her voice was cracking with distress as she said, 'Do you think it can be mended?'

'Shouldn't think so,' he said, grinning a twisted grin. It was easier not to care with Martha making such a fuss. 'I wasn't getting anywhere anyway. Don't get so worked up, Marth. I'll leave it by the bin.'

'NO,' she wrested it from him. 'Don't leave it behind. It can be mended. I know it can.'

The sunlight touched the rooftops as he watched Martha heave the useless guitar on to the rack with their cases.

And as if she was not part of this drama at all, as if she was not responsible for everything that had ever gone wrong in their lives, their mother waited silently for them to be finished, her thin fingers itching to start the car and be away. Perhaps she had driven away so often in her dreams she had really left long ago. This was the formality, Joss thought.

Martha lashed the last cord to the roof-rack. She'd stopped crying and was wearing the identical super-efficient expression Fran used when someone sliced the top off their thumb or started to have their baby on the bus.

'You can take it to be mended tomorrow,' Martha said with ferocious optimism. 'There'll be somewhere. I know there will. You can get it mended tomorrow.'

Then she got into the passenger seat and slumped, her face turned away, inscrutable behind the fall of wild russet coloured hair that was also uncannily identical to her mother's, leaving Joss to sandwich himself gingerly between two cat baskets; one emitting a continuous stream of unprintable abuse, the other eloquently silent.

'Thank God,' said Fran. 'Oh shut up, Ludwig! Say something soothing, Joss, for heaven's sake.'

His life shattered and she asked him to say something soothing to the cat.

'Valium,' he hissed. 'Librium. Mogadon . . .'

Martha glanced curiously over her shoulder then rolled up

her eyes.

He was still murderously intoning the names of tranquillisers and sleeping pills when Fran started the car so he didn't hear what she whispered, under the engine's roar, but he saw Martha squeeze her hand and give a watery smile.

Women. He hated the way they ganged up, the way they tried to make you pretend to like the miserable things that happened to you. Like Ludwig raging at his side he wanted them to know he was leaving under protest, howling in every fibre that his life had come brutally to an end. But he didn't have Ludwig's guts. Because even though he could never forgive Fran and Martha, they were all he had, now. Perhaps that was the worst thing of all.

Almost every inch of the back window was filled with their belongings. There was just one microscopic space. Because of the baskets fencing him in on either side and Fran's textbooks on midwifery sticking into his neck, it took a while to twist himself round enough to peer through it but he managed it before they reached the end of the road, nudging the space frantically with his shoulders to enlarge it.

To his disbelief handfuls of stones began to rattle down the back of his neck. Stones with a familiar suffocating chemical smell. Thrifty Fran had stowed the opened packet of cat biscuits with their luggage rather than leave them behind. He shook them bitterly out of his tee-shirt in a ludicrous rain of tiny grey herring.

By craning his neck, he could just see the attic window. But the rising sun shone full on the glass and he couldn't tell if his father was really standing there, watching them go.

Asha couldn't sleep. Sometimes pretending to go back to sleep worked and she fooled herself and dozed off but this morning her heart gave a mighty leap the moment she opened her eyes.

How would she get through the desert of time stretching between now and the first post? In term-time there was no problem; things to be learnt, revised, written out in neater handwriting. She could lose herself for hours. But school didn't start for two weeks. Today was all her own.

She couldn't even practise the piano. Madeleine and Isobel

10

loved to hear her play, but not at – Asha peered to read the dial on the bedside clock – 5.15.

She sat up, swinging her legs edgily, then caught sight of herself in the mirror; long white nightdress, glossy hair tangling around her face and shoulders. In term-time she slept with it plaited so it didn't take so long to brush through in the morning. That was something she could do. Give her hair a good brush, then practise French-plaiting it so she could wear it like that for school next term. Hair tied back with narrow ribbon, calf-length skirts, straight back, remote face, books under her arm. That was the way Asha McGillveray went around at school.

Ice maiden, the boys called her when she wouldn't go out with them. Frigid. If you wore short skirts and tight jeans like Tamar Tetley, they called you something else.

Asha preferred her camouflage. Inside her prim chrysalis she could secretly grow into whoever, whatever she wanted to be in her own time, in her own way.

Madeleine would be up at seven to make the most of the garden before she went to work. How could Asha make sure she got to the front door first when the postman rang? She needed to be on her own to open it. Her parents had never given her anything that was not exquisite. They never had anything in their house that wasn't perfect. Her mother wouldn't leave a flower in a vase if it had a faded petal. And this longed-for gift would banish the floating sensation she had lately when she thought about them. Something she could see, touch, hold in her hand . . . We love you so much, darling. You know how much we wish we could all be together.

For a while there had been trips home in the holidays. But they unsettled her too much, her mother said, meaning Asha. Too painful. And for a while there were letters. But Asha's father was busy and her mother said her brain became paralysed if she even looked at a pen and she could only think of the dullest things. Asha wished it was possible to say that she loved everything about them. Nothing about her parents could ever be dull or ordinary. She could still summon up the flowery fragrance of her mother's hand-lotion, the expression

11

on her father's face when her mother entered the room, as if the light had come on.

Brushing, brushing, until her scalp began to sting, Asha began to hum, just above a whisper, the tune of her latest piano piece, a Chopin *étude*. Discipline. Discipline. She wouldn't even look at the clock until she'd plaited perfectly from the crown of her head down to the furthest ends of her hair.

If only it had been raining, or snowing or blotted out with fog. Anything but this sun-dazzled day like something left over from a kid's storybook holiday. Azure skies, fluffy white clouds, torrents of birdsong. The works.

As Joss stumbled out of the cafeteria loaded up with cans of coke, chocolate and crisps, his legs rubbery from the drive, the sun hit him between the eyes with a force it hadn't managed once on the family's real (disastrous) summer holiday. The Greenhouse Effect, he thought. Disrupting the natural order, generating muggy winters, tepid summers, scorching Septembers. The planet was winding down. Just his luck to see it go. Just his luck to be born at the most depressing time in the earth's entire history.

Fran had laughed when he had said that. 'Rubbish,' she said. 'What we've got is a good old-fashioned Indian summer. A second chance. Wonderful.'

He could see her hunched over the counter, writing a cheque for the petrol, her hair a dry red-brown cloud full of static, her ethnic skirt all faded browns and terracottas. Joss's father hated that skirt so maybe that was why she was wearing it. An Indian skirt for her Indian summer.

She caught him up as he reached the car and put her hand on his shoulder. 'Doing okay?' she said lightly.

'Yes, why not?' he said, sliding away from her touch, averting his eyes from the roof rack. *Don't think. Don't think.*

Martha had found her way back and sprawled with her feet on the dashboard, eyes closed, headphones jammed on.

'You did a good job on Ludwig,' Fran added as she slid, wincing on to the hot leather of the driver's seat. 'God, how am I going to get out of this parking place?'

A sulphurous growl came from the back of the car and having begun went on, apparently without the need to draw breath.

'Great, Mum, he heard his name. Now he's remembered what's going on.'

'Did you get me a Diet Coke?' demanded Martha loudly, her eyes still closed. 'You should hear this group. Amazing.' She opened her eyes and held an earphone towards them. 'Listen.'

A tinny jangle filled the car.

'Amazing,' said Fran insincerely. 'Now let's drink up our additives and preservatives and get moving, gang. If someone will let us out, that is.'

'No, really, Mum. They're great,' persisted Martha. 'They're going to be really famous.'

'Diet Arsenic,' said Joss, doling out the rations. 'Poison Bars . . . Shut *up*, Ludwig, you can have some of my chocolate in a minute.'

He posted a squishy section of Mars Bar under the wicker lid and instantly snatched back his hand. 'Thank you Ludwig, old ally, buddy, friend,' he said bitterly, examining the vicious punctures in his flesh. 'I hope my tetanus jabs are up to date.'

'Actually they aren't bad,' said Fran, who'd been obediently concentrating on the racket coming from the headphone. 'Listen, Joss. What are they called, Marth? Bit like the Beatles aren't they?'

'They are nothing whatsobloodyever like the Beatles,' said Martha, snatching the headphones back. 'They're called Horse something and they're absolutely new and they care about the planet, not just about making money and getting stoned like *your* lot.'

'Whoops,' said Fran turning to Joss, making a face, wanting an ally as always. If she couldn't have Martha she would make do with Joss. But his head was full of lamenting guitars, unwritten songs, and he couldn't look at her.

There was still the afternoon post. Or it might come tomorrow, on the day itself. But that was cutting it too fine. They wouldn't do that. So unless Madeleine and Isobel had

13

been conspiring behind her back, hiding huge packages the moment they arrived, the sum total of her birthday was one battered airmail envelope from India, from Valli, her Indian godmother who hadn't seen Asha since she was a baby but who never once forgot. She hadn't opened it yet, but knew what she'd find. A card bearing some sacred Hindu design, a letter full of love and philosophy and a cheque for a pound or two. Asha's godmother was not a rich woman.

At least she could practise the piano now. Madeleine had gone to work at her volunteer bureau. Isobel was off to see a friend. With any luck she wouldn't come back until after lunch so Asha would be alone in the house for several hours.

'I'll be fine,' she nodded to her aunt. 'I can make myself a sandwich. I'll be fine. Honestly.'

Isobel wasn't herself this morning. She hung about as if she wanted to say something but didn't know where to begin, afraid to embarrass them both.

Asha made herself sit very calm, very poised, her eyes confident clear pools any adult could look into and be reassured. But it turned out Isobel was only worrying that Asha might find it boring being with the aunts on her birthday. Wasn't there anyone of her own age she would like to invite over to share her day tomorrow? 'I'm sure we could manage to take a bunch of you out to lunch, if you would like that?'

This innocent suggestion filled Asha with panic. Possible companions flashed through her mind at the speed of light. Terrifying Tamar Tetley in her micro mini dress, seven ear rings (at the last count) crowding up the lobe of each ear. Overweight Bethany Blessed whose parents belonged to a religious sect and never let her go on school trips because they didn't trust teachers to supervise things. Ghoul (originally Simon Goole) who dressed in black because the world was imminently going to end. She tried to imagine any or all of these seated round a table with her admittedly eccentric, but not that eccentric, aunts and failed.

'I'd rather celebrate at home with you two,' she said. 'Honestly. It'll be cosy.'

'Well, if you're sure, dear. But — oh well, if you're sure

that's what you really want.'

Asha lifted the lid of the piano and began to play.

Her aunt looked back through the open French windows at the chestnut hair shining, exquisitely plaited, the wide grey-blue eyes looking coolly ahead at the music, the small determined hands plunging through something surprisingly tempestuous for her niece's taste. Oh dear, she thought. If only she didn't feel she had to be so perfect. Give us such little trouble. But it's too late to tell her now.

Somehow the pattern had been set from the moment Asha arrived on the flight from Rio, nine years ago, looking like a Royal child in the old-fashioned camel coat, yards too long, the neat white socks and polished clumpy shoes. 'Will we get there in time for my bedtime?' she asked on the journey home. 'I'm always in bed by half-past seven.'

Seeing Isobel retreating, watching carefully without seeming to until her aunt was lost amongst the sunlight and fading roses, Asha released the breath she'd been holding. It was easier to wait now she was alone. Two hours, three at most.

Last year the present had come the day before. The jade horse that lived on the marble mantelpiece in her bedroom, its mane blowing back in an invisible wind, grace and power in every limb. The aunts had not quite seemed to like it, though Aunt Izzy said wonderingly, 'It must have cost a *fortune*, dear, though of course it is the thought that counts.' But Asha had fallen asleep with it clasped in her hands.

She had felt quite solid, entirely real for weeks after her last birthday. And it worked every year. It was not so much the gifts themselves, however beautiful and rare, as the feeling of joy and relief she had when they came. A kind of reality transfusion. Before her birthday she always felt like this, floating, almost transparent, as if she had to concentrate extremely hard to appear as solidly normal as everyone else. But this year she had waited as calmly and patiently as she knew how and in a short time, no time at all, she would have her reward.

2   The Earthworks

'Is this the Midlands?' Martha said in surprise, staring out at the shorn gold of harvested fields. 'I thought the Midlands was factories and things.'

'Some of it is,' said Fran. 'But where we're going is a real hotchpotch.'

'Naturally,' murmured Joss but Fran went on:

'It used to be very industrial. It's still got knitwear factories and so on but it's a country town too with a street market every week. And though the house is right in the town it's high up, so you can see the hills if you squint a bit. I used to love the hills here.'

'When did you used to be here then?' yawned Martha. She had abandoned her earphones and her stony composure and almost looked her age for once.

'I had an aunt,' said Fran. 'A proper country aunt. She put lavender in her linen cupboard and made elderflower wine. I loved staying with her. I borrowed her old bike and rode off on my own for hours and if you ever try to do anything so daft I'll be absolutely furious with you before you even say a word! Anyway things were different then.'

'No child molesters,' said Martha wisely.

'Well, I'm sure there were,' said Fran, laughing. 'Even in those long ago days. But I think people mainly knew who they were.'

'Why are you taking us this way?' said Joss suspiciously, as the elderly Saab toiled up a long hill. 'I saw the sign miles back. You could have gone directly from the motorway.'

'Because, smart-arse,' said Fran, as they finally reached the top, 'because I so wanted you both to see this place first.'

She was heading the car up a rutted track. A second wave of tiny herring surged down the inside of Joss's tee shirt. 'Oh what are you *doing*, Mum?' he said, almost beyond being angry.

'You have to get out to see it,' said Fran. 'You have to get out and walk the last bit. Some places, thank God, you still can't drive to.'

'But it'll take me ages to get back in,' said Joss. 'It took a shoe horn to get me in in the first place. It'll wake Ludwig and then he'll gouge me again. You and Martha go. I hate the country and I hate hilltops worst of all. They're always as windy as hell and then I get ear-ache.'

Fran was the limit. She had to have everything her own way like a middle-aged Anne of Green Gables. When she finally walked out on her long-suffering husband *she* had to do it at dawn. And she couldn't arrive at their new home straightforwardly. She had to make it into a bloody pilgrimage.

'Wear my headphones to protect your dear little ears, then,' said Martha heartlessly. 'Come on, Joss.'

Fran got her own way of course. Joss sullenly put on the headphones. They piled out, walked until Fran told them to stop, then stared down obediently exactly where she told them to stare. Even up here it was hot. Fran's skirt billowed out like a parachute in the wind and she staggered slightly, laughing, trying to keep her balance.

'Isn't it worth it?' she asked through clouds of whipping hair. 'I was so afraid they'd have spoiled it, but it's just the same. Isn't it extraordinary?'

'What is it?' said Martha, awed. 'I can see it's huge and kind of bumpy, but what is it?'

'No one knows,' said Fran. 'There's lots of theories. We just called it the Earthworks. Some people think it's a sacred site of some kind. I always thought it was the remains of an amphitheatre – look, the shape is right, like a vast bowl, just grassed over for – well, maybe thousands of years.'

'What do other people say it is?' Joss was surprised to hear himself speak, shouting in fact, the way people do with headphones on. Perhaps he needed to prove he was real, warm, breathing, maybe he needed the reassurance of their maddening female witter. It certainly didn't matter a hoot *what* she said. Nothing human mattered in this place. It dwarfed human effort. 'Look on my works, ye mighty and despair,' he whispered feeling his scalp creep.

'Oh, pick your loony,' Fran laughed. 'The wildest theory is that it was some kind of spaceport for UFOs back in prehistory times. You know, Superior Beings that watched over us and told us not to eat mastadon with our fingers. But whatever it was, people are getting fascinated with it all over again. When I was a kid I could spend the whole day here and never see a soul. But now people drive from London and Manchester to photograph it and crawl over it looking for ley lines. Last year some enterprising chap organised a rock concert here. Hundreds of people turned up. It could become a second Glastonbury.'

'Oh great,' groaned Joss. He made a mock-peace sign. 'Far out.'

'When was the last time *you* came, Fran?' asked Martha. 'When you came to look at the house?'

'Oh I can't really remember,' said Fran rather casually. 'Ages. When I travelled down last time I came on the train. Anyway, I wanted you two to be here with me.' She hugged Martha fiercely as if she needed the hug quite badly herself, her face a little bleak. 'We'd better get back on the trail, troops. Come on. We've got to fetch the keys before the van arrives.'

Suddenly she was bundling them back to the car as urgently as she had dragged them out of it. As if it had been *their* idea to go sightseeing, Joss thought. And this woman was his sole parent from now on. But she was unreliable, he thought. Absolutely unreliable and downright bloody secretive. She'd never told him she had an aunt in the Midlands.

He shivered despite the heat as Fran started up the car.

'Someone walk on your grave,' said Martha, who never missed a thing. He shook his head irritably, though he had felt something unpleasantly like that sensation, a dizzy telescoping of time and space. As if he had been there before or was fated to come again and for a second had collided uneasily with past or future selves.

She used to spend the whole day there, he thought. The whole day in this creepy place, on her own. She must have been thick-skinned even as a child. No one with an ounce of imagination could stand it for half an hour.

Within minutes the town swallowed them into its lower regions, all pretty much as Joss had feared; densely packed red brick, seedy, even stuffier in the heat, but the kind of town it would always be hard to breathe in. They picked up the keys from the estate agents, shopped for necessaries, got lost in the town's one-way system and still arrived an hour earlier than the removal van.

At least it was less claustrophobic in Chilkwell Street than lower down. Joss could see a line of distant hills, vaguely blue, if he screwed his eyes up. The house next door to their own end terrace house was newly painted, a rainbow sticker spanning one corner of the tiny front window. Someone was ruthlessly tooting a recorder in apparent competition with the raw screams of a young baby.

Joss tried not to look too closely at the front of Number 21 as Fran let them in, though he couldn't not see the peeling front door, its bell half-wrenched off the wall, loose wires dangling like lethal spaghetti. But the desolation seeped into him despite himself. Fran had assured Martha that the old lady whose house this had been, had not died in it. She had gone away to be cared for by kind relatives, she said. But Joss knew she was lying. She had died here all right. Of despair, he thought. Poverty, loneliness but most of all despair.

'There's a woodlouse in the bathroom,' said Martha carefully descending the bare staircase a few minutes later. 'A huge one. And the loo is all brown and yuck. Did you buy bleach at that shop?'

For want of somewhere more comfortable, Fran was crouching on the bottom stair, pale under her summer brown. 'I haven't ever driven that far before,' she said. 'I haven't ever driven on a motorway. I think my terror has just caught up. Do you think the electricity's on?'

As she made no attempt to find out or even move, Joss went rummaging irritably in the cupboard under the stairs, finding something with a huge lever which looked as if it might be important. Rashly he heaved at it. There was an alarming thunk and a whir, then the whole cupboard began to hum as if it had come alive.

Martha snapped a light switch experimentally and cheered as the bulb emitted a meagre gleam through its hideous plastic shade.

'Wonderful,' said Fran, still crouched on the stairs, her head in her hands. 'Could you dig the kettle out, Joss and the tea?'

'And biscuits,' said Martha reviving at once. 'Custard creams. And the lemon puffs. Have you noticed I'm into yellow food lately? Egg sandwiches. Sweetcorn. Lemon curd.'

Their mother moaned, apparently at the mere thought of food.

This was life with Fran Emerson, thought Joss. Better get used to it. Ripped everyone ruthlessly up by the roots then she couldn't take the strain and he was supposed to look after *her*.

'I'll let the cats out,' said Martha who seemed, as far as it was possible to tell, bossily normal for Martha.

'Who said,' Fran called plaintively to Joss as he hunted for a power point where he could plug the kettle in without electrocuting himself. 'Who said it's better to travel hopefully than to arrive?'

Ludwig, decanted from his prison, and inflated to twice his normal size, took a vicious swipe at Martha's ankles and fled howling up the stairs.

'Well, I'll tell you one thing,' said Joss. 'It wasn't Ludwig.'

'Oh, Fran,' said Martha, 'Fran come here, quick.' Her voice was trembly, unMartha-ish. 'Evie's had her kittens. Oh it won't be so bad with kittens.'

'Lovely,' said Fran, squatting down, marvelling into the blood-stained box, as if she'd never seen a kitten before, thought Joss, swallowing hard. 'I heard her ripping up newspaper. I thought she was cheesed off with travelling or having a private pee. Clever Evie. Beautiful Evie. Four babies,' she gloated. 'Perfect timing.'

The cat gazed back, purring, blinking golden eyes, coiled around her little family.

Joss averted his eyes from the box. It reminded him of butcher's shops. The damp ratlike heads he had unwillingly glimpsed did nothing to warm his heart. *Perfect timing*, he thought. Bare boards, lethal wiring, disgusting plumbing, nothing decent to eat or sit on, and she calls it perfect timing. He could imagine what his father would say. His father, back in their real home, where they still ought to be. Not here playing tree houses with Fran up in the Midlands.

In the house it was cool, the sun confined to the margins of rooms, tiger-like flickerings of amber along Persian carpets. But as she walked out of the house the heat struck like immense oven doors opening. She felt sick. She couldn't be ill. It was her birthday tomorrow. The aunts would worry if she was ill.

It was hard to breathe. Her skin stung. *Why is it so hot?* It wasn't supposed to be hot in September.

It would be cool in her music teacher's house. Patterns of black and white on the page, black and white rippling under her fingers. It was only the other side of the park. Five more minutes and she'd be there.

She didn't see the boy until she bumped into him.

It was a surprise to her that she was still solid enough to create an obstruction. He should have been able to walk through her like mist. 'Sorry,' she said automatically.

'My pleasure, darling.'

Flushing, she moved aside so he could carry on up the hill. He had been sticking posters along the wall that divided Gladstone Walk from the Park. She only registered the photograph after she'd walked past. Some local group beginning to make it in a big way. The Hoarsemen? She'd heard Spooky Ghoul raving about them and the name had made her shiver even though it was only meant as a joke. The original Horsemen in the Bible had been four nightmarish angels heralding the end of the world; Famine, Plague and what were the other two?

Her mind wasn't working properly. Thoughts flickered in and out with no sense to them and though rock musicians didn't interest Asha in the slightest, she found it curiously hard to get the Hoarsemen's faces out of her mind. Despite herself there was something about them that fascinated but also disturbed her. One in particular had a lovely face. She would be embarrassed to say it to anyone else but it was almost an angel's face, not a nightmare angel at all but a stern beautiful angel come to judge them all.

3   The Dark Arches

'—so we thought, why not have breakfast in the garden, the weather's so lovely,' said Aunt Isobel, meeting Asha at the foot of the stairs next morning. 'And Madeleine's made it look like something out of *Far From the Madding Crowd*, dear. Come and see.'

The aunts had set the table under the copper beech and spread the old embroidered Chinese cloth, washed and hung in the sun so often it was a pastel ghost of its former self. Madeleine had picked the last of the sweet peas and they stood in the vase she always used, fragile butterflies perched on elderly drought-thickened stems. There were fresh apricots, and coffee and by Asha's plate the festive pile of packages to which she herself added Valli's flimsy envelope.

I am sixteen, she thought.

But the thought slipped past her like water without touching her heart.

Sunlight fell through the beech leaves glancing along the silver and crystal, splashing across her white cotton dress. Everything had that brilliant edge which made things so unreal. People imagined dreams to be hazier than reality; soft-focus, slow motion like shampoo commercials but Asha's were too clear for comfort. In Asha's dreams there was nowhere to hide. People's eyes bored through her without mercy, their voices went on and on in her head like tolling bells. And she knew what was going to happen just before it did. Like now. Because before she was through the French doors she knew.

For there were the aunts hovering at either end of the table in floating summer florals from some long ago Liberty's sale, like benign spirits, beaming love and anxiety at her. She couldn't bear the way they felt so guilty. She could feel their concern fluttering around her like soft wings. If it would help them to feel better, she would smile and play the piano until her heart broke. Like the little mermaid she would swallow her poison and dance though her feet bled at every step, smiling, smiling –

'I wish it was more. Just a little thing,' Madeleine murmured as Asha unwrapped sprigged paper to reveal a sturdy schoolgirl's watch. 'I thought – when you have exams, you know. You might need – The little envelope is from me, too. Only a book token.'

'And mine is just so silly,' said Isobel, pinker than the sweet peas, her smile widening as her anxiety level increased. 'I don't know what you'll think, Asha. It's not a new thing at all, but a very special family thing all the same. It's just that Maddy and I were never really quite the sort – and Lucia went away before – well – I mean, if you don't like them, you can always sell them later, if you get hard up at university or something.'

It fell into Asha's hands like lead. It was all she could do not to drop it and scream. Blood-coloured stones set in gold so ornate and ominous it could have been dug from a pharoah's tomb.

'Let me fasten it so we can see it on you,' said Isobel. 'With your lovely hair –'

Obediently Asha let them do what they wanted, forcing her hands to stay in her lap when every instinct shrieked *take it off, take it away* . . . She couldn't breathe.

'I don't know what to – Oh, thank you both so much. Do you think I could take it off now? It's so grand I don't think it would like being worn with such an ordinary summer dress.'

She turned around in her flawless white, laughing, so they could unfasten the clasp, her mermaid hair flying out.

Take it off. Take it off. I don't want your love. I never did. I never asked to come.

A silence followed, during which Asha looked long and admiringly at the hideous heirloom before folding it up again in its layers of tissue, then she broke off a tiny piece of roll, buttered it and almost got it to her mouth, but sat and smiled around warmly at everyone instead.

'I'm so excited,' she said. 'It's all lovely. Everything's lovely. You're both so sweet.'

Isobel was looking agonised.

I told you, Madeleine signalled. Isobel shrugged helplessly, her colour deepening in her distress, her eyebrows arching into her hair.

'Has the post come yet?' their niece said, then, in a clear calm voice, her face smooth, untroubled, her eyes steady. The aunts looked away from Asha's hand, unconsciously crumbling her roll.

'Yes. Only a telephone bill, I'm afraid, dear. Quite a dreadful one.'

'This must be the last pressy then,' she said, laughing, borrowing a sharp knife to slit the airmail envelope.

The usual card, left over from last year's Divali. The usual two pieces of paper fluttering out. Except that it wasn't.

The cheque was a banker's draft from the Bank of India for twenty-five pounds. The letter was not from her godmother but in an unknown hand regretting that Valli Chaudhuri had passed from this life after a long illness, bravely borne, leaving instructions that this sum should be forwarded with love to her little English god-daughter.

Asha stared until the words swam. However often she reread them, she couldn't take in what they said. She tried shaping each word with her lips. The aunts half rose in their chairs, then sat down again, afraid to speak. After a while Aunt Madeleine whispered, 'Asha?'

'It's Valli,' said Asha at last, her voice harsh in her own ears. A parrot mimicking. 'She's dead. Will you excuse me, please?'

'Of course – Oh how dreadful – Is there anything – ?'

But she was gone, running into the house, jerky as a puppet. A door banged at a distance, then another.

Valli who fed her when her mother could not, who sang to her when her mother could not. Valli, whose name was a song in itself, whose hands smelled of cinnamon and her saris of sandalwood. Valli who gave her the sacred Sanskrit name for the hour she was born. Asha, meaning Hope.

Something was fighting to get outside her. Something dark

and hot. Asha clutched her mouth afraid she was going to be sick, but all that came out was a high sound that seemed to come from someone else. There was an ugly girl in the mirror, her face distorted, ill. She couldn't breathe. Something was tearing inside her. She knew she mustn't scream. The aunts would be upset.

Is my heart breaking? Why is it breaking over an old woman in India I haven't seen since I was three?

Then the whirlwind came roaring out of some furious dark place and the whirlwind shrieked so she had to listen even though she forced her fingers into her ears.

Because she remembered you even when she was dying, it said. *Because she named you and held you and knew who you really were, when your own mother didn't give a shit about you. Valli was the only mother you ever had. And now she's gone and you're on your own forever.*

Later, when it mattered, she tried to piece together what happened. All she could remember for sure was how important it seemed not to upset the aunts. The rest was a disconnected series of snapshots.

In one she had bundled up a great many peculiar things, and rushed out of the house, her pockets and school bag bulging. Then there was a jump like bad editing in a film and she was in the Post Office with her savings book, someone was pushing money across the counter and a lady in the queue was asking if Asha was all right.

Then there was another jump and a gap and she was running down the street, and inside her head the same words repeating like mad mantras: *Everything I have is not enough. Everything I have . . .*

Then she was tearing along under the old railway viaduct alongside the canal and into the long stagnant tunnel everyone called the Dark Arches, the dank chill striking through her summer cotton, bringing her briefly to herself so that she looked around in bewilderment to find herself here.

Torn black and white posters stretched, fluttering, ahead and behind her.

PLAYING AT THE APOCALYPSE CAFÉ

Four young faces, burning in the darkness, beautiful and

furious as the angel Gabriel.

The Apocalypse Café. She had forgotten it was here, amongst the rusting Victorian ironwork, the derelict workshops. The café was not a proper café at all but a roughly-renovated cellar where teenagers came to drink, pick fights, listen to live bands. Now it flickered in her peripheral vision: padlocked bars painted black and red. A dull despair hung in the air with the smell of stale beer. As she ran her shoe stuck in a gluey patch of something and she tore it free, sobbing with disgust.

Another clumsy cut in the film and her hand was on the door of the shop, closing it behind her, and with a dream-like knowing she knew at once it was here amongst the old clothes, broken radios, vinyl sofas and scraps of greasy carpet. Somewhere in the shadows; her true, her rightful birthday present.

'Need any help?' said the woman strolling out, from some even darker inner room. And then she said, her tone changing, 'Whatever you want from here it'll cost you and you'll have to organise your own delivery. We don't humour time wasters.'

'Oh that's fine,' said Asha. 'I'm not a time waster. I'll know it when I see it, honestly.' Her voice sounded forced in her own ears as if she had not spoken to anyone for years; as if she had been underground longer than she knew.

'Because some people,' the woman resumed unpleasantly, as Asha walked deeper into the gloom and began to poke around a set of Fifties G plan shelves, 'some people nowadays expect something for nothing.'

'Not me,' Asha assured her. 'Honestly.'

A girl's enigmatic face, her lips stretched in a curving mermaid's smile, her eyes haunted, swam towards her from the depths of a cheap dirty mirror.

It's me. It's only me. Asha.

Asha, meaning Hope and she had tried. Gone on and on hoping even when it was blindingly obvious to everyone else how hopeless it was. Shut herself in with the aunts and homework. Her bedroom walls filling up with certificates, prizes, commendations.

Her parents had dumped her in this room stuffed with

straw and she had valiantly spun her gold, sure if she was good enough, clever enough, beautiful enough, they would love her and take her home forever.

Asha. Of all the names in the world. People misheard it as Natasha, Sasha, or a sneeze. Then they said, 'What a fascinating name. However did you get it?'

Oh my godmother gave it to me actually. My parents couldn't be bothered. I was supposed to be a boy and they couldn't have another baby after me. I don't want something for nothing, you stupid cow. I want nothing for something. Nothing for everything.

But everything I have is not enough.

She rejected a plaster alsatian and a lamp in the shape of a pineapple and began rummaging in a plastic laundry basket full of grubby *bric-à-brac*. She was shaking. She had never been down here before, under the Dark Arches and couldn't believe she was here now. Whatever the furious force that had brought her this far it was spent, leaving her dazed and exhausted. But her birthday present was here. She would not leave without it.

'For a present is it?' the woman went on, in her grating voice. 'Because if it is, there's some nicer stuff over here. House clearance. Dad always gets in first. "We don't take the Best and leave the Rest." That's his motto.'

'No, it's not for a present. Well, only sort of. It's for me, really,' said Asha, concentrating, remembering.

Once, before her parents sent her away to England, she had played at divining for water, turning, turning, until the forked twig gave a lurch, almost dragging her arm down to the parched earth. Later the men had dug there and found a well everyone had forgotten about years ago. Remembering, how she had let herself be guided by something beyond her, something coming through her, she closed her eyes and circling slowly, stretched out her hand, blind, groping, *knowing*.

Her fingers closed. A dull shock ran up her arm, like low voltage current. Simultaneously something flared sullenly in the pit of her stomach.

Her eyes flew open. Dark, dumb and uglier than a gargoyle

27

it squatted on the tawdry shelf in front of her; a birthday present so hideous that by comparison even the pharoah's necklace was beautiful.

Her Box. Her Ugly Box.

She lifted it off the shelf, hardly believing and at once the dark whirlwind begin to spin again inside her, driving her on to finish what she had begun.

Heart hammering, Asha pushed her way past the rack of men's stale shiny second-hand suits and dumped her bag on the counter. But all the time she never let the Box out of her grasp. It was hers now and she was to have it. She had never been so sure of anything in her life.

'I want to buy this. How much is it?' she demanded, looking the woman aggressively in the eye.

The woman looked at her oddly, almost pitying. 'You would find that, wouldn't you, duck? One of the two most valuable things in this shop.'

'Look,' Asha emptied her pockets, then tore open her bag, spilling out most of its contents. 'Take it.'

Part of her watched in horror, as this wild-eyed girl shovelled almost everything she had of value across the counter; her post office savings, the sensible schoolgirl's watch, everything. She only knew she had to have the Box or die.

But the woman shook her head. 'Sorry, duck. It's a genuine antique. A collector's piece. Greek, as it happens. You couldn't afford it in a month of Sundays.'

'Oh that's not all,' gabbled Asha. She shook the bag until almost every item was out, the jade horse with its mane flying in an invisible wind; even the tiny pearl bracelet she had worn when she was a baby. And still the woman shook her head, in mock sorrow.

Then something broke inside her.

'Then take this,' Asha shrieked. 'And this. That's everything, everything I've got in the world.'

And from the bottom of the bag she took the package containing the heirloom necklace and from her pocket, the banker's draft, Valli's precious legacy; every penny scraped and saved, God only knew how.

Strangely enough the woman didn't look inside the envelope, just smiled a genuine, startlingly beautiful smile. She looked younger, suddenly. Softer. As if a weight was taken from her. Then she rapidly raked Asha's belongings towards her, heaping them in her grubby apron.

'Then it's yours,' she said. 'Take it. But you ought to know the truth. Only everything you have could buy this box, but believe me that wouldn't be enough if you were not the right one.'

She reached out then and seized Asha's hand so fiercely that Asha flinched away, but turning it over almost tenderly, the woman only traced the lines in its palm with her finger. Then, as far as Asha could remember it later, she began to talk in a dreamy sing-song that did not fit her grasping Midlands manner, but seemed to fit the smile.

'She's beautiful your mother but there's more mothering to be had in an empty house than from that one, my sweetheart. Look for love where it abides. Don't batter yourself at the door of that empty house like a starved wild thing. There's enough of everything and to spare if you aren't afraid. There's a power running from mother to daughter on this planet, and it's come to you now from ancient times down those motherlines because there's an older wiser mother that's been forgotten for too long, my bird, and she's chosen you and her power will come through you, Asha, if you let it. But will you pay her price? Can you pay it? For it is a dark one.'

Then a jump and a vague jumbled time until Asha found herself outside the entrance to the Dark Arches, a large brown paper bag dragging down her arms with a cold deadly weight. And she was repeating, bewildered, shivering in her thin dress, ' – but I gave you everything so what could – ?'

At that moment someone collided with her and she just managed not to drop the bag, pulling it to her protectively, her eyes widening with shock.

'Sorry,' muttered the boy, his dark hair flopping into his face. 'Sorry. Blind as a bat. Excuse me.' And he carried on into the stagnant sooty reek of the Dark Arches, his pale face thunderous, lugging the golden wreckage of a guitar.

4   *The Ugly Box*

That old guy at the crossing must have misunderstood when he asked for directions. What kind of music shop could possibly be down here? If indeed there was one at all in this dump. Still, this had to be the Dark Arches. Joss shuddered. He hated dark, closed-in places. He'd had to nerve himself to walk alone under the viaduct away from the light. The constant dank drip dripping from an invisible roof didn't help. Why hadn't he asked that girl while he had the chance? She'd have known if he was on the right track; she'd just come down the tunnel herself, presumably. She was pretty, too. No, not pretty. Something, though . . .

Worth checking out, as his old friend Bernie would say in his Yogi Bear voice, leering, thumbs jammed in his belt. (How did he *do* that and make it look so natural?) If Joss hadn't made a prize idiot of himself by almost knocking her in the canal, he might have had a chance too.

Liar, he sighed, to himself, liar, liar.

He had never checked out a girl in his entire life. He might lie to impress Bernie, but not to himself. The truth was, living for so long with Fran and Martha had turned him into a freak. Joss Emerson was a mutant. What was second nature to Bernie, and every other boy Joss knew, was daily torture to him. He dated it to when Fran went peculiar the first time and ran off to Greenham Common with some weird women from her Peace Group. After she came back, (and he was forced to admit it was a relief that she *did*, even if she was unwashed and hostile and smelled strongly of woodsmoke) he and his dad couldn't put a foot right. It was as if, just by being born male, they were responsible for every crime committed by their sex; starting with Herod and the firstborn to forgetting to put the loo seat down.

These days Joss was terrified to look at a girl in case he was unwittingly wearing the wrong expression. But if you didn't look at them, they might think you thought they were ugly (which was sexist because only women were judged by their looks, Fran said), or that you were plotting to leap on them when they were off-guard (which meant you were a sex-crazed beast). On balance, he preferred to give it a miss. He wished he could advertise the fact and spare himself the hassle. Please drive carefully, you are approaching Joss Emerson, a Sex-Free Zone.

A gust of stale air lifted the corner of a poster with a flapping sound. He peered, trying to decipher the Haunted House lettering. Norsemen? Oh, *Hoarsemen* and starring at the Apocalypse Café, too. Very witty. There were four of them of course. One looked Asiatic, his face as impervious as a face carved out of a cliff. The second musician looked like the member of some fierce ancient tribe, North American Indian perhaps, wearing an exotic kind of skull cap. The white drummer had the sides of his head shaved, a jaw you could break your fist on and a single long earring like a jet teardrop. The final member of the Hoarsemen was Black with short rasta plaits as well as several earrings, and scars on his face so elaborately symmetrical they were clearly intended for decoration.

A grim bunch of jokers, thought Joss uncomfortably, trying to deny the power those faces had over him. It simply didn't make sense that four guys could look like that and yet be somehow, there was no other word – *beautiful*. But what really magnetised him, filling him with a yearning he knew to be totally doomed, were the guitars. What wouldn't he give, for an hour, just one hour, with one?

He didn't much care for the Apocalypse Café when he reached it. The decor was of the Hammer horror kind; coffins. Mutants. Severed heads dripping blood. Perhaps it looked better after a drink, when the music got everything jumping but it was hard to believe. Joss found himself walking faster, the back of his neck prickling.

A minute later he had seen the range of shops on offer under the Dark Arches. They were all derelict and empty except one which was semi-derelict and that looked closed. Some kind of junk shop. He would have turned round then and gone home if he hadn't caught sight of the notice propped in a corner of the dirty window.

ALL REPAIRS.

It seemed a wildly optimistic service to offer, he thought, since it didn't specify what kind of repairs or indeed to what. It was hard to imagine anything coming out of this place in better shape than it had gone in. But he'd come all this way, why not give it a try?

He pushed half-heartedly at the door, not entirely sure he wanted to succeed but to his confusion it opened, propelling him into the shop. His heart jarred. Though he hadn't hoped for much he had hoped for better than this. Not so much a shop, more a graveyard for every shoddy, cheap and nasty object discarded in the last twenty to thirty years. And what was the smell that seized him by the throat? Damp? Rats? Rat poison? All three, he decided, sourly.

'Excuse me,' said the old man, strolling out of the gloom, 'let me save you the trouble of wasting your time. How unfortunate you should have chosen this particular moment. We really are extremely busy just now. I suggest you come back some other day.'

He didn't exactly bow at this point, but there was something suggesting the exhausted actor, reluctant to go back on stage.

'I – well, I just wanted to know – do you repair musical instruments?'

'I told you. Best to come another time. My apologies for your wasted journey.'

'But could you answer my question, please?' Joss persisted, baffled and angry. 'Just tell me, if I walk up that disgusting tunnel again and it's the right cosmic moment, would you be able to repair my guitar? I mean – what is it? Do you hate customers or something?'

The old man put his head to one side, as if listening to something too faint for Joss to hear. Not rats, Joss hoped. Then he gave a snorting laugh. 'Guitar, you say? I thought you said musical instrument. Give them a pencil box and a couple of elastic bands and they are all instant musicians today. Music? Who nowadays wants to take the trouble? Any fool can make a noise. Only an artist makes music.' He made a dismissive gesture.

An actor's gesture, Joss thought. He was agreeing to play the part after all?

Joss heaved the crippled guitar on to the counter.

'This is it,' he said, very carefully. 'It got smashed falling down the steps when we moved house with my mother yesterday. If it's possible for it to be mended here or anywhere at all, I'd like to know. If not I'd like to know that, too.'

He was proud of himself. Clear, to the point, in control. That was the way to communicate. That was how his father handled people.

The old man laid his hand tenderly on the curving wood. 'Quite an accident,' he commented. 'So we have to conclude you did not much like the idea of moving house. And who did you most succeed in punishing by this catastrophe, your mother or yourself, do you think?'

Joss drew in a sharp breath and was about to tell this interfering old buzzard exactly what he could do, when to his astonishment, the old man swung the guitar over to his side of the counter and stowed it out of sight.

'You're going to mend it?' Joss said, open-mouthed. 'You can really mend it?'

'Certainly. '*All repairs.*' You saw the notice. Why so surprised? Isn't that why you came?'

'How long will it take?' he said, his mind racing. It was a stay of execution. He could start learning to play again. He'd do it properly this time; systematically. Maybe he could even find other musicians to play with in some backyard somewhere. Before, he had always felt too self-conscious to expose his amateur efforts but if he could have his guitar back in one piece, perhaps he could have his old dreams back too, perhaps he could do anything, he thought. When he was small, before he started school, wild and wonderful songs came to him when he was trying to sleep. And years later, when his father first bought him his new guitar, he had dreamed of other songs, songs unlike any that had ever been written before, and he had longed for them to find their way down his fumbling amateur fingers. Perhaps the songs would come again. Perhaps it would be different now.

'Ah – ' the old man spread his hands. 'That's not so easy. You can't hurry a craftsman. The best I can say is, leave it with me. We'll contact you when the work is completed.'

'But how much –'

'Just leave it to us. All repairs,' the old man repeated maddeningly. He seemed to be hurrying him out of the shop. How did a small, bent old man manage to manouevre Joss towards the door so firmly without actually physically shoving him?

Then the weird thing happened.

'I wonder if perhaps, until yours is ready, you'd like to borrow this – ' the shopkeeper said, dreamily, then without waiting for a reply he went swarming up a flight of shelves like a squirrel up a tree trunk, and scrabbled perilously around in the darkness at the top, while Joss stood around, half angry, half wanting to laugh. What did the old nutcase think he was going to find? Someone's pawned ukelele?

He had found something though because now he was clambering down again, more slowly. Only, this was the baffling part, when the old man lifted whatever it was off the top shelf, raising clouds of greenish dust, Joss could have sworn the thing was, well, something very old. Old and distinctly mouldy.

It was stringed all right, but the shape was wrong; rounder, simpler. He couldn't put a name to what it could be, only that it didn't belong to Joss's own time or place. It couldn't have.

Yet on its bumpy trip down from ceiling to floor something happened to it. A shiver, like summer lightning.

And it came down a guitar. A blazing blue electric guitar.

Then everything was muddled. He could just remember trying to say, 'You're going to lend me *this*?'

And the old man saying hastily, 'Take it as another sign of our good will, young man. Unfashionable nowadays, but that's always been our way. Now I really mustn't take up any more of your time –'

And Joss was outside in the dripping gloom, open-mouthed, not sure whether to laugh or cry.

He didn't feel even slightly normal again until he was

walking up Chilkwell Street to Fran's new house. If it wasn't that he had left home with a broken accoustic guitar and come home with this extraordinary electric beauty, he would have thought he had dreamed the whole thing. It didn't make sense. People did not lend other people mega-expensive guitars while their broken ones were mended. Then he remembered.

He just let me walk out of the shop with it. And he can't contact me when the old one's mended. He doesn't know where I live. He never even bothered to ask me.

Asha thought it would be hard, going back to the aunts, but it was so easy, she was almost offended. If behaving badly was this easy why had she worked so hard at being good?

They didn't ask where she'd been. They didn't ask what she'd done with the watch or the pharoah's rubies and when she waved the paper bag under their noses, making no attempt to be convincing, saying brightly, 'Just look what came from Mummy and Daddy after all in the second post. What *is* it, do you think?' they only looked mildly at her as if they would have liked to stroke her hair perhaps, gently smoothing her back into the old Asha, the way they'd iron out a troublesome wrinkle in a frock.

Madeleine said she simply couldn't imagine; Asha really must tell them as soon as she found out. Then they drifted off to their own parts of the house like sorrowful ghosts and she climbed the stairs to her room, her heart hammering.

Now she drew the curtains and lit the scented candle she'd been saving for a special occasion without knowing what.

The Ugly Box was not a gift to be exposed to sunlight. Not yet.

'This is my birthday present,' she said to herself. 'It deserves ceremony.'

She set the Box down on the carpet and squatted beside it, and the part of herself that had been so ruthlessly pushed aside, looked on, aghast at what this new Asha had done and how she was behaving.

But all she knew was she had to 'get to know' the Box.

It didn't occur to her to try to open it. She simply stared in fascinated dread and wondered why she wanted it so badly if it made her shudder even to look at it.

It was so heavy, she thought. Cold and heavy. Not only in her arms as she carried it home, but in her heart. All the way home she felt its brooding, sorrowing heaviness inside her like a sickness. The Box was aware of her from the beginning, she knew, not as if it was completely awake, more the way unconscious, seriously ill people still know what is going on around them.

God, that made her feel even more frightened. As if like a wintering toad, at any moment it would open a yellow eye and focus on her.

Antique, the woman had said. Greek.

'But I think it belongs to the beginning of the world,' Asha whispered to herself. 'And those weird-looking words or signs or whatever they are, if they are Greek, it isn't the human sort.' Then she clutched her head confused by her own thoughts. Who would use language, if not humans?

The gods of course.

The words presented themselves matter of factly as though dispassionately tapped out on a computer screen. Oh sure, visitations of the gods were commonplace in her part of the East Midlands. She really must be going mad but she mustn't think about it. She must concentrate, concentrate on the Box. The heavy stuff was probably lead, she thought. And it was not square but octagonal, a shape which made the Box seem stranger still.

It was the grotesque figures embossed on the dull metal that frightened her most because they didn't stay the same for long enough for her to know what she felt about them. One moment they were abstract swirls, meaningless lumps and bumps. The next they had a malevolent life of their own with grinning gargoyle heads and swarming spiteful hands.

Stop it! she scolded herself.

If she let herself become frightened she was finished. It would be like falling into a whirlpool. She would lose herself. Then she wouldn't learn what she was meant to and it would all be to do again.

She frowned. What was *that* supposed to mean? The

strangest thoughts kept coming into her head as if they were her own.

But how could you tell when thoughts were your own? Perhaps these *were* her thoughts. Perhaps it was the thoughts about having to get As and not upsetting the aunts that were the alien ones.

'I can't find out what it *is* by looking with my eyes,' she whispered. Again as if guided to do what she had to do next, she closed her eyes, stretched out her hands, directly over the Box at first then delicately probing the space around it, carefully keeping her fingers about six inches away, as if its true dimensions extended beyond its physical form.

Her fingers began to tingle as she knew they would. It was the next thing she didn't expect. The peace that slowly enfolded her, the gentle but distinct warmth spreading through the crown of her head, down into her shoulders until it was flowing strongly throughout her body, yet travelling further and further beyond it with every breath until the whole room was shimmering with it.

It was so easy she wanted to laugh with joy. With no more effort than breathing out and breathing in she could send this wonderful warmth surging through the whole house, and into the street. She didn't even have to stop there. She could reach out into the town, into the country beyond, she could stretch up with her mind until she touched the sky, skimming the stars. She was limitless. Why had she never understood that before? Why had no one told her?

Behind her closed eyes, about the size of a sunflower seed, light was forming. Soon it was larger than a candle flame and still expanding. Her skull was filling up with light. Under her hands there began a vibrant humming like dragonfly wings but she was scarcely aware of her body, she was soaring, soaring –

That's enough! someone said firmly, yanking her back by the hair from wherever her spirit sailed, like a kite that had slipped its string.

That's enough for the first time. Don't let her overdo it. We've made a good start. Leave it at that.

Asha was opening her eyes into the premature twilight of

her room. Her head ached.

Then her eyes fell upon the Box and she knew it for what it was; a fake antique knocked together for gullible tourists, as phony and mean as everything else in that shop. And as this sank in she found herself remembering, dully at first, then with growing fear, that it was her sixteenth birthday and that this year, for the first time, her mother and father had not even bothered to send a present. And that all along she had known they would not.

Then the pain flooded in. That was why she had snatched up everything she owned in the world and torn out of the house. That was why she had to buy the Ugly Box to punish herself for being a mistake no one meant to bring into the world. It had made some kind of dreadful sense at the time. Except that she had been out of her mind.

And now she had nothing. Nothing and no one. And that was how it was going to be from now on.

Then she was crouching on the floor like a small child trying to make itself even smaller, rocking herself in her own arms, repeating over and over in a thin wail: 'Valli's dead. Valli's dead. Oh Valli's dead. Valli's dead.'

5   At the Apocalypse Café

JUDGEMENT!

The message blazed from the church as Asha crossed the road on the first day of term. For some moments she found herself unable to pass it.

Judgement could not be escaped. That's what Bethany Blessed's parents believed. Bethany's father sold judgement door to door like brushes. He believed the end was coming and only the righteous would be saved. He changed the family surname and renamed their bungalow *Shores of Galilee* so God would make no mistake when He came in the night to destroy the wicked. Normal people laughed at him.

But if these were not the shadows of judgement flickering across her wall night after night, what were they? War, plague, famine, drought. Fire and flood. Every night the same horrors in the same unalterable sequence until dawn released them both.

Asha could neither break nor endure the terrible enchantment which she knew she had brought upon herself. In her madness she had summoned the Box out of the world of the gods, calling it back to the world of human suffering. Now it was neither awake as she guessed it longed to be, nor free to return to its sleep outside time and space, but like a feverish child tormented them both with its nightmares.

When she was not blaming herself, Asha blamed the Box. After the third night she tried to get rid of it, bundling it secretly out of the house pretending a visit to the library, walking instead to the grimmest end of town with that familiar weight dragging at her heart. For almost an hour she crouched on the low wall of the council dump, trying not to breath, watching the erratic shimmer of flies in the heat.

If she sneaked it into the piles of garden rubbish it would be snatched up by giant grabbers, carted off within minutes. No-one would know. No-one could blame her. She could free herself as easily as walking away, just go back to her old life at Wintergrove as if nothing had happened.

Asha didn't have a revelation. She didn't hear voices or see presences, apart from flies and gulls, and a shirtless man delving amongst the garbage. She simply knew that if she allowed the Box to be flattened and buried beneath stinking mounds of waste, she would condemn herself to be both its gaoler and its prisoner forever. Her only hope was to go through with it, whatever that turned out to mean.

It was then that the voice spoke. '*If you had thrown it away, Asha,*' it said, '*you would have destroyed the world.*'

She jumped, glancing fearfully around. But there was only the man, whistling, rooting amongst pieces of old carpet and it was a woman's voice which had spoken. It was a woman before, she thought, the mad time she had tried to 'get to know' the Box. Since then there had been other voices, though she had tried to ignore them. She suspected there were four of them at least. Each with her own voice, her own personality.

But who were 'they'? And what was the Box, what on earth was it, that it was watched over by these disembodied witchy guardians? Why did her sense of it so come and go, blinking on and off like signals pulsing from a far-off star. Sometimes she thought she understood. Images exploded in her head: treacherous female fingers plucking fruit, prying open secrets. Poisoned clouds. Angels with blazing swords and blazing faces guarding the way back; the longed-for place you could never re-enter. Torn posters flapping in the wind. But it was like trying to grasp smoke and in the end it always eluded her.

Asha didn't try to lose the Box again but certain her sanity could not stand another night like the last three, jammed it deep into a drawer amongst her underwear in the hope of silencing it like some cheap alarm clock. She even tried to insulate herself from the relentless tick of its despair by surrounding it with crumpled layers of old newspaper. But she was beginning to understand that the Box couldn't help itself. That it was compelled to run obsessively through the world's darkest fears in much the same way Tamar Tetley tormented herself watching late-night horror films.

The Box was not malevolent, but was itself haunted and trying to exorcise itself. Like Asha, it only wanted to be free. And, in some obscure way, needed something only Asha could give to it.

At three this morning she had given in. Shuddering with the weakness of physical exhaustion, she got out of bed and lifted the Box from its drawer. 'I don't need this,' she muttered to herself. 'I just don't need this.'

On her bedroom wall a section of rainforest flared lividly, falling into charred ruin.

'Ssh,' she said to the Box, her teeth chattering. 'Hush now. I've got you.'

Cradling the thing in her arms like a goblin child, she climbed awkwardly back into bed. 'Hush now, sleep. It's all right.'

The wall flickered. A woman with burning holes for eyes stretched out skeletal hands for food.

'Sssh, I'll sing to you, Box. Rest. Sleep.'

She began to sing, scarcely above a whisper, a half-remembered song in Hindi that Valli used to sing; stroking her damp hair, rocking her string cot on the shaded verandah. And as she sang, Asha, shrinking from the horror of all the Box knew and could never forget, feebly stroked its gargoyle sides to comfort it.

'I know I am mad,' she said to herself. 'I am stark-staring mad and I must never tell another soul.'

But the twanging tension that for nights had lashed her room into dark spirals like a demonic humming top, lulled, as if the Box was listening.

It needed something to take its mind off horrors. I must remind it of something beautiful, something peaceful, so it can rest, she thought. Then perhaps Asha, too, could sleep in peace.

'Once upon a time,' she whispered to it. 'Once upon a time, Box, there was a world. A world so beautiful and new, no-one had invented words to describe it. It hung in the sky like a blue-green jewel, and all around it the air shimmered clean and new as a lark's song.'

She stole a rapid look at the wall. There seemed to be nothing worse than a tide hypnotically lapping. Perhaps it was a polluted tide, a radioactive tide, for all she knew, but even so it rocked gently, like an old-fashioned cradle, like the old string cot on the verandah in India.

'And on this world,' she yawned, 'there were many wonderful . . .'

The water lapped. The cradle rocked. The Ugly Box and Asha slept . . .

'Judgement,' Asha whispered, staring up at the forbidding walls of the church. But it was too large a word in every sense. Like Time, Space, Love . . .

'Ay-up!' Tamar Tetley caught up with her and whacked her on the back in greeting. Tamar had had her nose pierced since she had seen her last. Asha had to admit it suited her exquisite brown face, perfectly complementing the little galaxy of studs and sleepers she wore in her ears. Tamar surveyed Asha with the expression Asha always took to be sadistic. Tamar found

Asha a source of endless entertainment.

'Judge not that ye be not judged,' quoted Tamar comfortably, looking up at the hoarding, dismissing it with her considerable powers of contempt. Then she nudged Asha ungently back on to the pavement. 'And standeth not in the midst of the road neither or thou shalt be flattened by a bus.'

'Thanks, but I was perfectly all right,' said Asha frigidly and shouldering her school bag began to head into the flood of teenagers making their way towards a distant pair of gates.

'*Nice* summer, Ms McGillveray?'

Tamar stuck to her side like a burr. Asha wished she wasn't so imposing in every sense. Tamar was not especially tall but she had devastating long legs that gave the impression of extending to her throat. Today she wore a primrose yellow mini-dress that showed off most of them.

'Oh yes,' said Asha distantly, wondering why the deep-freeze-treatment never worked so well on Tamar as it did on other people. 'Lovely thanks. And you?'

'Oh yes *lovely*,' mocked Tamar, scowling her familiar scowl. Then to Asha's amazement she leapt high into the air and came down in a war-like crouch, barring Asha's way. She followed this with peculiar passes through the air, some graceful, dancer-like, others unmistakably aggressive as if she were wringing necks in loving slow motion. At the last moment, with a blood-curdling shout she shot out her fist, stopping it inches from Asha's face.

Despite herself Asha flinched and Tamar doubled up with shrieks of laughter; the famous Terrifying Tetley trademark.

'Well, what do you think? Are the ballet classes paying off?' she hooted, then, disappointed in Asha's lame response, she roared off towards the gates, skinny bare knees scissoring, a manic blur of primrose.

Deposited at the school gates by Fran on the way to her first day at work, Joss saw Tamar Tetley hurtling towards him and backed away as fast as he was able. But Martha, staring, didn't budge. A wistful expression appeared in her eyes.

'You'll be late,' Joss prodded.

'If I don't hassle Mum about having my ears pierced after

all,' Martha said slowly, still yearning, 'do you think she'd let me have my nose done instead?'

'It's through *that* gate,' said Joss.

'I wouldn't have an actual jewel in it,' his sister said, 'just a tiny little stud.'

'I'll meet you here at going-home time,' Joss carried on. Martha was famous for her obsessions. You just had to be firm. 'Just for today because you're new, understand? After today you're on your own.'

'The same goes for you,' said Martha, sweet as poison. As she walked away, Joss expelled his breath with a hiss. Martha never gave an inch. The last he saw of her she was drifting with the tide of other kids, thoughtfully fingering the side of her nose.

He found his way to his own school and after a few false starts, his own classroom. The primrose maniac girl was there, talking to a tall skinny boy dressed from head to foot in black. Even his sticking-up brush of hair was a dyed lifeless black and from his unhealthy ear lobe swung a silver skull with tiny amethysts for eyes.

'Look, they're brilliant, Tetley,' he was saying. 'There's no one to touch them, right. When the Hoarsemen play it's – it's like all the accumulated pain of the planet, like all its *agony* pulsing out of the music. You've got to go and see them. They're off down south next month, they've got a huge contract and a tour of the USA and everything. You'll never have a chance like this again.'

'Ghoul's right,' said a boy in a sweatshirt with a monk's hood which gave his head a sombre, skull-like look. 'They are just going to be so big – ' he mimed infinity for her. 'If you miss it you're going to hate yourself for the rest of your life.'

Tamar nodded but she looked bored, Joss thought, her thoughts elsewhere.

'At the last gig the sound system was so powerful, when they switched on the amps one of the security men passed out!' The monk's hood boy laughed a humourless bray, shaking his head. Sandy tufts leaked out of his hood, flopping around his forehead.

'Thanks but no thanks,' said Tamar sedately. 'I don't want

any more brain damage than I've already got listening to you two, Gunny. But Asha might go with you.' She flirted her eyes towards the girl sitting by the window, sorting through a file, and laughed a quiet, diabolical laugh.

The girl looked up, glancing warily across.

Joss recognised her with a flash almost of pain. Of course she wasn't pretty. He was an absolute mug. She was beautiful. But too pale. And – he struggled for the right word. Haunted. Yes, haunted. At that moment she saw Joss too and it was obvious she remembered their near-collision under the Dark Arches. Her eyelids flickered in alarm and her mouth opened but before she could say anything Ghoul also spotted Joss and said in his toneless voice, 'Well, maybe this is a man who appreciates a once-in-a-lifetime offer.'

He was holding out a ticket. Even from where Joss stood the words flared at him like a migraine:

APOCALYPSE CAFÉ.

Another boy, a grass-green shawl of a scarf wound around his neck despite the warm weather, pushed his way silently through the group and sat behind the girl in the window. There he appeared to tune out, behind his gold-tinted lenses, absently drumming beige-brown fingers on the table.

'Well?' demanded Ghoul. 'Do you like good music?'

'I think so,' said Joss defensively. 'Depends what you mean by good.'

Ghoul began to reel off names. Joss caught at one or two groups that were familiar, mainly from Martha and her cronies. 'But none of them,' Ghoul concluded, 'none of them remotely measures up to the Hoarsemen. You know what's really amazing about them? They tell the *truth*. Everyone else has lied to us from day one – isn't that right? But not them, when they sing you just know what they're telling you, right in here,' he banged his own chest. 'And the Hoarsemen aren't just a rock group, believe me, once you've heard them, man, they're a way of life. It's like you've got no choice, you know. Once you've heard the truth, you just have to follow. They may have started here in this one-horse town, ha ha, but they won't just change the face of this town, will they, Gunny. I don't know how, yet and I don't know when but they're going to change the face of this freaking planet.'

Gunny began to laugh, pumping his shoulders up and down, but there was no energy in the laughter.

'I like the blues,' said Joss suddenly. 'Mostly I like blues.'

The boy by the window stirred in his seat, but when Joss looked directly at him, he was still vacantly staring, silently drumming. Joss had spoken the truth. Lightning Hopkins, Big Bill Broonzy, Brownie McGhee were his heroes. His dad had a vintage collection of blues 78s. Priceless. But Joss was also thinking of the blue guitar and the music he would coax from it if only he could get hold of some amps.

'Well do you want the ticket or not?'

'I might.' Joss sauntered to a vacant table across from the haunted girl and socked his rucksack down, claiming the space. 'But I'm broke,' he said. 'I couldn't pay you today.'

Ghoul shrugged, miming – You've blown it, you sap. 'No money, no dice, man,' he said. 'I really wanted you to be part of it, you know. But it's got to be your choice, right.'

'You're new, aren't you? What's your name?' asked Tetley who turned out to be called Tamar to rhyme with jar. Joss told her, though secretly he was talking for the benefit of the pale girl whose presence filled the room like a faint troubling perfume.

'We're all maniacs here,' said Tamar. 'Except Asha, hey Ms McGillveray?'

'What, even Bethany?' jeered Gunny, fluttering sparse sandy eyelashes. He dragged his hood even further over his head tying its drawstring tight, making himself more skull-like than ever.

'Don't mock. Bethany Blessed has profound religious convictions,' said Tamar.

A third girl had come quietly in. She was plump and dressed for camouflage, even occupying space as if she had no right to it, walking close to the wall like a stray cat. But her eyes flashed as she said in a surprisingly deep husky voice, '*I* don't have them, Tamar. My parents do. It's not contagious. You shouldn't get us confused.' Flushing, she took a magazine out of her bag and began to flip through the pages.

The room filled. When the teacher came in Tamar stormed

to the back of the room, slumping ironically against the radiator, eyes narrowed, gum in place, her primrose dress falling off one skinny shoulder; the class bad girl. The school day began.

Joss got through it. That was the best that could be said. At break he hung around on the edges of Gunny, Ghoul and their crowd but their sole topic was the Hoarsemen's forthcoming farewell gig. At lunch-time he made a feeble attempt to find a free computer but every machine in the lab was occupied by hostile kids in chains and leather, any one of whom looked tough enough to splinter Joss like a chicken bone if he drew attention to himself. So he slid out again and wandered around by himself, cursing Fran for putting him through this.

He read a notice board or two, pretended to admire some sculpture in the foyer, drank water in the cloakroom and had a meaningless conversation with a man in a beautiful suit who seemed equally at a loss.

It was after he came back out into the corridor that he heard the music. It was not the blues, oh definitely not the blues but music of the deepest blue it still undoubtedly was. *Indigo music*, he thought; shading into the purple you get at twilight. Torrents of twilight, pouring down the school corridors and no-one but Joss seemed to notice.

The upper part of the door to the music room was screened with mesh and the room faced into the sun, so that when he saw her it was through dusty golden honeycomb; playing her heart out on the crummy school upright, alone in the sun-dazzled room.

He stayed, drinking it in, until the doors began to slam violently in sequence like the doors on a train, and footsteps and voices came hurrying. Then he fled before anyone could catch him. He didn't know why.

In the afternoon, he heard Bethany Blessed say, 'You're ever so pale, you know, Asha. Are you all right?'

Asha hesitated before she said lightly, 'Oh, I'm just tired. I never sleep well before school starts.'

'Nor do I,' said Bethany, delighted at the coincidence. 'Isn't it silly? Like a little kid. I keep hoping I'll grow out of it, but I suppose it's too late now. I'll be leaving soon if Dad has his way. Mr Larch talked Mum into letting me try A Levels but Dad doesn't really believe in them for girls and he usually gets his way in the long run.'

Her voice had a hungry note as if she was hoping for more crumbs of conversation but he didn't hear Asha's voice again.

At the end of the afternoon, while Joss was gloomily reloading his gear, the boy with the scarf came up, checked no one was in earshot, whipped off his glasses and said urgently, 'Were you serious? About the blues I mean?'

Without the smoky lenses the boy's eyes were a strikingly pure green, a colour startling enough with his golden beige skin and gold-brown curls, and even more startling against the fringed silk scarf. Joss could not read his expression but something warned him not to joke. This kid might be weird but he was the most human, most promising person he'd met all day. So he just said, 'Yes, I'm serious. Why?'

Still unsmiling the boy demanded, 'What do you play?'

Joss's heart began to speed up. 'The guitar,' he said, 'but mine's –'

'Electric guitar?'

Joss took a deep breath. 'Yes,' he said, 'but –'

'I *knew* you played,' said the boy and although he still had not smiled Joss could tell he was pleased. 'Come back with me tomorrow,' he said. 'There's a couple more of us. Sax and guitar. They go to Riverside, not this dump. We've got a perfect place to practise and everything. But we need another guitarist. Come and show us what you can do.'

Joss opened his mouth to protest that he was a beginner, that he only had a borrowed guitar, and worse, a guitar without any amps, but the boy, tinted lenses back in place, was drifting away before he remembered something. 'Oh, Joss,' he called, over his shoulder, 'my name's Otis. Otis Underwood. See you tomorrow.'

Martha pounced as soon as Joss came out of the gate. 'Dinner was disgusting. I'm starving – you've got to buy me something.'

Martha was vicious company when hungry and it was a long walk home. Joss groped in his pocket.

'Does it have to be yellow?'

'No,' she snarled. 'Just big.'

Walking through town, refuelling rapidly with chocolate, Martha began to mellow.

'Your school is crappy. Riverside is much better, you get a real education there. That's where I'm going when I'm fourteen. At your school they're all Geeks and Nerds.'

Against his better judgement Joss steered her out of the path of a bus. She was devouring a tube of sherbet now, talking fast through a sticky blizzard. Joss discovered that Ghoul and Gunny were Gothics and the toughs in the computer lab were Geeks. Joss himself was probably a Nerd as he'd been known to wear an anorak and wore glasses for reading.

Joss decided that Martha was fated to be a sociologist. In a single day she had the town's teenage sub-culture sussed and knew exactly where everyone slotted, including herself. Joss wished he could say the same. He felt exhausted, as though he had spent the day travelling through a foreign country. Oh, for a school where kids were simply kids and friends fitted as predictably as old shoes. Bernie, Spike; Alex Greenwood.

'What's Tamar, then?' he challenged his sister, hoping to catch her out.

Martha furrowed her brow. 'What does she wear?'

'The loony girl with her nose pierced.'

Martha's face split into a sticky white beam. 'Oh she's wonderful. Did you see her mini-dress? She'll go to Art School when she leaves, I bet you.'

'Why bother working on a portfolio,' mused Joss. 'Save yourself the trouble. Just buy a mini and get your nose pierced.'

'Look, I just *know*, clever clogs,' said Martha. 'I can tell about people.'

'What about a girl who wears –' he stopped to think. What had she been wearing? All he could capture at first were her grey, haunted eyes, the glossy red-chestnut hair plaited close to her head, but slowly he reconstructed her. 'A dark skirt, almost to her ankles.'

'Ethnic with fringes and mirror bits?'

'No, I don't think so. Plain. Simple. And a white blouse

48

with a lacy kind of collar.'

Martha looked baffled. She lifted her face, tipped her sherbert tube down her throat and finding it less empty than she thought, turned purple. 'Sounds like Mary Poppins to me,' she gasped once she'd got her breath back. 'Don't bash me any more. I've *stopped*.'

'She's not at all like Mary Poppins,' protested Joss. 'She's absolutely b – ' he stopped himself at once, but not before light dawned greedily in his sister's eyes.

'Oh, Joss,' she shrieked. 'You're in love. You are! You're in love. Wow! What's her name? You've got to tell me her name – Hey wait! I'll tell Mum – I'll tell Mum if you don't wait – '

Minutes later, brother and sister arrived at their blistered front door yelling furiously, then fell abruptly silent.

The baby was crying again. Fran had already been round for coffee with the neighbours, (or, Joss thought with disgust, probably herbal tea). Fran said they were dears. The man did the housework and looked after the baby. When he went out for the day he carried the baby's necessities in a large embroidered shoulder bag. Joss, cringing at the very thought, instantly christened him Harry the House-husband. The woman was an artist. Naomi. The baby's dreadful name was Orchid. Fran didn't know the name of the older one, but she thought it, too, was a girl. Joss had no desire to meet any of them, except perhaps the nameless one who tooted its recorder at six every morning.

'She said she'd put the key in the shed,' said Martha. 'Till she's had some more cut.'

They let themselves in, drifting through by degrees to the kitchen which by its very awfulness, like the negative of a photograph, conjured up their real left-behind kitchen with its scrubbed counters and glowing dials. It was worse, Fran not being there. Joss tried to imagine her whisking around expectant mothers in her midwife's blue and breezing home, later, full of her day, bringing the house back to life, but he failed.

Fran and Martha had done what they could, the last two weeks. Hopeful female touches, dried flowers, rugs and books. It made things worse than ever, in Joss's opinion, showing up the damp and desolation, the impossibility that this could ever be anything but a slum.

Ludwig appeared, howling his blood-curdling 'Milk' miaow. He was getting another abscess, out of sheer spite, Joss thought. Martha gave the yowling beast a saucer of milk without affection.

'And now shut up, you smelly cat,' said Joss bitterly, 'or I'll spin you round till you're dizzy and shove you outside to get lost.'

The cats were still forbidden the outside world. Evie, wrapped in her family of four, scarcely registered the loss but Ludwig, deprived of the great outdoors turned feline poltergeist; swinging from curtains, abseiling along the underneath of sofas, manifesting on top of the television like a reproachful household god, yellow eyes blazing.

'We're to make supper,' said Martha. 'She said she might be late. She said we were to do potatoes in their jackets.'

Unconsciously they had moved closer together.

'It will look all right,' said Martha, 'when the man's been. He sounds brilliant. He does everything. Naomi told Fran about him.'

'It won't ever look all right,' said Joss. 'And even if she makes it look all right, it will always *feel* all wrong.'

He kicked his bag viciously across the kitchen, spilling what was left of Ludwig's milk, splintering the saucer.

Martha stared, hypnotised by the dirty liquid spreading across the cracked clay tiles. Her eyes filled. Her mouth dragged itself down, twisting out of shape. She drew a huge sobbing breath and he was for it.

'I hate you, Joss Emerson,' she yelled. 'It could have been all right with just me and Mum. But it will never be all right with you. You won't let it. However hard we try to make it nice, you'll just *smash* everything up and ruin it. I wish you were never born!'

Then Martha pounded upstairs to her uncarpeted, uncurtained bedroom, presumably to torture her teddy bear or cut up Joss's baby photographs, both activities she favoured under stress.

Joss climbed the bare staircase, her screams scouring his

ears. He had claimed the attic room, as his own and Fran had let him have it too. Bribery, pure and simple. But it wouldn't get her anywhere.

The blue guitar was stowed under his bed, wrapped in a piece of balding blanket. For a long while he sat, cradling it across his knee, his eyes unfocussed. He was watching another Joss Emerson step into a smoky spotlight. He didn't wear anything flashy, just blue jeans, an ordinary workmanlike shirt open at the throat, the sleeves rolled back. But this simplicity only made him more charismatic. His one touch of theatre was the hat, black, battered, slightly melancholy, which he now pushed to the back of his head as he smiled the sad smile for which he was justly famous. Then he struck a deafening chord on the blue guitar and in its vibrant rainbow-coloured aftermath, began to play a song of his own composing; the kind of music that had never yet been heard on this planet . . .

Even when he half-heard Martha guiltily clumping back downstairs, to scrub potatoes for supper, he didn't move. He was listening too hard, listening to that unearthly musician playing and singing the blues.

6 *The Awakening*

After school Asha's routine was unvarying. A cup of tea with the aunts; piano practice, supper, then homework in her room. Sometimes the aunts asked if she didn't find life dull with no-one for company but two stuffy old women. But Asha resisted their well-meaning efforts to tamper with the flow of life at Wintergrove. She didn't think it was dull. It was safe like the reassuring ebb and flow of tides. If she could not be happy, she could at least be safe.

But this afternoon, the moment she turned her key in the lock she knew something was wrong. The shock-wave met her in the hallway, unmistakable as the smell of burning. It emanated from the top floor in jerky electrical pulses. *The*

Box! Before she could race upstairs to see what had happened Aunt Isobel appeared in a state of high excitement.

'We've been so busy, Asha. We started cleaning out the kitchen cupboards, then we realised how dreadful the rest of the house looked.'

Speechless, Asha followed her. The downstairs looked as if it had been burgled. Drawers hanging out of chests, their contents scattered everywhere, chairs piled on top of other chairs, precious rugs dragged back anyhow.

'We've been living in a slum, dear, frankly,' said Aunt Maddy, clambering over the chesterfield to greet her. She had tied up her hair in a large red duster and rather resembled a pirate, Asha thought. 'I felt so ashamed when I climbed up and saw the tops of the cupboards. Would you believe there was some kind of terrible whiskery mould growing up there? Asha, I'm sure one could have cured *cancer* with it!'

'But what made you decide to do it now?' asked Asha, tripping over a carved footstool, not sure she liked these new, wild-eyed aunts.

'Goodness knows,' said Isobel, who had a smudge on her nose, her arms dripping with *bric-à-brac* at every step. 'It can't be Spring Cleaning, can it? Is there such a thing as Autumn Cleaning, Maddy, dear?'

'*Equinoctial* cleaning,' suggested Madeleine. 'Would that cover it, do you think? We wouldn't want to be thought eccentric.' And both aunts went into fits of giggles.

Asha was suddenly inspired. 'Did you go out to lunch?' she asked. 'Shall I make a pot of coffee?' Neither aunt had a head for wine, but when they ate out they insisted on 'doing things properly, dear,' and usually tottered home in a taxi, with bird-bright eyes and flushed cheeks.

'Certainly not,' said Madeleine. 'We had a cheese sandwich and a cup of disgusting Darjeeling that got left in the pot too long, didn't we, Izzy? We've been much too busy for gadding about. You won't mind beans on toast, will you, Asha? If you want to practise the piano there is a large pile of books on it at the moment but I expect you could find somewhere else to put them. I would make you a cup of tea, but we seem to have mislaid the – ' She gestured helplessly.

'That's okay,' said Asha. 'I'll do my homework first. I've got loads.'

However much she wanted to soothe the aunts it was hard to radiate her customary calm. She was frantic to get to her room.

Half-way up the stairs she understood the aunts' spring cleaning urge. Her own skin began to prickle with excitement. The soles of her feet itched with excess energy. At the same time her head felt marvellously clear, as though every step was taking her further into fine blue mountain light; dry, mountain air. Her pulse beat so strongly she could have run miles without tiring. The aunts had got it right. This was spring energy, this was the force that drove the green shoot so irresistibly towards the light, it would split a paving stone that got in its way.

She threw open the door of her room and rushing to the window, threw that wide open, too, with the vague idea that like leaking gas, this feverish effusion would do less harm if she could let at least some of it out of the house.

She could hardly get near the chest of drawers. The vibration was not just uncomfortably intense at close quarters, it was audible; a sweet high chiming that ran disturbingly up and down her spine. Somehow she got through the singing force-field and dragged out the drawer, impatiently shaking out the layers of rubbish she had used to insulate the Box.

An overpowering smell of forges and hot metal filled the air. The debris of its violent transformation littered the bottom of the drawer. The Box was unrecognisable. Like a cold-blooded reptile, it had shed its skin.

Now it was as plain as a young girl's jewellery box, made of dark unfamiliar wood, lovingly crafted for all its simplicity. It was oiled rather than varnished and the oil not only made the wood glow ruddily but gave the Box a faint, pleasantly musky fragrance. Asha ran her fingers along the glowing grain, sniffing at the perfume that came away on her fingers, then blinked away a fleeting revelation of an ancient tree in a sundrenched overgrown garden. The tree from whose wood this Box had once been made or would be made or was still being made, she thought. There was no time in that garden, only change, only creation.

This Box was satin-smooth to her touch. There was only a faint patterning, the glowing darkness of the wood shot through with ghostly gold, like marks made by sea water; only the faintest patterning, she thought, suddenly tense, tracing it with her fingers; it was scarcely there at all, yet it was there, persistent as an ancient spell, winding around the box like a thread, like a twisted friendship bracelet one child makes for another.

But once Asha had seen it she knew what it was and could not shake off what she knew. The patterning was not accidental, a trick of time and weather. The artist had known what he or she was doing. It was a snake, a golden snake closing the deadly circle of itself, biting its golden tail. It was a warning, and Asha knew it.

'She's called Liana,' said Martha on the way to school next morning. She had met the recorder-tooting infant on a neighbourly visit with its mother. 'It means "garland of flowers". Naomi says she was given the name during meditation before Liana was born.'

'She should have given it back,' said Joss.

Martha giggled. She had forgiven Joss for last night or else she had forgotten. Joss found he couldn't forgive or forget so easily. In her rage Martha had leaked the truth and the truth was brutally simple. Joss had never wanted to come to live at 21 Chilkwell Street and Fran and Martha hadn't wanted him either, it seemed.

So why was Joss still here?

By the time he woke, after a night of confused dreams, to the familiar squawk of *London's Burning* from the neighbouring attic, he had a plan. He was going to phone his dad and ask if he could go home. He would make it clear he didn't need looking after. He could make things easier for his dad by helping out with the chores. They would rub along fine on their own, he knew. Two men, respecting each other's space, the way Fran and Martha could never understand in a thousand years.

The core of it was that Joss had never understood why Fran left. She never gave any explanation for breaking up the family. It was all looks, hints and deadly meaningful silences as if she expected him to understand her warped thought-processes by telepathy. He knew there had been rows, when he and Martha were supposed to be asleep but they didn't mean a thing, he was sure. All families quarrelled. Fran was always one for over-reacting. His father was a good man. Everyone didn't gush their feelings over you like a hot spring. Fran thought hers was the only way to love but Joss's father cared for his family in the way he knew best, in a way that felt far less smothering to Joss, frankly, a solid, dependable down-to-earth way. Richard showed his feelings through what he did for his family, half-killing himself to pay the bills, while feckless Fran flitted about like a hyperactive butterfly, never sticking anything for long, always yearning for something out of reach. Joss's dad had a grip on reality. He knew life was a hard lonely business and just got on with it without all Fran's song and dance. Presumably the Florence Nightingale bit would go the same way as *Frances Emerson Designs* and her blighted attempt to get a degree with the Open University. Fran wanted to have her cake and eat it. She was like the women who whined on late-night phone-ins, wanting to know where the magic had gone, demanding weekends in Paris. Frankly, Joss thought, his mother was a case of terminal time-warp, stuck fast at seventeen years old. The Love Generation. Yeucch.

'She's nice actually,' said Martha.

'Who?' asked Joss, dragging his mind back.

'Naomi,' said Martha. 'She's funny. I like her. But I don't actually know what meditation is, do you?'

'Just a fancy way of making your mind blank,' said Joss. 'I suppose it's a bit like praying, only instead of talking, you listen.'

Martha was silent for a while before she said, 'Do people still pray, then? I mean, normal people?'

'No,' said Joss carelessly. 'Not normal people. Just batty people. Religious people.'

'Why don't they?' she asked. 'Why was it just in the olden

days they prayed?'

'Why? Because praying doesn't work,' he said angrily. 'Because prayers are stupid. Because when you come right down to it, there's no one to hear them, is there?'

They were at the school gates but Martha showed no sign of departing.

'Mum prays sometimes,' she said at last. 'She prayed for peace at Greenham Common. Women prayed all over the world. And now – '

'Look I haven't got time for this,' said Joss exasperated. 'And nor have you. You'll have to get yourself home, Marth, I'm going to see someone after school.'

He didn't know why he still planned to go home with Otis Underwood when he would be packing his bags, going back to his real home. It was as if there were two Joss Emersons. The one who was leaving and the other one, the one who was almost tempted to stay and see how things worked out. Only almost.

'Okay,' Martha said, then she brightened. 'Oh – is it that Mary P – '

'No,' said Joss, making a threatening gesture. 'It isn't. Now shove off.'

His second school day was much like the first except that now he knew some of their names. He was mildly surprised to barge into a couple twined in each other's arms in the stock cupboard after break. He remembered then that there had been quite a few boys and girls holding hands around the school this morning, snatching furtive kisses. It wasn't as if it was Christmas. Ghoul was still flogging tickets for the gig at the Apocalypse Café inviting anyone who wanted, to come along at lunch-time and listen to a pirated tape of one of their concerts. Joss thought he'd go along out of curiosity, but Otis headed him off with surprising vehemence.

'Believe me, you don't want to hear it. Their sound may be the best thing since the Beatles but they're sicker than Plutonium. Tyke, one of the guys in our band, calls it Eine Kleine Vulture Musik. If you take a good look at their fans it makes you wonder if the Hoarsemen give away free lobotomies with every record. It's creepy, Joss, honestly.

Normal kids, well, if you don't count Ghoul, – turning into pathetic little zombies. Come on – we don't have to stay in this dump. Did you actually stay in all yesterday? What did you find to do?'

As they pounded down the back streets to the nearest chippy, Joss filled Otis in on his dreary hour, missing out the indigo music but including his encounter with the lost-seeming man in the beautiful suit. Otis was impressed.

'You were lucky to see him,' he said. 'Some people never see him the whole time they're at his school. Some people even refuse to believe he exists. They think he's a myth to frighten naughty children, like the Bogeyman.'

'Who is he then?' asked Joss apprehensively.

'The headmaster,' said Otis. He made a face. 'What a poser. Should have been a film star. He's usually out spreading his charisma around the community, conning businessmen into coughing up cash, getting his picture in the papers, telling everyone what a progressive school this is.'

'Progressive?' said Joss, remembering the couple in the stock cupboard.

'Yeah – couldn't you tell by the abstract artwork in the foyer? We're big in Friendship Skills and try ever so hard to become Racially Aware. Not many kids get GCSEs but they're all *extremely* racially aware. It's wasted on me naturally, as being radically cool from an early age I was racially aware by the time I was two, but I give the rest of them a few tips.'

Apparently Otis was only silent in class. Once you got him on his own he talked a blue streak.

'I bet my mother knew this was a progressive school,' Joss said bitterly.

'What the hell,' said Otis. 'All school is a waste of time. Progressive. Repressive. Radioactive. Who cares?'

Joss kept finding himself warming to this boy then remembering with a pang that it was pointless to make friends.

I won't be living here. This time next week I'll be back home with Bernie and the gang.

'Now,' said Otis, when they emerged from *The Seagull* with

their scalding parcels seeping grease, 'Let's cut the superficial crap. Let's talk about music. Who do you like?'

For the first time since her headlong flight to the Dark Arches, Asha almost had a normal night's sleep. But next morning she felt, if possible, worse than ever. The reincarnated Box had revealed a side to its nature so bizarre that, as if life wasn't complicated enough, she now had the worry of how to protect the aunts from its new, most unwelcome manifestations.

In the end the only thing she could think of was to take it to school with her. At least it looked fairly innocent in its present form but she still felt like a terrorist getting on the bus, with the Box ticking subversively in the bottom of her bag. Nothing happened, thank goodness. She thought the driver leered a bit when he called her darling but he was new to the route and it could have been perfectly normal behaviour for him. She was probably being over-sensitive. She might not have noticed ordinarily.

This was Asha's dilemma. Having cast off its layer of lead, the Box had stopped filling her room with its fears. It seemed to have blasted itself clean out of its hibernation phase and now the Box no longer needed Asha's comfort.

It wanted love. Not motherly love, brotherly love, or sympathy and understanding but Love. And it became clear from the heartshaped fantasies wafting out of the drawer all evening like escaped Valentine's Day balloons, that the Box believed in thinking big. By love it meant Romeo and Juliet, Cathy and Heathcliff rolled into a single ecstatic experience. It wanted to float through cornfields in slow motion. It wanted sobbing violins, the scent of white lilacs and the moon in June. It was cornier than a True Love comic. Asha couldn't stand it. But frighteningly, she wasn't strong enough to fight it either.

Again and again in the middle of a sticky translation Asha wrote down a perfectly innocent sentence in French, only to turn crimson when she read it through. Determined not to give in she switched to taking notes for a history essay but found herself plunging alarmingly into the steamier details of Oliver Cromwell's private life when she sincerely meant to write about the Diggers and St George's Hill. In the end she settled down grimly with her maths, which she guessed would prove harder for the Box to infiltrate. By now she was as vigilant as Cromwell himself, and managed to stop herself before she dreamily drew the second heart in the margin. It wasn't crude graffiti style at all but surprisingly artistic with fancy Celtic-looking knots worked into the design. True lovers' knots. Catching herself gazing admiringly at her handiwork she scribbled it out in angry black zigzags.

All night the Box filled the house with its unreasonable longings.

And it didn't confine itself to the house.

Once Asha, waking to see the silhouette of a boy and girl twining together upon her wall like summer honeysuckle, heard the screech of cats under her window and groaned with appalled comprehension. Evidently the Box's broadcast of lust was travelling through and beyond the Victorian walls of Wintergrove. The local cats, too, were having a second spring.

She dragged the pillow over her head to blot out the noise, diving back guiltily into the dark.

At breakfast the aunts were unusually silent. Once Isobel volunteered, with a faraway smile, that she had had the most vivid dream about 'someone I knew years and years ago. Most extraordinary!'

But Aunt Madeleine just muttered something about a headache and said she really must get a plumber to fix the downstairs loo.

Asha, who was beginning to suspect the Box had even wilder surprises in store for her, didn't dare to imagine the effect a second transformative burst of energy would have on the tranquil melancholy of her grandfather's house. She might come back to find Madeleine had eloped with the plumber. She couldn't go on like this. It was like being trapped on some nightmare roller coaster with no idea if she would ever be allowed to get off.

Why don't you ask us to help then? said a voice chattily in her head as she stepped off the bus.

It was the young one. The wild one. There was something uncomfortably healthy and pushy about her. Asha visualised her with a suntan, in indecently short shorts, toting rucksacks in and out of air terminals.

Do you always sit around waiting for things to happen? Take matters into your own hands for once. We can't help you if you don't ask, you know. It's in the contract, I'm afraid. I'm bending it now, frankly.

Asha gritted her teeth and silently told the voice to shut up. She wasn't about to start holding conversations with invisible persons, especially pushy invisible people who reminded her unpleasantly of Tamar Tetley. She preferred the motherly one or the one she thought of as Beauty; they made her feel soothed, in harmony with herself. The pushy one made her feel wrong-footed, a wimp; the way she felt when she was ten and came last in the sack race.

You'll be sorry, said the voice. *You're going to need all the help you can get today.*

'Oh shut up,' exploded Asha, to the alarm of an old lady passing by. 'Not now, all right,' she hissed into her collar, simultaneously trying to smile reassuringly at the old lady. Fortunately an earsplitting whistle distracted them both.

'Hey, gorgeous!' called a window cleaner from his ledge, two floors up. 'What are you doing tonight?'

Asha ploughed towards school affecting indifference to the whistles, catcalls and kissing noises erupting bewilderingly from all directions.

'You dirty old man,' jeered the window cleaner's mate from ground level. 'I'll tell your missus.' But he couldn't resist gazing after Asha. 'She is lovely, mind,' he sighed. 'What a peach. And still at school. It shouldn't be allowed.'

By the time Asha arrived in the classroom her face was flaming like a peony. Gunny grinned unrepentantly a scant few inches behind and Mr Larch the history teacher was barking, 'If I catch you doing that again, my lad, you'll go straight to the headmaster,' and Bethany Blessed whispered to Tamar, 'Pinched her, right on the stairs, in front of everyone.'

'On the stairs,' said Tamar ironically. 'Oh dear me.'

Before the history lesson was over, Asha had been leered at, winked at and passed crumpled notes by almost every boy in the class except Otis Underwood (and everyone knew he lived on another planet) and the new boy, Joss, who seemed not to know she was in the room at all. She never caught him looking at her anyway. Even Mr Larch seemed to have difficulty keeping his concentration on the English Civil War.

By lunchtime the school resembled an episode from an inferior soap opera.

'You'd think it was spring,' said the secretary wistfully watching couples wander on to the school field, their arms draped round each other. Half-heartedly she tapped another few keys on the typewriter then looked up. 'What were you wanting, Mr Larch? – Ooh, Mr Larch!'

'Ted,' he murmured into her hair. 'Please call me Ted.'

Under the old mulberry tree by the school kitchens, Bethany Blessed was hardly daring to believe her ears; 'Go out – you mean with you, Carl? But you're in the seventh form.' Adding silently, and you're glamorous and American. And I'm fat and boring and my parents are both nutcases and everyone in this town knows it.

'The perfect age difference, Bethany,' said Carl, his cornflower blue eyes blazing sincerity. 'And I can tell you're a sensitive person who just needs bringing out of yourself. Say you will. Just a walk and a talk. What harm could it do?'

She couldn't look at him, was terrified to let him look into her eyes and read her feelings there, and so she looked everywhere else quite desperately, before he finally coaxed the promise from her. When the bell rang and he left her, she couldn't move, just stood, touching her lips to the place on her fingers where he had clasped them. The most beautiful boy in the school and God had given him to Bethany. It couldn't be true.

Asha spent her lunch hour in the girls' toilets. It seemed the only safe place.

Now do you believe us? said the pushy goddess as Asha emerged from her cubicle at last and bent over the washbasin, splashing cold water on her face and wrists. (Asha had at least half-admitted to herself by now that it was goddesses she was dealing with.) *This is strong stuff. This is very real power. If you're going to do what you must do next, you need our help. Will you trust us?*

The bell rang. Asha peered cautiously down the corridor. A first year girl and boy were disappearing around the corner, trotting along, hand in hand like babes in the wood.

'You're right,' she sighed. 'It's too dangerous. Tell me what to do and I'll do it.'

Well first, came the unwelcome reply, *you go even deeper into danger.*

7 Joss and the Furies

'What's the matter?' said Tamar in the cloakroom, long after school had ended. 'You're usually gone before this. Waiting for gorgeous Gunny?'

'I've lost my purse,' said Asha, hunting through her bag. 'I'll have to walk home if I can't find it.'

'Probably someone's nicked it,' said Tamar. 'I've got ten pence left from dinner if you want.' She began to delve alarmingly in today's mini-dress, which was fake leopard-skin with a wobbly home-made hem.

'Thanks,' said Asha. 'But I need more than that. What are you doing here so late, anyway?'

'Detention,' said Tamar. 'Insolence in Home Ec.' She crossed her eyes. 'Hey do you think they put something in the water? Everyone's sex-mad today. Actually I really fancy that Carl Lieberman even if he talks like a problem page, but I asked him out and I think that frightened him off.'

'I thought Americans invented liberated women,' said Asha.

Tamar screwed up her nose so that Asha feared for the jewel. 'In theory,' she said. 'In practice they want Madam Butterfly.' She flapped her arms, rattling copper bangles and huge zebra-striped earrings. She was too much, was Tamar Tetley. She was a female piranha. No wonder the American boy felt overwhelmed.

But the pushy goddess was beaming approval. *Now that's*

something like a girl.

'I've got to go,' said Asha. 'It's a long walk home.' She hoped Tamar couldn't hear her heart pounding. She was doing what the goddesses told her to do but she didn't like it one bit.

Joss put down the borrowed guitar. His hands were wet but he didn't want to wipe them in front of everyone. Silence thickened the air. He felt as if he was breathing soup. Otis was too carefully not looking at him. Christy knocked spit out of his sax. Tyke retied his shoes; both of them.

Joss fought down the apologetic phrases that floated into his head; *I haven't practised for months. I was really nervous. It would have been better if we'd been jamming all together not me playing alone in front of you as if it was a bloody audition or something . . .*

The only thing he could do was put them out of their mutual misery.

'Thanks for asking me, anyway,' he said to Otis. 'It wasn't your fault I was crap. I've got to go now.'

That ought to let Otis off the hook with his mates who looked stricken like people playing statues. When he left they would unfreeze, he thought, hoot with laughter, holding their stomachs; 'Bloody hell, Otis, where did you dig him up?'

Otis just nodded and said neutrally, 'Sorry it didn't work out. Thanks for coming. See you around.'

To Joss's dismay Otis's mother was in the tiny kitchen blocking his escape, unpacking vast quantities of groceries. A clutch of yelling kids grabbed at crisps and cans of fizz. She smiled tolerantly but before she could say anything, Joss mumbled the first rubbish that came into his head and barged out of the house.

He had known this would happen if he took his music seriously. If he tried to mix his dreams up with his life. Once you said out loud what you secretly longed for, you might as well strip naked for everyone to jeer at. Once your dreams collided with reality, once you spilled them into the harsh glare of other people's opinions, you had nothing left to keep you going. You were empty inside.

He hoped Fran would be satisfied. Another one of her happy little myths exploded. 'You can do anything you want to, Joss, if you want it badly enough.'

Now perhaps she'd accept that he was fated to be one of life's background people. Some people had to be, didn't they? Fran was one herself only she wouldn't admit it. There were two kinds of people. The inexplicably golden ones, like the Hoarsemen, who got the breaks, and the mediocre majority, who watched enviously from the sidelines. Look how hard his dad worked. Where had it got him? Working at it, wanting it badly didn't make a blind bit of difference. It was that golden rain. It either fell on you or it didn't.

Oh he had been scared. Joss had been so scared. His fingers had turned into numb strange fruit that just happened to be stuck on the ends of his arms. He could scarcely play a note. He had started out wanting to throw up and ended up wanting to die. And I did, he thought. I died, right in front of them. He was never going to put himself through that again as long as he lived.

He didn't actually know where he was, he realised. His feet had simply pounded away from the little council estate as fast as they could cover ground. Now he seemed to be heading back towards school in an elaborate loop, through eerily empty streets. Where *was* everyone? The next turning brought him past the blind backs of houses into the unmistakable reek of the canal, reminding him uneasily of the Dark Arches, a memory he tried to push away because he had never been able to make sense of it.

He might as well walk along the canal as anywhere else, he thought; the dirty water slopping at the side of him, brambles and elderberries overhanging dog-haunted nettles and willow herb like a despairing memory of real countryside. If you felt this depressed you might as well rub it in. There was a satisfaction in knowing just how bad things were.

At least his life was straightforward now. In the last half hour it had simplified with the brutal precision of an equation. There was no longer anything to stay for.

Then he heard the girl's voice pleading, against a confusion of male jeers and wolf whistles and someone saying, 'No, leave her, can't you see she's scared?' and another shouting shrilly, 'They always say no when they mean yes, don't you know anything yet, Kenny?'

Joss began to run, though it was the last thing he wanted to do, jogging tensely down the towpath as though he had been ordered to. The next bend brought him into open space.

There were four of them he saw to his despair, the kind of thugs who probably tore the sleeves out of their leather jackets with their bare hands; beefy lads of sixteen or seventeen, crowding round, trying to pull her bag away. For a moment he thought, wanting to believe it, they're teasing. Just mates fooling around.

Then he saw who she was; her face, pinched with fear, her haunted eyes enormous, her beautiful hair slipping out of its plait and without knowing he was going to, he began to run in earnest, calling her name ridiculously as if he had been on a long quest and found her at last, 'Asha – it's okay. Asha!'

'Let her go,' screamed Kenny. 'It's her boyfriend.'

'It's a wimp, you mean,' jeered another, swinging round, his face a mask of hate. To Joss's surprise he didn't feel the blow when it landed, though he staggered from its impact. The punch that hurt, for some reason, was the one he actually delivered. It must be something about jawbones. He felt betrayed; it never looked painful in films. He wanted to hop around howling, sucking his fist like a two-year-old but apart from the dignity side of it there wasn't time. Another boy was charging him across the fallen body of the lout he had so astonishingly felled.

Then things became dreamlike. For some reason Asha started shouting. The words didn't sound like English though he was in no state to be sure. At the same moment her bag sailed up into the air and before it had time to hit the ground, something came flapping out like a huge ungainly bird, and then another and another until there was a storming flock of them. Whatever they were the longer they were in the air the less Joss liked the look of them. When they had climbed beyond tree-top height, they went into a dive that made his stomach lurch, and the air filled with a vibrating whistling sound which wasn't bat, bird or insect, but resembled a malevolent combination of all three, put through a powerful synthesiser.

These were things Joss didn't have time to think about but would not have liked if he had. He stumbled backwards with a moan of protest. So did the three youths. Obviously they had seen something too, perhaps even more horrifying than his own vision because they went greenish grey and threw up their hands to ward the something off, before they fled, gabbling with fear, leaving their companion on the ground. For a few moments the winged things hovered hornet-like and several above the scummy water, until becoming small and single again by invisible degrees, it acquired solidity, grew corners and sharp edges and plummeted like a brick.

Asha rushed to the canal's edge and dipping down her hands into green sludge, fished out the plain wooden box that bobbed there. She shook off the sludge and that was strange too, Joss thought, because the box was neither wet nor slimy. Then, her eyes closed, she hugged the box for a second before stowing it back inside her bag.

Part of Joss's brain was obviously still working because he understood quite lucidly that he must get himself and Asha away from this place as soon as possible. He was pretty sure he'd only stunned the lout but he didn't want to hang about and meet his big brothers.

'This way,' he barked, hauling her up the bank and through a broken fence. They ran doubled up under the hedge of someone's respectable back garden, emerging in an avenue of bungalows incongruously jumbled alongside Victorian warehouses and seedy second-hand car outfits. There was no sign of the youths but Joss wasn't chancing it and dragged her down another couple of alleys, determined to put as much distance between them and their enemies as possible. But as they ran, gasping now, turning left and right and left along the narrow grid of terraced streets, another part of his mind reeled with the horror of what he had seen.

The trouble was he had no language for them. Disembodied faces with wings? Ghosts? Angry spirits? They had hung in the air, an avenging elemental swarm and the sound of them made his skin crawl.

Furies, he thought illogically. Furies. That's what they were. But it wasn't me they were after, that's why I didn't feel scared of them, just scared *by* them.

Then this brief flare of knowledge deserted him and he remembered he was clutching Asha's hand with his own injured one and that there was, strictly speaking, no urgent reason for holding it now, so he dropped it, genuinely shocked to find blood and torn skin congealing on his purpling knuckles. They had stumbled to a halt by some boarded-up houses. Weeds grew out of windows. Circus posters, religious-nut posters were plastered everywhere. An American evangelist was coming to save the sinful. Bethany's mob, perhaps.

'Your face,' said Asha, pointing shakily as if she was afraid to touch. 'He hurt your face. You're going to have an awful black eye. I'm sorry. It was my fault.'

To his dismay she began to cry. 'I can't go home,' she wept. 'The aunts will know I'm upset and I can't possibly tell them about this. Do you think we could find a café or something – oh, no, I forgot I haven't got any money,' she almost wailed. 'Oh dear, I don't mean to be pathetic, I'm so sorry.'

Joss could see she was completely done-in.

Behind her on a boarded-up shop-window, a familiar poster. **Farewell Performance Apocalypse Café.** Some wit had scrawled across the blank and blazing faces of the Hoarsemen – *Greatest Show on Earth. Last Chance to be Saved.*

'I've got money,' said Joss quickly. 'Don't worry. We'll find somewhere.'

And they did as if they had conjured it up by needing it so badly. *Pinocchio's* said the painted sign. The puppet on the sign had evidently just told a lie because his nose was longer than a school ruler and a bird was perching impertinently on it. *Pinocchio's* looked tacky from the outside and proved incredibly smoky and greasy inside, but the woman behind the *cappuccino* machine politely passed no comment on Joss's swelling technicoloured face as he paid.

'No sugar,' said Asha quickly, covering her frothing mug with her hand.

'You should,' he told her. 'For shock.'

'If I had sugar,' she said. 'I might stop being shocked but I'd be sick instead.'

'No sugar then,' he agreed. 'I got one of these dire little packets of biscuits between us. I think they might be rather old but the Eccles cakes looked worse.'

They had to make themselves heard through the sound of drilling. Planks were propped against a wall and wood shavings lay around under a stepladder. A stocky man in overalls with dark hair sprouting rather creatively out of his ears (to compensate, Joss thought, for the minor loss on his head), stared fiercely at the wall, a rawlplug between his teeth, a pencil in his hand, as if imagining fantastic landscapes.

Asha shook her head at the biscuits. 'I couldn't,' she said, swallowing. 'This has been one of the worst days of my life. I couldn't begin to tell you.'

'Me too,' said Joss, then seeing her face fall, said rapidly, 'Oh I don't mean the fight and you and everything. It was before that. I made a total prat of myself. If those boys hadn't been annoying you – if I hadn't bumped into you and got myself beaten up, I'd have probably drowned myself in the canal anyway.'

Why had he told her that? What a stupid thing to do. Why should he trust her, a girl and a stranger? But when he looked into her wide grey eyes he knew everything about her; her honesty, her loneliness. Everything except why she was mixed up with a spooky box that generated its own Hammer horrors special effects. In this café, amongst the nonstop steam and gush of *cappuccino*, the sound of drilling, the lacklustre ebb and flow of hardup customers, it was as hard to believe in a box of furious elemental spirits as it was to believe in Tinkerbell.

There was just too much to think about. Minutes earlier he was sure he had lost everything worth living for. But now, through some wild intervention of the gods, he was in this charmed if sordid space, talking, actually talking to Asha. He had rescued her, he realised. He had held her hand and she hadn't objected. Despite the pain of his swollen eye and knuckle and the seething confusion of his brain, he was so happy he could hardly speak. Now she would tell him what haunted her and he could help her. He had saved her and in return she would save him. He was dragged back to the present with a stab of alarm to hear Asha speaking his thoughts aloud.

'We saved each other's lives then,' she was saying slowly. 'That's quite a responsibility.'

'Why?' he asked, disconcerted. 'What do you mean?'

The drilling started up again.

'Well, when you save a person's life they're honour-bound to do something extraordinary with the life you save, don't you think?'

Honour-bound? Did anyone really say things like that? He didn't like to laugh. She seemed so deadly serious.

'They weren't going to kill you,' said Joss. 'They were just – ' but he didn't feel comfortable with this and finished lamely, 'I'm sure they weren't.'

'And you weren't really going to throw yourself in the canal, either?'

'No, of course not,' he said uneasily. Then he found himself looking out through grimy windows at the sunlit street saying, 'But there's more than one way of killing yourself, isn't there?'

That's when it happened. The supernova explosion in his head as if the world shifted on its axis. Then everything became unbearably beautiful. It was that simple. One minute the shadowy world in which Joss had been stumbling around, mistaking it for the real thing. The next someone switched on the lights and he saw how blind he'd been. *Pinocchio's* was paradise.

There was a rusting white Sherpa van half on the pavement outside; the carpenter's presumably. The name on the van was MIDLANDS LIGHT AND POWER. This was not a name, Joss realised, but a poem, a song distilled into four words. Inches from the van, a fledgeling sparrow was taking a dust bath in the gutter but to Joss a phoenix could not have been more beautiful.

And Asha answered! She said, 'I know,' so quietly, he wouldn't normally have heard, but for this moment it was given to Joss to see everything, hear everything, know everything. It was the most extraordinary moment of his life.

Then Asha said in her normal voice, 'I will have a biscuit now if you don't mind,' and he shook himself free of enchantment. The world shed its phoenix colours. His rational mind put itself back into gear.

If he was going to help her, he had to know what he had let himself in for. He needed to know what was going on.

'You shouted something, when that thing — those things — flew out of your bag. It didn't sound English.'

She shook her head. 'I don't remember,' she said. 'But it wouldn't surprise me. Anything can happen around the Box. I think it's haunted.'

It was startling to hear her use that word. Then, even more extraordinarily she said, 'And I have to look after it, so I suppose I'm haunted too.'

'Could you tell me about the box?' he asked gently. 'I mean, just now, were there really those – '

'It really happened,' said Asha.' They were real. Or at least I saw them, too. But I don't know what it meant. It's never done that before. I mean, I can tell you what I know but you might not believe it and you might not be any wiser afterwards. Some of the time I think I'm going mad. Coping on my own has been – ' she didn't finish the sentence, but shook her head, tracing a finger around the rim of her mug for a second before she went on, 'But it feels all right to tell you. In fact, I'm sure it wants me to tell you. At least, I know *they* do. They *meant* you to be there to save me – ' She stopped, seeing his outraged face. 'I'm telling it wrong,' she said. 'I suppose I'd better start at the beginning.'

8 *Birds of Light*

Asha only meant to tell Joss about her birthday and the junk shop under the Dark Arches but the more she tried to explain, the further back she had to go to make him understand. And for some reason she needed Joss to understand how despairing she was, the day she and the Box found each other.

'I am fond of the aunts,' she said, 'but I wanted my mother and father. I wanted them to want me with them. For years I pretended to believe they wanted what was best for me, that they'd only sent me to England for my education, for my health, but suddenly I couldn't pretend any more. My father wanted a son you see and my mother shouldn't have had children at all. She was the youngest Gladwell, born years after the aunts. When my grandparents died, my mother was only twelve. Isabel and Madeleine were already in their twenties. My aunts gave up their lives to look after her as if it was the obvious thing to do, and brought her up by themselves as well as they could. She'd always been dear little Lucia, my grandfather's favourite so it was natural to go on spoiling her, putting her first. Maybe that's why she grew up never thinking of anyone but herself. When she was seventeen she met my father at a party in some country house, and ran off with him a week later. After that they lived abroad because of his work. I was born while they were in India. A few years after that they went to South America.'

'What does your dad do, exactly?' asked Joss. 'He sounds like something left over from the British Raj. Pith helmets and polo.'

'Oh, no,' said Asha. 'He does big projects for different Aid organisations. Stuff for the U.N. and charities trying to save the rainforests. That sort of thing.'

The café's owner picked her way through the wood shavings. 'More *cappuccino*?'

'I'm afraid I haven't – ' Joss began, embarrassed.

'On the house,' insisted the woman. 'Come in when you are rich and order a big *Pizza Margharita* and we'll call it quits.'

'Oh,' said Joss touched. 'Thank you.'

Over their second cups of *cappuccino* Asha sketched in the rest; her life at Wintergrove, the old house overflowing with memories of her grandparents' life overseas. By the time they returned to England, Isabel, Madeleine and their mother swore they would never leave its shores again.

'They wanted to put down roots and live ordinary lives. But my grandfather never settled. My mother's birth was the one compensation for what he'd lost. So he fed her on his dreams, never stopped telling her how much more magical her life could be if they could only take off again to some far-flung place . . . the aunts feel guilty about my mother. That's why they try so hard with me . . . I suppose they're scared I might turn out like her. But I won't. I'd rather die.'

Joss was hardly breathing, letting her tell her story in her own way, spinning threads between them, drawing them closer. He understood the despair that had sent her under the Dark Arches. He couldn't pretend to understand what happened there nor what it meant but that didn't seem to matter. After a while Joss found himself telling his own story, as if his was part of hers, as if it needed two voices to carry the secret song of it; the loss of his home and father, his smashed guitar, the impossible substitution of the blue guitar for his own.

'So you can't play it?'

'Not unless I get some amps from somewhere. Anyway, it was just a stupid fantasy. I'm useless.' And he told her about today's humiliation.

To his surprise she didn't respond with much interest. And when she spoke she didn't express the sympathy he secretly hoped for but asked a weird question.

'Isn't there anything unusual that happens around your guitar?' she asked. 'Like there is around the Box?'

'No,' he said, feeling wounded. He had taken a huge risk – sharing his worst-ever disaster and she didn't even notice. 'It's just a flash guitar. What could happen?'

'I don't know,' she said, looking down. 'It was only a feeling.'

Feelings again. Women's intuition. He had enough of this from Fran and Martha.

'The feeling's wrong then,' he said abruptly.

'I've got to go,' she said, gathering up her things. 'It's late. Thank you for being so kind.'

She was backing off, he saw, aware she'd offended him; like an anemone withdrawing delicate tendrils, beyond hurt and harm. If he didn't say something –

He fidgeted. 'I didn't mean – ' he said. 'If I sounded rude – '

'Of course not,' she said smiling her school smile, a smile so dazzling it blinded the onlooker, making her true self invisible. Then, (and he could see the struggle she had to risk another attempt), she said tentatively, 'It's just, well, they told me I'm supposed to work *with* the Box. I have to learn how it's meant to be used. I thought your guitar might be the same. That's all.'

'I don't think so,' he said, brushing aside that baffling 'they' again for now. 'Honestly. But it's a nice idea.' He smiled too. Quite a genuine smile that he prayed would not show the terror he felt, that he might lose her, having only just so astonishingly found her.

Then she did the most electrifying thing. She reached out and put her hand lightly over his own, the one that didn't hurt, fortunately. Asha McGillveray, the school Ice Maiden!

And she said, 'This is hard for me to explain. I know it sounds batty but the g – *they* told me they need us *both* to spend time with the Box. I don't know why but it isn't just to do with us, they said. It's the planet. The Box is important to it for some reason. I know it sounds loony but I don't think we can afford to risk being wrong just because it's embarrassing. Could we meet again, after school do you think, or at the weekend? Just go for a walk in the park or something?'

Seeing his incredulous expression, she said, 'No I don't know who or what *they* are. But they're terribly powerful and they came with the Box but everything that happens around the Box isn't them. Most of it is the Box itself, being haunted and trying to get itself free, and sometimes *they* try to talk to me, to help me, to make me more – useful to them, I suppose. I've only just admitted that to myself. They *do* know what the Box is for but they don't want to tell me more than I can cope with. Frankly I'm not sure I can cope with any of it.'

She took her hand away from his then and began to tuck escaping wisps carefully back into her plait. She was very faintly blushing he saw. As if she didn't make a habit of grabbing hold of boys' hands and asking them to go out with her, even on the pretext of saving the planet. She wouldn't have done it then, he thought, if she wasn't even more afraid of something else.

'Just a walk in the park,' she repeated stubbornly. 'If that would be all right.'

'Yes,' he said, reeling. 'Yes, yes that would be – fine.' His own face was stinging. He was glad he couldn't see what colour it was.

They left *Pinocchio's* together. The carpenter was piling his gear into his rusty Sherpa. He nodded as they passed. 'You'll want to get that eye fixed,' he said, 'that's going to be a shiner in the morning.' Then added surprisingly, 'Shall I look at it for you?'

Joss said with freezing politeness that he was perfectly fine. The man didn't seem in the least offended but called after them irrepressibly, 'Glad to see you got the girl anyway! She looks worth at least one black eye.'

God, adults! Had they no memory? Joss was furious. His life was always lurching into farce. But when he darted an agonised sideways look Asha looked perfectly at ease. Amused even.

And when they were safely out of earshot she said wickedly, 'Maybe he's doing a correspondence course in surgery.' It was the first time they had laughed together and it felt more intimate than when she had covered his hand with her own. He had to look away. She was a bright light, hurting his eyes.

He left her in the town centre, heading home as fast as he could. Fran would be worrying. He wasn't looking forward to explaining his eye. Fran thought her life was complicated enough. She'd think he'd done it on purpose. An adolescent cry for help.

Something else was worrying him. He hadn't told Asha the truth about the guitar. He hadn't lied intentionally, it was just that he didn't know the right words for the dreams; not the ones that came at night, which easily dissolved in daylight, but the daydreams, visions, almost. The figure so like Joss himself but not Joss. The boy who was both bright and dark, like the dark twin to the candle flame that comes when you stare at it very hard. This figure was at the heart of the music, came with the music as if he was both its source and its

74

expression and he burned with an energy so fierce, so inexhaustible, it scared Joss to death.

A haunted box, a haunted guitar; and he daren't think about either of them. But he didn't need to think about them, he thought. And he didn't need to think about Otis and his lousy backyard band either or the stark awfulness of his new home and how he wasn't wanted there.

As he let himself into the hall he heard laughter. His heart sank. Fran and Martha were irritating in their giggly moods. But today, to Joss who knew them too well for his own comfort, there was just the faintest air of performance about it. Oh, not the female charm routine, he thought.

Next moment he heard a light amused male voice say, 'What did you say you call the other cat?' and knew he had been right. Oh hell's teeth, it was old Embroidered Shoulder-bag from next door. Harry the house-husband himself.

'Not so much a cat as the family ghoul,' said Fran invisibly clattering crockery. 'When Ludwig's really pissed off with us he skulks on top of the wardrobe in Martha's room hoping we'll come and coax him down with sardines. He looks exactly like the Cheshire cat, perched up there, except if Ludwig vanished it wouldn't be his smile that got left behind but his glower.'

'Just like Joss really,' said Martha darkly.

'Oh, Marth,' scolded Fran, though her voice sounded tickled, Joss thought. 'Poor Joss is having a hard time at the moment.'

'Hi, everyone,' said poor Joss, timing his entrance, enormously enjoying his mother's confusion.

'Oh, Joss, this is Luke from next door – there's some tea in the – Joss, your eye! Your hand! Whatever happened to you!'

'Perhaps I should take Orchid home,' said Embroidered Shoulder-bag. 'She needs changing anyway. It looks as if you've got enough to deal with at the moment.'

Actually he didn't look as bad as Joss had thought, rather home-made and crumpled, but taller than Joss had fantasised (as though staying at home with babies automatically lopped inches off your height). He wasn't particularly long-haired either. Joss's dad would have had something to say about his baggy multicoloured jumper, though and the enormous jade green shoes at the fraying ends of his jeans.

'Nice to meet you, anyway, Joss,' said ESB, and bending he scooped up the infant who was lying cheerfully kicking on a blanket. It was funny. Joss needed to despise him but when he saw Luke pick up his mousy baby, and laugh into her little blotchy face as if she was the most beautiful child in the world, something happened in his stomach; a blaze of longing. Then it was gone, the furnace door slammed shut.

'You forgot your handbag,' he said coldly, indicating the object dangling over the back of Luke's chair. Luke grinned, winked and came back for it like a man. 'Couldn't manage without it,' he said. 'By the way, if you need arnica for the bruises, we've got plenty next door.'

Martha, her mouth hanging open in shock, clutched her squirming kitten so tightly, it squawked.

'Were you mugged?' she asked, her eyes huge.

'Don't be stupid,' he snarled back. 'You watch too much TV. It was a scrap, that's all. Nothing to fuss about.'

Then Fran bore down on him with something brown in a bottle and did something so sadistic he would have preferred to be struck by lightning.

That night, stiff, bruised, amazed, he lay for hours staring at stars through the slanting attic window. Each time he closed his eyes the dark-bright musician rose up before him, the guitar blazing in his hand, wanting to tell him something but Joss didn't want to hear it. His real life was hanging out of reach, like a coat he could not put on until he saw Asha again. At the weekend they were going for a walk, a walk in the park. Just the two of them.

When he dozed off finally, he was alone with Asha in a beautiful if neglected garden, walking in the shade of infinitely wise ancient trees and she was showing him how to make a bird, a living bird, saying delightedly, 'Look, it's easy. You just call light to you and it obeys, it wants to, it really does.'

He saw then that her hands were brimming with light, and out of this light the shapes of birds were forming, issuing effortlessly, playfully from her hand; winged, joyfully singing.

But his own attempts were hopeless; lumpy, without life, like a child's botched models in plasticine. Fatally afflicted with gravity they toppled sideways off his sweating palms and hit the ground like stones and he woke shouting and shaking to find he had only slept for two hours.

But it didn't matter. It didn't matter. The only thing that mattered from now on was this miracle, there was no other word for this event which had swept him up on the darkest day of his life, sailed off with him like Elijah on his blazing wheel of cloud. Hijacked by love. Headlong, hopelessly, head-over-heels in love.

9   *New Lamps for Old*

When Asha walked in, Isobel was beside herself with anxiety, her eyebrows arched so high they were invisible, her eyes themselves enormous.

'He actually phoned, he was so worried about you, Asha. And I had to tell him I'd *no idea* where you were. Have you any idea how dreadful I felt?'

'I'm sorry,' said Asha. 'I honestly couldn't help it. I had to stay late at school and then I lost my bus money. I'll phone and apologise to him for missing the lesson, I promise. Don't worry. I'll do it now, if you like.'

'It's not like you not to let us know,' said Madeleine, her thinner paler face drawn with anxiety. 'You're always so – '

'Good?' said Asha. 'Predictable? But that wasn't really me was it? Don't pretend you liked it. I've seen how you look . . . Oh look, *listen* – both of you. Please don't worry. I'm honestly not going to take up drugs or shoplifting. I just missed one piano lesson. It's not a very dreadful crime.'

'I know, dear. Of course not. It was just so out of character. We were afraid something terrible had happened to you. You hear such – ' Isobel wrung her hands, speechless with the horrors she'd been imagining for the last few hours and Asha flew to her, hugging her so fiercely that both aunts gazed at each other over her head in amazement. Asha had only ever hugged anyone to be polite, to please, even as a small child; just as, until today, she had been punctual and utterly reliable. What had come over her?

'Oh, Aunt Izzy, I'm fine,' Asha was saying. 'Do you need any help with supper? Then I'll do some homework for a bit until it's ready.'

When she got safely to her own room she was so tired she couldn't even take off her jacket, just sat on her bed, clutching her bag in her arms.

At least the Box seemed calm; neither brooding, lamenting nor lusting for the time being. Perhaps she could safely leave it at home in future after all.

'Haven't you even tried to open it yet?' Joss had asked, after they left the café. She wondered why, confused as she was, she had known from the start she must not.

It has to ripen, she thought, like an apple. If you pull an apple off the tree before it's ready you get ill, eating it. Only it wouldn't just be me that suffered. She knew that too. She pictured the snake holding the glowing Box in its coils and how it had seemed to warn her. A dark price, the woman had said. It had all happened before of course and the whole earth had paid a dark price that time. Was paying it still. But now perhaps, just perhaps, it could happen differently. That was why the goddesses were watching over it so carefully, like a precious egg getting ready to hatch. That was why they were trying to teach her what she needed to know, so she would be strong enough, wise enough, when the time came.

What had Joss really seen when it burst out of her bag? Even then the Box had not actually opened. What had come out had issued *through* it like ghostly vapour. Her tormentors had seen something terrifying she knew but Joss, too, had staggered back into the bushes, shocked and pale and she had felt sad and sorry for him.

She had wanted him to share her vision: the star-like beauty of them, flaming in the air. Star people flown to earth. Remembering now, she felt a burning place in her own heart, as if one of them had left a searing fingerprint of light there, a distant memory of where she had once lived long ago and might one day return. Homesickness, she thought. But a homesickness that made her happy; gave her hope.

Hope again.

Is that why Valli named me? To keep hope alive even when it seems insane?

She had thought it a bad joke, she remembered, that day in the Dark Arches. Now she wasn't sure of anything. Meeting Joss had changed absolutely everything.

She liked Joss. She liked him very much. She liked his eyes, which were dark and sad, and his hands which were thin and quick with nervous electricity. A musician, she would swear, though he hadn't mentioned music, not real music anyway, just some backyard rock group he thought he wasn't good enough to join.

But it had been so embarrassing, practically forcing a promise out of him to see her again. The goddesses were relentless about it, coarse in fact, laughing like celestial drains at her discomfort. *Look dear girl, just do it. Some girls would be glad. Is it so hard!*

Hard? She blushed to think of it. What must he have thought of her? 'Just don't ask me to wear leopard-skin minis like Tamar Tetley,' she warned, sensing Beauty assessing the contents of Asha's wardrobe for Saturday's walk in the park and finding it severely wanting. 'Even goddesses can push their luck.'

Waves of appreciation shimmered through her room. If she soft-focussed her eyes it was visible as a tender blue-green fluorescence, like the haze in a bluebell wood. Bewilderingly, they liked her best when she misbehaved, when she was stubborn. She had never been rewarded for fighting back before.

She drew the Box slowly out of her bag, hardly daring to look, in case the canal water had damaged it after all.

Now you can start work, said the one she thought of as the Motherly One. Like all of them she didn't stay the same for long so sometimes she was younger than the others, but always a presence so loving Asha wished she could crawl into her lap and sleep, bathed in that compassionate blue-green haze, lapped in a waking dream, the blissful sensation of someone stroking her hair; perhaps she'd never have to grow up, be alone again . . . But they were shaking her. There was no time, no time. The Wise One was speaking. The Winged One. She had owl eyes, Asha thought, fierce owl eyes, and there was an impersonal feel to her, as if she flew over high cold places and saw Time spread out in all its ebb and flow, what had happened and what might be to come.

Don't worry, tiredness soon goes with this kind of work. Remember the breathing we taught you, the first time . . . ? Well now we're going to take it further . . .

'But why are you going out, why?' Martha dragged the cushion from under her jumper where she had squashed it in an improbable bulge, gave up trying to imagine what she would look like if she should ever be pregnant, and clenched her fists. It was Saturday and Joss was going to meet Asha.

'To see a friend.'

'But you haven't got any friends,' yelled Martha. 'Anyway, it's not fair if you go out. I'll be all on my own until Mum finishes.'

He was about to yell back when he realised there was genuine panic in her eyes. 'You'll be all right,' he tried to soothe. 'Make a cake, then we can share it when I come back.'

Martha's cakes were famous. She'd been making them without recipes since she was seven.

'There was a spider,' she said. 'In the kitchen. I can't go in while that spider's in there.' Her face was stark with tragedy. It was Martha's secret shame that she lost all control at the mere thought of spiders.

'But that was this morning, Marth. It could be anywhere by now. I'm not spending all day tracking it down. Spiders are part of life. Better get used to them.'

Before his eyes his sister became Medusa whose scowl shrivelled heroes by the boatload, her eyes blank black tunnels. Against his will he found himself trying to placate her.

'What about your knitting –'

Not having the right needles she and Naomi had improvised with one thick and one thin, and wool unravelled from a jumper. By now Martha had turned out loopy yellow miles of it.

'It's gone wrong. I need someone to pick up the dropped bits. Naomi didn't show me how.'

Thwarted in his attempts to comfort Martha, Joss now found he wanted to hit her extremely hard and wisely left. But he felt guilty leaving her in that cheerless house with a tarantula at large, miles of doomed yellow knitting forming round her ankles.

He forgot her though as soon as he reached the park gates. Asha was waiting by the pond. She looked different. Softer, warmer. Hardly Ice Maidenish at all.

'It's changed again,' she said. 'I couldn't tell you at school. Come and look.'

They found a bench, screened by willows and she opened her bag so he could peer into it. He frowned, feeling stupid. 'I can't tell. I didn't see it properly before.'

'It looks just the same,' she said. 'But it *feels* different. It's not so heavy. It weighed a ton before and in the beginning it made me feel cold inside just being near it. But it's not that. Put your hands around it here, inside the bag, and shut your eyes.'

He did as she said. 'Hey,' he said, backing off.

'No, it's all right, I got pictures in my head too. What can you see?'

'Er,' he said, not wanting to say. It made it worse that he knew he was blushing violently.

She sighed. 'This is going to be impossible if you're going to be so proper. This is the Nineteen Nineties, you know.'

'All right,' he said touchily to cover his panic. It had shaken him to see the garden of his dream even if the figures in it were from a dream far older than his own. 'I can see a man and a woman in a very overgrown garden. They haven't got a stitch on and they seem extremely friendly to me.'

His insides were melting with the conflicting desires to look again yet deny the compelling power of what he had seen.

They were so bloody happy. So beautiful; their bodies flecked golden in the drowsy sunlight that scattered through the canopy of flowering creepers, as if they'd been dusted with pollen. It was nothing like the photos Bernie brought to school. It was peaceful. It made him want to weep with longing. It made him want to run a mile.

'Keep looking, it's a story.'

'I bet,' he said, still scarlet. 'Are you sure the park is the best place for this?'

Like a film flickering across his inward eye it ran for about five minutes, paused and began all over again. Joss rubbed his eyes, letting them adjust before he opened them fully into the afternoon light, struggling back from a great distance.

Twin boys in identical anoraks and thick spectacles cycled past.

'No honestly, Simon,' chirruped one, 'If you threw up now and stuck a piece of litmus paper in it, what colour would it turn?'

Joss caught Asha's eye and they burst out laughing. She looked amazing when she laughed. But it was hard to look at her for long after what the Box had showed him.

'Okay I've seen the story,' he said, striving to be cool. 'The Paradise Peep-show. Nicely directed. Downbeat ending.'

'It's remembering,' said Asha. 'Trying to make sense of where it all went wrong.'

'But that isn't history,' he gestured towards the Box still half-hidden in her bag. 'It's a fairy story, a myth. Not even vicars believe *that* any more.'

'It's not like that,' said Asha. 'The g– *They've* been trying to explain it to me. Listen, listen –,' she leaned forward so intimately that for a dizzy moment he thought she was going to seize his hand again. 'Myths are the doorways truths come through. Different times, different truths. When myths are new they are like – new suns, so bright and blazing everyone sees the world new by the light of them. There's a great burst of energy. A whole new lease of life. New myth. New world.'

Joss was silent, remembering the rusty van, the sparrow quivering its wings in the dust, how, for one shining moment, he had seen through the eyes of a god. And he wondered if it would be okay to take hold of *her* hand.

'But as time goes on, truths wear out or get half-forgotten or distorted and the world – the old world, Joss, wears out *with* them. Isn't that what's happening now? Doesn't everyone secretly believe everything is winding down? Petrol, food, ozone. The planet's even running out of room – But isn't it really our imagination that's running out, our vision, – our – our joy?'

Asha's imagination didn't seem to be running out, he thought, only away with her. She was so incandescent with her theory you could have lit the street by her.

'New lamps for old,' he said, sing-song. 'Change your story, change the world. Rewind the video. Adam and Eve scuttle backwards into paradise. Fig leaves stick themselves back on the tree. Fallen angel gets sucked back up into heaven. Woosh. Everybody loves everybody else. Taraa! War and famine disappear overnight.' He shook his head. 'You market the computer game and I'll buy the tee-shirt if you want but it's not real, Asha, what you're saying. What about science? What about history? Are you going to throw all that out of the window for this – tosh?'

Asha didn't answer. She didn't look offended or disappointed. In fact she looked unnervingly detached and intent as if she was listening.

'What?' he said edgily. 'What is it?'

'They just said to leave it for a while. You're not ready.'

'Oh,' he said. 'Did they, now?'

'They said we need to take our time. Spend a few minutes every day to start with, you and me, working with the Box. That's it for today. Just being together with it will help, they said. It needs us you see, they think it needs the combined energies of the two of us, before it can make its next big change. They said just forget about it for the rest of today. We can do whatever we like.'

They were silent for some moments after she relayed this message from beyond. He felt obscurely angry. He supposed he should be glad of any excuse to spend time with Asha but he didn't like the ground rules. To begin with it would have been nice to know who or what was setting them. He knew he had seen something by the canal, that Hammer horrors stunt, but that wasn't enough to base anything on. He wasn't sure they weren't both the victims of some bizarre delusion. Joss was hurt too. He wanted her to want to be with him, to need him, Joss Emerson, not as her companion on some supernatural planet-saving mission, but for himself.

'Well what do you want to do, then?' he asked when the silence had grown long enough to make his palms perspire.

'Go home with you to meet your mum and your sister,' she said cheerfully. 'Could we do that? I'd love it.'

This had not been at all what Joss had in mind but if he was honest he hadn't given much thought to how they'd actually spend their time together. Apart from a few fantasies, that is, and he had known they were fantasies even at the time. The truth was he had looked forward quite desperately to his Saturday with Asha, but now it was here he felt empty and annoyed and had perversely begun to wish it was over almost as soon as it began. What had he imagined for heaven's sake? Well certainly not being in a haunted threesome with the box. And not taking her back home to be given the once-over by hawk-eyed Fran and Martha either.

He sighed. The responsibility for making the afternoon a success weighed on him like a cement overcoat. Her idea was as good as any, he supposed. 'I warn you, Martha will be unbearable. She usually is. But I suppose you might like the kittens.'

'You've got kittens!' She beamed like a little kid. She almost skipped a step.

'There's four. Three weeks old. The one Martha likes best is a thug already. He's got enormous back feet like Bugs Bunny.'

'I wish the aunts would let me have a kitten,' Asha mourned.

'I'd rather show you our old house,' he said as they set off. 'This one's a slum, the perfect incentive to be a teenage runaway . . .'

When he opened the front door into the hot vanilla smell of cake baking, Martha was blundering uncertainly round the living-room with her drippy friend, Nicola. Both had their eyes screwed shut, their hands outstretched like sleepwalkers.

'We were trying to imagine what it's like to be blind,' said Martha sheepishly. She was staggeringly well-behaved when she saw who had come in with him. She didn't giggle or even stare but said 'hallo' perfectly normally when he introduced her.

'I can't keep up with Martha. She was pregnant this morning,' Joss grumbled. 'Only with a cushion,' he explained hurriedly.

Drippy Nicola was soon packed off home. Martha was far too intrigued by Asha to want to share her.

Asha's favourite kitten was the tabby.

'Has he got a name?' she asked.

Martha shook her head. 'Not one that sticks. I called him Harriet until we found out he was a boy!' She roared with laughter at the very idea of a boy called Harriet.

'His markings are beautiful. His face is like a sweet little mask, like a monkey's face. And he looks so wicked. He could be Hanuman, the Indian monkey god, full of tricks.'

'Hanny for short,' said Martha, charmed.

'Highly mythological,' said Joss.

'Make some tea, Joss,' said Martha. 'The cake's ready. We can eat it hot. It rots your guts but it tastes mega. I want Asha to help me name these two. She's brilliant at names.'

By the time he came back from the kitchen, the remaining kittens had satisfactory names and Fran was home, shoes thrown off, feet tucked underneath her in her favourite armchair, looking ten years old in her working clothes and rather woebegone.

'Oh I could kill for a cup of tea, Joss. Cake as well! I sneaked off early. I wanted to get back before the man came.'

'Fran's man,' Martha smirked.

'To start sorting this house out,' explained Fran. 'If it's not beyond the powers of mortal man, that is.' She sighed, then said, 'Oh, don't take any notice. When I'm tired I think buying this house was a horrendous mistake. Then after a night's sleep I see its possibilities again.'

As Joss might have guessed, Fran and Asha took to each other at once. After tea and cake Asha was borne off to see if she could tempt Ludwig down from Martha's wardrobe where he was doing his vulture impersonation, and he didn't snarl or turn his back or anything; just sniffed her hand, musingly, scanning it for cake crumbs. Then Asha was given a tour of the house, and implored to say what she thought could be done with it. Fran always asked people for sensible advice and then wound up doing something totally bizarre she had thought up all by herself, Joss thought. Asha was shown a skirt Fran had bought in a sale, and even asked if Fran should henna her hair again.

'I helped last time,' said Martha with relish. 'It's green and gritty and you slap it on like mud. Mum looked like a swamp monster and she had to sit on the loo with clingfilm on her head for *hours*. But she said it didn't come out the right red.'

'And my grey bits went yellow,' mourned Fran. 'I'd forgotten that. Perhaps it'd be more dignified to go grey.'

Asha had to go. 'I didn't mean to stay so long.'

'Oh stay for supper, why don't you, I always cook far too much.'

'Well –' said Asha wistfully.

Joss, who had been close to passing out with boredom, struggled out of his coma and tried to look pleased. 'Yes,' he said. 'Stay. Why don't you? We'd like you to.'

'No,' she decided. 'Better not. I haven't let the aunts know. I'll come another time if I may.'

No sooner had she decided to leave than Joss felt an illogical pang. He wanted to keep her with him. He needed to know how soon he could see her again, not as a part of this cosmic mission crap, but because she was so lovely. Because it was amazing that he, Joss Emerson, had the chance to go out with her when she had turned down every other male at school. He couldn't understand why he had been so jealous and grouchy. As if Martha and Fran had stolen her from him. When it was only because of Joss she had come in the first place. It was Joss she liked. She was only being friendly with them because she liked him. She was only being polite.

He had to do something, say something that would show her beyond doubt that he cared for her.

'She could have one of the kittens, couldn't she?' he blurted. 'When they're old enough. She could have one.'

'Hanuman the monkey cat,' shrieked Martha. 'You can have Hanny, Asha.'

'I'd love to,' said Asha. 'But I'll have to ask the aunts.'

'I'll walk back with you,' Joss said, at the door, as she put on her jacket, freeing her long hair from under the collar in a fluid gesture that made him go weak at the knees.

'No, I'll be fine,' she said. She was so contained and calm. She didn't need him at all.

'I want to see you again,' he said. His voice cracked with urgency. He couldn't help himself.

'Come to tea,' she said. 'Come to tea tomorrow. We've got to meet every day, remember. And you can meet the aunts.'

I meant alone, he thought. Why must she involve other people all the time? Mothers, sisters, aunts.

'Your mother is lovely,' she said. 'So young! And Martha. Martha's amazing. It must be nice to have a proper family. I often imagine what it must be like to be in a family.'

'Over-rated,' he said. 'I would say. Definitely over-rated. Anyway it feels all lopsided now we don't live with Dad. It isn't a proper family at all any more.'

She shocked him again then. Just reached up and kissed him lightly right beside his mouth as if it was the most natural thing in the world. As if they were lovers already.

'New lamps for old, Joss,' she said. 'That's all it is, you know. Not better or worse. Only new and strange.'

He wasn't listening. He wanted to catch hold of her and kiss her back but he didn't dare.

Joss heard it then, faintly at first, then louder and nearer, and he could see Asha heard it too. Instinctively they both moved into the shadow of the doorway.

There were about a dozen of them, heading towards the town; dressed in black, skull earrings dancing; half singing, half chanting hypnotically, over and over, 'Omega sound. Omega sound'. Ragged dull voices, blank pale faces. Joss felt his throat ache watching them go. Even when they were out of sight, their despair still lingered like a toxic cloud, clinging wherever it touched.

'Omega sound?' he repeated.

'It's the concert tonight, remember,' said Asha. 'That's their latest record. I only know because of Gunny.

'Omega sound, Omega sound,
Every kid's a walking wound.
Earth your poisoned burial ground . . .

'He was singing it all through Art. I put in less Omegas. There are actually a lot more. They repeat it like a mantra. It made me feel peculiar, and not just because he can't sing in tune. There was something dark about it. Not rich and dark. Dark and empty like a grave waiting for a corpse. It reminded me of when the Box was leaking nightmares into my room all night. I can't explain it very well, Joss, but I knew *I mustn't* listen to it – I had this feeling that if I did the sound had the power to sort of – paralyse me. As if it's saying it's no use, it's no use, don't even try to fight the awfulness. Like the way you're supposed to feel when you lie down in the snow to die. It's not that it's an ugly sound, there's actually a sort of terrible sweetness to it that seems to want to wrap itself around you. I sang a bit of the Brahms Requiem in my head to immunise myself. I saw some of their posters, the Hoarsemen, and I thought they looked like fallen angels. Can you believe Bethany's going? With Carl? If her parents find out they'll go beserk.'

Other people again. What did he care what boring Bethany did with that pseud Carl. He didn't want her to keep talking about other people. He wanted her to kiss him again in that heartstopping natural way and talk to him and be kind only to him always.

He watched Asha till she was out of sight and stared at the empty street for a little longer, but before he could close the door a rusting white Sherpa with a depressingly familiar legend on its side MIDLANDS LIGHT AND POWER roared up and braked violently outside the house.

'Oh, no,' said Joss. 'I don't deserve this.'

'Eye's healing nicely then,' said the driver, also depressingly familiar, leaning out of the window, grinning broadly. 'What it is to be young and healthy! Is this your house? Would your mother be Frances Emerson, by any chance? I've come to see her about doing some alterations.'

10   *Prophecies and Pyramids*

'Sorry I couldn't come,' said Joss grabbing Asha by the sleeve, as she walked past in the early morning crowd, without seeing him. 'It was Fran's fault, she'd fixed up for us to have supper with the people next door and hadn't bothered to tell me.'

'That's okay,' said Asha. 'You phoned. Look I can't stop, Joss, I've got Art. Perhaps we could meet at lunchtime. I brought the Box in case. Oh I forgot to ask – did you have a nice time?'

She was dancing backwards, the red and gold in her hair catching fire in the sharp September light, laughing over the heads of the first years.

'Brilliant,' said Joss. 'Fantastic. Liana gave us a recital of *London's Burning* on her recorder.'

'I can't hear you,' she yelled.

'It doesn't matter,' he said, not even bothering to raise his voice.

She vanished into the crowd and Joss too went moodily into school.

The Box. Whoopee.

She had changed, he thought. In a matter of days she had lost the haunted air that had drawn him to her in the first place; made him want to protect her, help her, sure she was a loner like him. But now she glowed with life and confidence. Was that anything to do with him? He wished he could even half-believe it, because what it felt like was that as fast as he got close to Asha she took a step away into some bewildering landscape where he couldn't, daren't follow.

He was distracted by a moan of fury and the spectacle of a boy banging his head on the cloakroom wall. 'Just because I didn't have the money!' he was yelling. 'I could kill myself. The best thing, the only thing that ever happened around here and I missed it.'

He was only slightly faking it, Joss thought. The frustration was genuine enough. A fifth-year girl, wearing some kind of black gauze bedspread, comforted him. 'They'll come again, Alan,' she said with a strange enigmatic tenderness. 'And that will be the all-time greatest show on earth. You only missed the beginning, you know. They've promised we'll all be there together at the end.' Her face shone with something Joss might have mistaken for ecstasy if she wasn't so pale, so tired, so *emptied out*, he thought.

'What exactly did he miss?' asked Joss quietly as an unusually quiet Tamar brushed past him. 'Do you know? Did you go?'

'You're kidding,' said Tamar. 'I've heard their songs. I don't like what they do or who they are. That last one – ' she shuddered. 'No thanks! But I heard about it on the grapevine. If half of it was true, it was weird enough.'

'Like what?'

Tamar had shadows under her eyes, he noticed and she'd left the nose-jewel out today. Dressed in a subdued sweatshirt and jeans she looked almost ordinary. The sight was strangely shocking.

'They made things happen,' she said. 'Impossible things. And they – promised things, to people, people who . . . believe in them.' She could hardly drag the words out.

'Believe – in the Hoarsemen? Have I missed something? Since when have they been a religion?'

'Not just the Hoarsemen,' said Tamar wearily. 'Look I don't want to talk just now. I've got enough on my mind, Joss. Some other time, okay.'

She trudged off leaving Joss uneasily looking around him. A hell of a lot more kids were dressed in black this morning, he realised; floating, flimsy black. Funny hair too, sleeked back otterlike so it hardly looked like hair at all. Had they been wearing those medallions before? They must be souvenirs of the concert, a rip-off probably, a PR stunt; those fallen angel look-alikes blazing out from mass produced lockets of red and black.

His uneasiness grew as the morning went on. What had happened to everyone? Not everyone, but every fifth or sixth person he ran into. It wasn't just that they had the same hair styles, the same clothes, the same tacky medallions, they were wearing the same expression, dazzled somehow, as if they'd all been gazing too long into some fierce light source.

'As if they were dreaming the same dream,' Asha said later.

Joss couldn't believe it when he saw Ghoul. Even his funereal mug was transformed; it might have been blissful if it hadn't been so yearning; the pale eyes slightly out of focus as if they were still looking at something so beautiful they couldn't bear to tear themselves away.

'Good concert was it?' said Joss, to cover his discomfort.

'Yes,' said Ghoul fervently. 'You should have been there. It's only if you're with them you can really know.'

'Yeah, you have to be in the actual presence,' agreed Gunny, nodding his skull. 'Some things you can't talk about, right, Joss? So we won't even try. But it was beautiful. Absolutely beautiful. And one day they'll come again and everyone will know what we know. They promised.' Then he grinned a crazy blinded grin and corrected himself, 'Not promised, prophesied. That's what their first LP's going to be called, you see. *Prophecy.*'

Joss mumbled that that was nice and got away as fast as he could to Computer Studies. The back of his neck was creeping and he didn't want to know why.

Nor did he get time to think about it because something else had happened the night of the Hoarsemen's farewell performance. By lunchtime it was all over school. Bethany Blessed had disappeared. She hadn't been seen since Saturday night. The police came into school in the afternoon asking questions but no-one seemed to know anything. Carl Lieberman had flown back to the States with his family.

'Where would she go?' asked Asha when Joss met her in the music room. 'She doesn't have any friends, at least I don't think so. What can have happened to her?'

He shrugged. 'Happens all the time. Runaways. Sign of the times. Like dumping dogs beside the motorway.'

'I feel awful,' said Asha. 'She was always trying to make friends with me.'

'She seemed very boring,' said Joss.

Asha shook her head. 'She was very scared. Very lonely.

Not boring. Something's really wrong, you know.'

She practised part of a scale one-handed and then stopped. 'Have you seen that thing they're drawing?'

'What do you mean? Who?'

He didn't want to hear this. He wanted her to make him feel better not worse.

'Since the concert. That sign. I thought it looked like lots of little linked pyramids with antennae, quite complicated. Gunny was doodling it. Then I saw a girl tracing it on a table in spilled coffee at break. They had this sad little smile on their faces while they were doing it. As if they were hypnotised. I hate it.'

Joss couldn't stand the way she kept talking about things that scared him, the way she kept talking about people who didn't interest him. The two of them, that's what he cared about. Frankly he wouldn't care if a tidal wave came racing inland and swept the rest away tomorrow. And he couldn't stand the way she was still so matter of fact as if nothing had happened. Didn't she care at all?

Suddenly he was so desperate that without knowing he was going to he blurted out, 'Why did you kiss me, Asha? Didn't you mean it?'

Asha's hands were motionless on the keys. He couldn't read her expression but he thought it might be dangerous.

'Did I *mean* it?'

'Were you only – ' He couldn't say it. 'Sorry, I don't know what I'm saying,' he said. He looked away. He couldn't bear her to look at him.

'No I wasn't *only*,' she said. 'I can't explain it, Joss, I didn't plan it, you know. It was the look on your face. That's all. You looked lost. I suppose I just wanted to – well I just *wanted* to. But if I'd known you were going to be so upset – '

'Not upset,' he said quickly. 'Just muddled. I didn't want there to be a mistake.'

He had turned back to her now. He could hardly breathe.

'What kind of mistake?'

'If – if I kissed you back.'

She started to say, 'Oh I see,' but never finished. He didn't grab her the way they did in films, to shut her up. Nothing so pushy. It was just that when she saw his expression she went very quiet and in that thickening silence the distance between their faces seemed to narrow without anyone actually moving.

It wasn't an expert kiss but he didn't make a total fool of himself either, didn't bang her nose or catch her hair on his wristwatch. It was a strange feeling, doing what he had wanted to do since he first saw her. But strangest of all was the bewildering ache inside straight afterwards that told him he hadn't solved a single thing.

'Are you sure I was supposed to do that?' Asha asked the goddesses when she was alone in her room.

Didn't you enjoy it?

The Bossy One, of course. Tamar Tetley writ large, not in her air-terminus gear today, but something vaguely Amazon and definitely indecent, involving a leather kilt, a great deal of thonging and a couple of glittering knives ready for action.

'That's not what I meant,' said Asha already feeling stupid as she always did with this goddess. 'I like Joss. I more than like him. But he seems to need me in some way, not just, well, *like* me, but *need* me and it scares me – as if he thinks I can save him or something. Maybe I used to feel like that, wanting someone to rescue me. But since, since we – whatever this is we do with the Box – I feel different, stronger. And I know you said he's important but what if he gets hurt? I don't want to use him, you know. I don't care how important it is. You shouldn't use people.'

The Motherly One manifested the way she usually did at these times, not physically exactly, but on the borders of the physical and did a brisk soothing something that intensified the rippling blue-green haze around Asha. She felt herself calm down immediately.

Just believe us. It is necessary. You aren't using him in the sense you mean. We are teaching you and you are teaching him. Everything is working perfectly. The Box is getting ready to change again. Can't you tell?

This was Beauty, her beauty not of the film star kind, but freer, wilder. Beauty was lovely to please no-one but herself and her joy shone out infectiously like an apple tree breaking into blossom.

'Are you sure?' Asha passed her hands across the glowing wood and sniffed her fingers for the sweet, disturbing muskiness. 'It doesn't feel tingly and restless like it did last time.'

That's because it's a gentler, more natural change. The last changes would once have taken – maybe decades, but matters are too urgent to work on that scale any longer. Everything is speeding up. From our region the speed of change is actually visible. Can't you tell? You're changing too. These last days you have changed beyond recognition.

'I think so,' said Asha. 'Yes, I know I am. I don't worry all the time. I don't feel so awful when I'm with people.' She laughed. 'I don't even absolutely hate Tamar Tetley any more.' She was silent, thinking of other surprising, not unwelcome changes, and asked anxiously, 'And it's all right about Joss? He won't be hurt?'

It was the Wise One who answered her, the Winged One.

He may be hurt, was the unemotional reply. *But that isn't your affair. You can't do his learning for him. Only your own. Speaking of which ...*

'I know, I know,' said Asha and drawing a deep breath she began again to practise the latest skill the goddesses had taught her.

And so Joss and Asha were a couple.

And somehow, since the kiss in the music room, everyone knew it without being told. Unless Tamar Tetley had spread it around. She was famous for knowing everyone's business by some kind of uncanny osmosis. But Joss, who couldn't believe it himself, was astonished how naturally everyone else at school accepted it. He could only think it didn't loom that large alongside the disappearance of Bethany Blessed and the mushrooming phenomenon of the Hoarsemen.

His next hurdle was going to meet the aunts. The very thought made him feel haunted. But when he turned up outside the imposing front door of Wintergrove in his cleanest jeans and newest sweatshirt, Isobel and Madeleine's panic was so endearingly obvious, he quite forgot his own, helping Asha put them at their ease. He was shown round the old house and treated to the stories of its treasures for half an hour or so, prompted by Asha when necessary. ('Go on, Aunt Maddy, tell him about the Maharani's carving and what the Buddhist monk said.') Then as the weather was still scorching they had tea in the garden, so at least he didn't have to worry too much about crumbs and tablecloths. To his surprise, Aunt Izzy asked what he thought about the Greenhouse Effect, then listened with her head on one side, murmuring agreement while he explained as simply as he knew how. Asha knew her aunt's bird-like super-attentive expression meant she was thinking of something else entirely but didn't give her away. The aunts had been trained long ago to coax men for their opinions on all serious issues. Serious, to the aunts, usually meant boringly incomprehensible.

'But what do I know about plumbing?' spluttered Joss when they were on their own.

Asha had her head under a cushion, apparently weeping. 'You're male,' she shrieked at last. 'You are the pinnacle of God's creation. You were *born* knowing about science, technology, the insides of cars and – and blocked lavatories.'

'I'm going to tickle you until you stop being so disrespectful,' he warned, flexing his fingers.

'It was just when Aunt Maddy took you into the downstairs cloakroom,' Asha wailed. 'Your expression! Don't tickle me Joss – it's my worst thing! I've recovered, truly. Oh, poor Maddy. Oh you were good not to laugh right in her face.'

'I like her,' said Joss showing her he had put both hands unthreateningly behind his back. 'I like them both. They're brilliant. I wish they were my aunts. Before I go I'll give them Mike Zamirski's phone number.'

'Mike – ?'

' "Fran's man" – remember, MIDLANDS LIGHT AND POWER? He's knocking our kitchen to pieces at the moment but everyone tells Fran he's really reliable and won't rip anyone off.'

'There you are, you see,' said Asha wickedly. 'The aunts' touching faith was justified. Men *know* these things!'

'That does it,' said Joss. 'No mercy! Absolutely no mercy!'

And so the weeks settled into a familiar rhythm. Later Joss thought they had a painfully happy quality; walking the streets of the dull little town, talking the hours away, in the park, in *Pinocchio's*, in Fran's kitchen. It was a golden time all right, like living inside a delicate golden bubble. Yet a shadow hung over their happiness from that first day. Secretly, he knew it was too magical to last.

The Hoarsemen, now in London, brought out a new single called *Kaos* and appeared on TV for the first time. Joss missed it but everyone was talking about it at school. The video was wild, apparently. Racing time-lapse storm clouds inter-cut with scenes of children dying of hunger, tiny blank-faced babies in rows and rows of cots in a nightmare orphanage in Eastern Europe somewhere. The kids of one Islamic country dressing up to get themselves killed by the kids of another Islamic country. Homeless twelve-year-olds in Birmingham and London. Gunny insisted the lyrics were written in a kind of code but only the people who'd been to the concerts could understand. He said it wasn't the same if you saw them on Top of the Pops. You had to be in the presence to know.

No one knew what had happened to Bethany Blessed.

'It's as if the ground swallowed her.' Asha said to Tamar one day at lunch-time. But Tamar, whose spirits had not yet resumed their old cauldron bubble and boil, only piled another veggy burger on her plate and said tersely that sometimes people disappeared for their own reasons and it might be best to let them.

Joss was immune to all of this. He was still wrapped in his frail golden bubble, trying furiously not to think about what would happen when it burst. Everything outside the bubble was remote, unreal.

At the house in Chilkwell Street, Mike Zamirski put in a damp course, dug up the old kitchen floor and laid a new one. Then he put in cheap but convincing-looking pine kitchen cupboards and Fran whizzed up curtains on an ancient sewing machine she borrowed from Naomi. Fran felt kinder towards her new home since she had discovered (from Naomi of course) that the name Chilkwell referred to an ancient chalk well, reputed to have healing powers. 'Just think – it could be in our garden!' Martha spent an entire Saturday searching for it but all she came up with was some old chicken wire and boring broken crockery. Like Fran, Martha was happiest when she had a myth between her teeth, thought Joss; the sillier the better.

Luke and Naomi gave Fran a large pear-shaped crystal as a housewarming present. Joss was relieved when his mother hung it in the kitchen window where no one but the milkman could see it.

Sometimes Joss thought the new house might actually be all right; one day. But he wished his father would write. He wrote himself once or twice. Fran said Richard was probably too busy to write back. 'I expect he'll write when he's more settled,' she said. 'It's been a big change for him, too.'

Once Joss picked up the phone and dialled his old number, but crashed the receiver down as soon as it rang. It shook him, imagining it ringing in that too-familiar house. For a moment he had been scared a ghostly Joss would answer. The Joss who stayed home.

The scorching September became a stifling October. The leaves hung wilting, uneasily yellow-green until freak hurricanes turned the lot black and sodden, then brought them down in droves to plaster roads and roofs like some sinister plague.

After that it rained for weeks. Mike Zamirski had to interrupt work at Chilkwell Street to do emergency repairs elsewhere.

'I've never seen storms like it,' he said when he finally turned up one day, accepting the tea Martha had made for him. 'Out of my tool bag, you nosy cat, you.' He scooped the kitten out and dumped it casually on his own shoulder where it balanced for a moment, tail waving wildly, before it settled on its haunches, shoving its nose into his hairy ear, purring.

'Beano likes you,' said Martha, who liked Mike too because he made her laugh and let her help so long as she did what she was told.

To no-one's surprise Martha had got her way and

persuaded Fran to let her keep the hooligan kitten. As the aunts nervously agreed to let Hanuman live at Wintergrove, only two of Evie's children had to be found homes elsewhere.

And whenever it was possible, after school, Joss and Asha found time to 'work with the Box'. This, like the ritual visit to the aunts, was at Asha's insistence so, on the grounds that he loved Asha and wanted her to love him in return, Joss tolerated it. He didn't honestly know how he felt about it. He couldn't seriously share her romantic conviction that they were working together to Save the Planet.

Sometimes he believed the things Asha said she was learning. Sometimes he even believed he was learning them, too. The exercises were rather fanciful but he felt less restless afterwards as if he had been connected for a brief while to something. Connected to what exactly he didn't know. On those days he was spared his monotonously regular nightmares about the blue guitar, still wrapped in its blanket under his bed, still unused, unplayed. But his mind veered away from making sense of that. He told himself that all he cared about was being with Asha, and that what they did with the Box was an enjoyable game, a game of pretend. Asha insisted the Box was in the process of changing again because of the time they spent 'working' together and that the goddesses (her name for a meddlesome bunch of Cosmic Aunties), were 'pleased' with them both.

The Box looked the same as it always had to him. He had never seen it in its gargoyle incarnation. His own vision of the Furies, vengefully swarming above the canal had faded with time, like his equally bewildering visit to the junk shop under the Dark Arches. And the Box had never given a repeat performance of the Paradise Peep-show. He supposed the Cosmic Aunties would still say he wasn't ready. But he could see with his own eyes the change in Asha. There was a little song Fran used to sing when Martha was a baby.

> 'You get brighter every day
> and every time I see you.
> Scatter brightness on your way
> and you taught me how to love you.'

98

Soggy hippy stuff that Joss despised. But she was, brighter every day. Sometimes, in contrast he felt himself growing darker, shadowier. As if the clearer she became, the more confused and lost Joss was forced to be. But he couldn't talk about it. It sounded so stupid. Besides there were no words.

Sometimes he buried the confused bursting angry feeling by putting his arms around her and kissing her hard, as though, if he could only hold her tight enough he might struggle through to some kind of peace. She always looked bewildered then and pulled away. Then, feeling guilty he would sulk and accuse her of not loving him.

It got worse the nearer it got to Christmas. He'd hated Christmas for the last four Christmasses. He hated the way people went collectively insane every year buying stupid things for people they didn't even like. His dad hated it too. But Asha was like Fran. She spent hours choosing 'the right thing' for someone, then took almost as long to choose the paper and ribbon to wrap the thing with. There was no reasoning with her.

They had their first quarrel in the middle of Debenhams when she demanded to know what was wrong with him and he said didn't she realise she'd just bought half an acre of rain forest that would only be dumped in the bin on Christmas morning.

'But I love Christmas,' she said. 'It doesn't matter what other people do, Joss – if they buy hideous things and cards with Xmas on them and believe Christmas is about how much money you splash out. It doesn't have to spoil it for us. We don't have to do it like that. The aunts don't do it like that.'

He didn't remember what he said next, just how angry and trapped he felt, the need to relieve his misery somehow, anyhow. But he didn't expect her reaction. She just marched off in the middle of the store, her back poker-straight, her face white.

At first he couldn't believe she meant to leave him there. As it sank in, he began to run through the crowds, crashing into overstuffed yuletide carrier bags, tripping over pushchair wheels, knocking over toddlers for all he knew, blind with fear, calling out her name like a maniac. At last she turned, and by some miracle stopped, waiting for him. When he reached her, she saw at once that he was sorry, saw the naked unhappiness in his eyes and forgave him instantly. Kissed him right in front of everyone as if he had given her back all her daffy happy Christmasses.

That was the trouble with Asha, Joss thought. She was never taken in. She wouldn't accept anything less than his true self. But being your real self with another human being all the time was exhausting; worse, it was terrifying. He wasn't sure he could stand the strain. He wasn't sure it was even necessary.

On Christmas Eve the Box began to shed its skin for the second time. Asha rang him, ecstatic.

'I'd just come back from the candlelit carol service. I was feeling so happy, Joss, and suddenly I knew something was happening, not like last time, but peacefully, and I ran upstairs and the whole room was – I can't describe it – the atmosphere, it was so clear, as if it was ringing and ringing with some beautiful bell-like sound just out of human range. And – are you still there, Joss, are you okay?'

'Yes,' he said tiredly.

Fran and Martha had put tastefully toning decorations on the Christmas tree. The friendly clashing ones had been left behind. There was a turkey in the fridge, brazil nuts in a bowl; Christmas cards crowded every possible space. Fran made friends quickly it seemed.

In his pocket was the card from his father. It was signed 'from Dad'. There had been money, too, though he hadn't looked at it. Fran and Martha were warming up mince pies for Mike who had popped round, very suspiciously Joss thought, for a Christmas drink.

'Don't you want to know what it looks like now?' Asha sounded querulous, her excitement flattening to meet his own depression.

'Yes,' he said. 'Sure. Tell me what it looks like now.'

She hesitated before she went on, 'Well actually it looks a bit of a mess, because it's still partly wooden. But the new bits look as if they might be some kind of crystal. Shan't be a minute, save some punch, Aunt Izzy! Just saying Happy

Christmas to Joss – it's not transparent, you can't see into it. But it's got a kind of – oh I can't describe it. You'll have to see it – it's going to be beautiful. And what a lovely day for it to happen. Christmas Eve!'

'You should check outside,' said Joss. The card had got crumpled. He tried to smooth it out but the paper was flimsy and tore. The picture showed a circle of holly around a lighted candle in a Dickensian brass candlestick. The kind of card you get in an economy pack from the supermarket.

His dad was hurt, that's why he hadn't bothered, that's why he hadn't said 'love'. He wasn't about to let himself be rejected again, after his whole family had walked out, was he?

'Outside?' Asha sounded bewildered.

'For the shining star over Wintergrove. Why, lo! Even as we speak three strangely wise figures may be wending their way up your path.'

He put the phone down before he knew he was going to.

That time in the music room before he kissed her it had been hard to breathe. But this time it was something terrifyingly close to hatred. Not love at all.

Fran was calling him. 'Joss, did you hear what Mike said? He knows where he could pick up amps for your blue guitar. What about that for a Christmas present? All I've got him is a jumper from Marks and Sparks, Mike. What's that poem about the blue guitar? Something about "playing things as they are"?'

She had hennaed her hair in the end. Cut it shorter too. It looked nice but it didn't look like Fran, it didn't look like his mother at all. She didn't look like anyone's mother any more.

'That's nice,' said Joss. 'But you'd better give the amps to someone else. I don't play the guitar any more. It was only a teenage phase. You know the kind of thing everyone goes through, like acne. Anything on TV?'

Someone was trying to steal the Box –

Asha sat up in terror, burying her face in her hands, keeping her hands cradled there while the nightmare slowly ebbed away.

She lifted up the corner of her pillow. The Box was still

there. She had taken it to bed for comfort after that dreadful telephone conversation. 'Oh, Box,' she said. 'I'll try to take care of you. I promise.' Her eyes filled. She had no idea why the Box that had once repelled her had become so precious. Troublesome though it was, she was learning to trust it and somehow the trust was becoming mutual. She had no idea what the end of this bizarre partnership could be but if there was such a thing as destiny, then hers and the Box's were linked forever. She stroked it, wondering if more of it was crystalline since yesterday or if she was imagining it. This time its transformation was as slow and invisible as the unfolding of a rose.

Then she realised the dream assault on her window was real and continuing; a persistent rain of tiny stones. Someone was calling her name.

Joss! She pushed open her window and peered down, her breath flying out in spirals.

'What are you doing? It's not even light yet.'

'I've brought you something, your real Christmas present.'

'You've already given me the scarf. It's lovely. Go home and don't be silly. You'll wake the aunts.'

Even in the half light his expression pierced her.

'All right, I'll come down for a minute – '

She let him into the kitchen. He was gibbering with cold, hadn't even thought to put on a jacket before he set off across the town. For the first time all year the weather was on target; ice hanging from every bush and drainpipe, the windows dimmed with frost flowers.

'You idiot,' she said. 'And the heating isn't on yet so I can't warm you up except by hugging you.'

He didn't seem to hear. There was a kind of force field around him that she couldn't cross with words or by touching him.

'I couldn't sleep. I was so stupid on the phone. I hated myself. I had to – here – ' He pushed something into her hand.

She unwrapped the tissue having to concentrate her mind to do it. She knew she had that crumpled look people wear when they've just woken up.

'It's a pomegranate! Joss, where did you find a pomegranate?'

'I stole it from the family fruit basket. Fran bought some from the market. I wanted to give you something silly. If you eat even one of the seeds you have to stay with me at least part of the year, oh lovely Persephone.'

He almost reached out for her then but she saw him control the impulse, draw back at the last moment as if it would hurt him to touch her. He was shaking. She didn't think it was just with cold. He looked brittle. Just holding himself together.

'And since when were you the murky old King of the Underworld?' she said as gently as she could, knowing that if she threw her arms around him the way she badly wanted to, it would be wrong. He would hang on to her again in that desperate resentful way; then both of them would drown and the planet would drown with them. She didn't need the goddesses to tell her that.

The space between them was electric with the kiss she had not given but she could not move or speak, could not rescue him this time.

'I feel like him sometimes though,' he said painfully, trying to smile at her. 'Cranky old sod. Nothing to do except abduct the odd innocent maiden from her flowery meadow. Well,' he put on a drawl, 'Guess life gets kind of limiting underground.'

There was another silence before he said, 'I'd better get back. Martha will be disembowelling her Christmas stocking by now.'

She was turning the fruit in her hand. 'I love it. When you cut them in half, they look as if they're lit up from the inside, like little lamps.'

'Did you hear from your mum and dad in the end?' he said. 'I never asked you.'

She shook her head. 'I had a card, that's all. It didn't even hurt so much this time. It's as if they've evaporated somehow, like an old story I don't need to tell any more.'

'When I see you next time you can show me how the Box is getting on,' he said. 'If the Cosmic Aunties agree of course.'

'Go home and get warm,' said Asha. 'Happy Christmas, idiot!' Then she half-whispered, 'Joss – will you be all right?' And he nodded without answering.

She watched his hunched figure thread in and out of the

frosty shrubs until he was out of sight, before she went upstairs, shivering violently herself by now, and climbed back under her duvet, the strange little fruit clasped tightly in her hand.

'I don't know if I can bear this,' she said aloud. 'Do other people bear this? Is loving people supposed to be like this?'

But no-one answered. The goddesses, like other people, seemed to be off duty on Christmas Day.

11 *Snake Dance*

And all Christmas holiday Joss was having nightmares.

It got so he dreaded sleep; creeping downstairs to watch TV with the sound down low. It was almost always horror films at that hour but they were welcome light relief to the company of the demon guitarist, who blazed out the second Joss loosened his grip on consciousness.

He avoided going to his room in the daytime now. He loathed being with Fran and Martha but he was afraid to be alone.

This meant he couldn't listen to his blues tapes. (Fran and Martha hated jazz.) In fact he hadn't been able to for weeks. The music was hijacked after the first chords, the demon strummer using it to home in, as if he was lying in wait for the opportunity to catch Joss off guard, the chance to take him over completely. Sometimes he succeeded and Joss found himself transported to that spotlighted space, ferociously playing his guitar as if his life depended on it, as if everyone's life depended on it; music never yet played in this world; torrents of music pouring through him, consuming him, burning him up, using him up until there was nothing left.

One day he couldn't stand it any longer. He was spending half his time hanging around Fran and Martha downstairs. If it went on, his mother would give him left-over pastry to play with the way she did when he was four. He'd wind up watching *Rainbow*.

He could hardly bear to touch the guitar now, but on the pretext of going to see Asha he got it out of the house in its insulation of grubby blanket, then headed for the Dark Arches.

It wasn't just that he wanted to get rid of it and its unwelcome demon tenant. He wanted his own guitar back. Even if it was broken, even if he could never play a note. It was all he had left. The only connection with his old life, with his dad.

He almost ran down the last few yards of the tunnel. He felt so light. Things were going to be all right! It wasn't too late to put it all right.

But he could see the shop was empty the moment he came out of the tunnel. All he could see when he pressed his face to the filthy glass were scraps of paper blowing across the floor. A torn poster with haunted house lettering. Even through the dirt he recognised the blazing angelic faces. *Last Performance at the Apocalyp –*

'You look awful, Joss,' said Fran, that evening. She was hunting for something and making a lot of noise doing it. 'Have you had a quarrel with Asha?'

'No,' he said, flipping channels irritably. 'Everything's fine with Asha.'

'Worried about exams coming up?' She delved down the sides of the sofa fishing out an old hairslide of Martha's.

'You're kidding. Who worries about exams at a progressive school? I'm fine, honestly. School's fine. Everything's absolutely fine, finer, finest.'

Finding her car keys at last Fran registered what Joss was watching.

'Joss, for heaven's sake, this is *Neighbours*. Switch it off before I throw up.'

'They're getting married today,' he said furiously. 'I want to see it.'

'God Almighty, is every teenager in this town a mutant?' Fran yelled. 'Glazed morbid faces as if you all live underground like mushrooms. *You'll* be dressing in black next, chanting this Omega garbage.'

For a second the genuine distress in her voice dragged Joss

back, anchoring him to the familiar room. He almost allowed himself to rest, float in this lit space, with Fran's rugs, plants, dried flowers, almost convinced himself there was no world outside hurtling to destruction; all landmarks swept away in the tide of global despair. He clicked off the set, turned blindly towards her, let her put her arms round him for the first time for months.

'I won't, Mum,' he said. 'Honestly I won't. I hate that stuff.'

'But this Hoarsemen things worries me,' said Fran. 'It's growing so fast. Someone was telling me it's the same in London. It's happening everywhere. They went to the States and everyone went wild over them. They even loved them in Japan, for Heaven's sake. Some of their fans are so young, but they look like druggies, Joss. Or religious freaks. Only it's not drugs or a guru. It's the music draining them, like a parasite. They smile but they don't see you, they're stupefied by the music in their heads. When I think Martha said she liked them – thank God *she* didn't get sucked into it. They look like human beings and they walk around like human beings but they've stopped living human lives in any real sense. And it's the music, Joss. That's what's doing it.'

'Don't be daft, Mum,' he said uncomfortably. 'The Hoarsemen are just a jumped-up local rock group. They're just the flavour of the month, that's all. No-one will even remember their name next year. You make them sound like – how *can* it be the music?'

'I don't know. I just feel it.'

She picked up the *Radio Times* and stashed it somewhere; twitched the curtains across the window, started tidying coffee cups and plates. Being busy always calmed Fran down, even though it made everyone around her feel much worse, thought Joss. Then, trying to lighten things, winding him up for the fun of it, she said, 'Must be women's intuition,' pulling a face.

'Oh, that old crap,' he said, grinning back.

'I've got to go to work now. Martha's staying at Nicola's tonight. Don't stay up till all hours, will you? It's so stuffy again, Joss. Not like Christmas at all.'

'Asha and I might go for a bike ride tomorrow,' said Joss, casually. 'If it stays this warm. As it's still the holidays.'

'Anywhere nice?' She made some quick adjustments to her hair, faintly smiling in the mirror as if she half-approved of what she saw there. He didn't remember seeing her do that before.

'The Earthworks,' he said. 'Asha's never been. We might take a picnic. Spend the day.'

She didn't move an inch. She looked totally natural but Joss felt her anxiety level rise from the other side of the room.

'Oh, Joss,' she said, 'that might not be such a good idea.'

'Why not?' He heard his own voice, shrill like a whiny kid's. He could have kicked himself.

'You're so young,' she said. 'You and Asha. And so – vulnerable. Sometimes I worry that you –'

'It's okay, Fran,' he interrupted, grinning edgily. 'I promise I won't let her have her wicked way.'

She shook her head, half angry then looked up at the ceiling. 'Oh God, I don't know how to handle this bit,' she said aloud, but not, Joss thought, particularly to God. She was silent again for a moment, then shrugged and said, 'Well, have a lovely time, both of you.'

'Thanks,' said Joss ironically. 'It's nice to know you trust me.'

'Oh, Joss,' she said. 'You can be such a bastard when you want, just like – ' She bit the words back.

'Richard,' he supplied. 'More compliments. Well done, Mum. Two males with one stone.'

'No, not Richard, actually,' Fran flashed back. 'Your father is not the only bastard in this world as I'm sure you'll discover one day.'

She slammed the front door when she left and the tacky little house shook as if it wanted to fall down around him in a shower of rotten plaster. It was all the worse for coming after the other part; the hug, the moment of understanding, when he let himself float in the lamplit ark of her room. Now it was only a matter of time before he drowned.

* * *

107

False Spring. That was what they were calling it on the news. Primroses in January. Outpourings of birdsong.

The hot sun on their backs forced them to shed jackets and sweaters long before they began cycling up the long hill to the Earthworks. It took longer than Joss could have imagined to reach it. Even the little unmade road seemed longer when you had to push your bike along it, but the view was spectacular. He experienced a surge of delight just being here with Asha in the sun and wind, in having left the suffocating little town behind, in simply achieving this high lonely place. So what if it wasn't true spring but global warming? This place had been here forever. It would always be here. The earth was going to stick around for a while yet with its roots and stones and rushing waters, whatever people did to it. It hadn't given in yet. It had staying power, he thought.

The wind was fierce on the hilltop. Like Fran, Asha had to hold down her skirt as the wind tugged at her, whipping her hair across her face. She hadn't put her hair up today, only tied it back loosely with a green ribbon. While she gazed over the weird terrain, Joss gazed at her equally baffled, wondering what the hell she was thinking.

'Well, what's your theory? Martian service station? Neanderthal hypermarket?'

She didn't answer. She was wearing the listening expression that unnerved him because it shut him out so absolutely. Then she shook herself, and he saw her arms were prickling with gooseflesh despite the warmth.

'Let's go down there,' she said, 'by that hollow near the little rowan tree. There's even a stream, look, and we'll be out of the wind. Come on. It's not far.'

Joss trailed after her. The back of his neck was creeping again. He wasn't sure he wanted to walk any deeper into the Earthworks. Its emptiness which had seemed so beautiful minutes before, suddenly set him crawling with anxiety. He remembered how he had hated it when he came with Fran. Perhaps it wasn't just because he'd been in a lousy mood. He'd thought of Ozymandias and dying. He'd lost his bearings. Who he was.

'Do you like it?' he said. 'Do you actually like it here?'

'In a way. I know it's eerie. But powerful.'

'Powerful? Powerfully what?'

'Don't spit your scorn so snarkily at me, Joss Emerson. Powerfully powerful. It's a place of power. There ought to be snakes here.'

'Snakes – I bloody well hope not. I shouldn't think it's likely in this part of the world.'

'Not poisonous snakes,' said Asha. 'Sacred snakes. They had them in temples of healing. Sick people came to sleep and the snakes brought them healing dreams.'

'I bet they did,' said Joss. 'Where did you get hold of this healing temple stuff? Have you been reading backnumbers of *Prediction* or something?'

She blinked hard. 'I don't know,' she said. 'I think – because this is a healing place too. And I don't know how I know that either so don't ask.'

They walked the rest of the way in silence. He had to admit she'd chosen the perfect spot. The stream was only a trickle, it hadn't rained since the autumn storms, but it caught the sunlight as it skittered over the tumbled stones and made a peaceful soothing sound.

Joss threw himself down on the grass, taking a wary look round first in case there really were adders lurking. 'Bone dry,' he said. 'How can grass be bone dry in January? And skylarks. Listen to that one. Its batteries will be worn out by the time the real spring comes.'

'I brought the Box,' said Asha as if she'd been dying to tell him this. 'Do you want to see?' She began fumbling with her bag.

'No thanks,' he said. 'But I'll have one of your sandwiches unless you want one of mine.' He hadn't known he was going to say it but there was a harsh satisfaction in setting her straight.

She stared at him for a long time, her eyes taking up more and more of her face.

'You really said that, didn't you?' she said at last, her voice cracking with hurt. 'Why did you want to come here, Joss? Why did you ask me to come if you don't even like being with me? If you never believed in the Box for one minute? You didn't, did you? You were humouring me all the time.'

'I do like being with you,' he said, reaching for her, unable to bear the look in her eyes, unable to bear his incomprehensible need to punish her. 'That's the whole point,' he murmured into her hair. 'I do want to be with you. Really be with you, Asha.'

His words hung in the air. Now they were out they sounded seedily insinuating even to him.

She didn't want to understand. 'I am with you,' she said, pulling away. 'Most days. For hours and hours.'

When he didn't answer her face went stony. 'Oh, I see,' she said. 'And your next line is going to be – if I really loved you I would, is it? God how corny can you get.'

He wanted to grin at that. Her truthfulness got him every time. He had to act sulkier than he felt to cover it. 'You are so cold,' he said. 'You are so selfish. I don't think you love me at all.'

'Wrong,' she blazed. 'Quite quite wrong. But I'm beginning to love me and I'll need myself all my life. It's you – you don't even like me half the time, Joss Emerson, but you feel scared and empty and you think *this* might work, don't you? If you can get me to do it with you that might fill your emptiness. And when it didn't then you'd think it might work better with some other girl or – leave me *alone*, Joss, don't you dare touch me!'

'Don't, oh don't,' he pleaded almost in tears. 'Please don't be like this. Just kiss me and we'll have our picnic and we'll look for the stupid leylines or even the sacred snakes if you like. But don't be like this, Asha.'

'But if I kiss you, you'll only – ' Her voice trailed away. She didn't want to quarrel. She never did, he thought. Nor did he. But they quarrelled all the same.

'I won't. I promise I won't. It will just be to make the peace. I can't bear it if you don't trust me. When you look like that I feel as if I'm turning into a sort of monster to myself. It scares me.'

She let him move closer, only tensed a little, but she was searching his eyes the whole time, looking for the truth in them when all he wanted was to hide from himself, bury his confused hideous feelings. She did kiss him though, and he could tell she meant it after her first hesitation, her fingers fastening on his sleeve and then her hand in his hair, the wind blowing over the two of them as they clung together in that vast emptiness, as if they were the last people in the world, or the first . . .

'Oh God,' he said, 'Asha please –'

'Don't,' she said very gently. 'You promised.'

Then when he wouldn't, couldn't let go of her she shoved him, actually shoved him away with surprising force so he fell sprawling, banging his head on a tree root.

'There was no need to –' he began, humiliated, but she had sprung to her feet, talking so fast there was no space to interrupt, to explain.

'Listen, Joss – I don't know who you think I am or if you ever even saw me as a real person at all but try to understand. One day I will have a lover, yes I will, a lover, don't look so prim because I'm a girl and *I'm* naming names. And we will do the things lovers do – okay? *In my own time*. When I'm ready. Not because I'm bullied or blackmailed or made responsible for your emptiness, your boredom, your bloody cowardice – yes, I do mean cowardice. Don't you think I know what it's like to be scared? What do you think it was like for me, night after night alone with the Box, seeing all those – *things*, scared I was going mad? But you, you won't even unwrap that guitar from its blanket and play a note, not a bloody note in case you get it wr –'

'You've said enough,' he said very quietly. 'You've said enough now.' He was on his feet, white as a sheet, blood trickling from the graze on his forehead.

'Yes, I have. I've said everything I should have said before. I should have finished it before. But it's over now. I am sorrier than you'll ever know, Joss. But it's finished.'

'Thus spake the goddesses I suppose,' he said softly. 'The good ole Cosmic Aunties.'

'No,' she yelled. 'Watch my lips! Nobody bloody well spoke but me. Now go away and leave me. Go on! Leave me!'

He stumbled away like a drunk. As he unlocked his bike and blindly trundled it back along the unmade road he scarcely saw the van nudging past him, only half-registered the strangely familiar faces dimmed by the smoked glass windscreen. He was living through the worst nightmare of his life. Nothing would shock or even reach him again. He knew for certain now what he had always vaguely suspected; nothing was too terrible to happen and in the end, all the terrible things happen to everyone. Some people lived with that. He couldn't.

He didn't see a single landmark on the way home but rode through a sun-dazzled blur, heading in the right direction more by instinct than anything.

When he let himself into the empty house he couldn't believe how little time had passed since he had left it. He had to track through moulting Christmas tree needles to get to the stairs. He only wanted a few things. He wasn't going to leave a note. He wondered if he should phone ahead and say he was coming but he decided not to. He could explain better face to face. Anyway there was nothing to explain. Half an hour later he was in the cab of a lorry heading down the motorway and his mind still hadn't caught up. He thought it probably never would.

She had known the snake would come to her under the tree. She had seen it in her mind's eye, while she was looking out over the ancient bowl of earth and stone but there was no way she could share mysteries like that with Joss. There was no way she could share anything with him any more. She couldn't grieve yet for that, just sat under the tree waiting, the Box beside her; part milky crystalline, part strange glowing fragrant wood. She knew the tree it came from now, understood the knowledge that shut those two innocents out of their green garden. Not sex, not nakedness, but true sight. Seeing things for what they were, no matter what others tried to make you see. And once you'd seen you had to walk your own path, however far it took you from the safe places, green gardens, sheltering trees.

She saw the Hoarsemen too. Saw them arrive and walk around, then leave as if they'd seen all they needed for this visit at least. They weren't alone. There were the hangers-on who took measurements, snapped a Polaroid or two. One had a dowsing rod. It was natural they should know about the lines of power that intersected here but she was amused, almost pitied them that they couldn't find them for themselves. She could have taken them to the right places blindfold. That was something to thank the goddesses for.

She could see this place would suit their purpose perfectly. She couldn't feel afraid. They were part of the Box's destiny and that was that. But it wasn't time. She had to be patient. She had to have courage. And so she waited on alone and sometimes she found tears running down her face so she supposed she was sadder than she knew but whether she was sad or not didn't seem the point any more.

She was almost asleep in the heat, her head pillowed on her stiffening arm, when it came gliding out under the tree roots, so beautiful it took her breath; a gold earth-tawny creature of immense, impervious power.

In that borderland between sleeping and waking it was easy for Asha to accept that this was the guardian spirit of the place, so she was careful not to move or make a sound that might disturb her. The snake-spirit seemed intent, knowing exactly why and where she was needed and though she brushed Asha's hand with her scales in passing, dry, neutral as a windblown leaf, it was not Asha she had come for but the Box. Asha understood now that such moments only come in solitude and can't be shared but she wished Joss was there to see the snake flicker her forked tongue over the Box in loving salutation. She wished he was there to see the gold-tawny coils weaving over and around the Box in a hypnotic flowing figure-of-eight dance, a dance of welcome, of celebration that went on and on until her head began to spin and her eyes close . . .

And later, much later, when she woke, she yearned for Joss to be with her to see the perfect octagon of milky crystal, shining on the rabbit bitten turf like a fallen star. But not even the goddesses were with her to share its beauty. She tried sending out her mind as they had taught her but there was no answering shimmer.

Asha was alone again. Not because she had been

abandoned this time, but because she had sent Joss away. Because she wouldn't let him pretend love was a safe unchanging place you crawled into to hide from your own life. If you gave up your life and your dreams for love then it wasn't true love she thought. Two true selves loving and living their true lives was what she had wanted. And that was what she had thought the goddesses wanted for them too. But she couldn't have it. It wasn't possible. Joss couldn't bear her way of loving. It scared the hell out of him. He wanted to use her to make him feel better as if she was some kind of tranquilliser. He wanted her to be a character in some confused play in his head and it scared him to death when she acted like a real person with ideas of her own.

She had wanted them *both* to be real. It was the real Joss she loved, the person she glimpsed in his eyes sometimes, with a shock of delight, when he suddenly burst out laughing or talked about things that mattered to him. But most of the time Joss hid his true self from her and like the persistent bride in the old story she had insisted on the truth, the truth, holding up her lighted candle, dripping her hot wax on his vulnerable sleeping face, and like the enchanted prince he had gone away from her forever into a far far country. She might never see the real Joss again.

He had hurt her badly she knew but she would never know what pain she had caused him.

He had stumbled away from her, hating himself, believing himself a loathsome monster. All because Asha had chosen truth instead of lies, instead of the love he offered, and even through the numbness of shock she could feel the pain that lay waiting for her like a seeping wound in her heart. For in sending Joss away she had also chosen loneliness. Truth and loneliness.

A dark price, she thought, trying to remember the words of the woman under the Dark Arches. A dark price to pay. But I never dreamed. Oh I never dreamed anything could hurt so much.

12 *Going Home*

His first lift took him almost half way. He sat in the cafeteria, counting the money he had left after the chips, wondering if he should get the coach. He'd been lucky to pick a truck driver who didn't ask questions, didn't in fact say anything much, just jounced along with Radio One full blare, but it was easier to be anonymous on a coach. It was strange how parts of him still functioned and others had seized up utterly. A woman struggling back to the car park, her head down against the sudden easterly gusts, exclaimed and asked Joss if he didn't think the weather had gone insane, and hadn't it turned terribly cold, funny how you didn't notice it in a car, and he couldn't muster a polite word, not even a nod.

There was a coach it turned out, but not for an hour and a half. He thought he would go barmy waiting that long. It was late afternoon, effectively evening, the light dying, a vague fog shutting off distance. At the bus station an old man was already sleeping across one of the seats, wrapped in heavy duty polythene against the increasingly bitter wind. He coughed repeatedly, a rattling chesty cough.

A few yards away a group of kids were kicking a litter bin as if they'd rather kick a person instead. When they got bored with that they set it on fire and capered around until the rubbish charred to ash. Their faces looked unnervingly tribal by the light of that brief unsatisfactory fire. An angry tribe cheated of a homeland. Joss himself wanted to be home so badly he could have wept. Only he didn't know where home was any more.

He kept trying to imagine what his father would say when he saw him at the door, how his guarded face would break into a smile, how he would welcome him, gather him in. But each time he reached this part of the fantasy the front door slammed in his face and went on slamming again and again. Why was his imagination punishing him, his nerve failing now he was so near? When he should have done this months ago.

Someone sat down next to him, only marginally altering the weight of the bench. He edged away not wanting to share his space, dreading having to talk.

Why had it turned so cold so quickly?

To the east behind the thin barrier of fog, the sky glowered dull yellow. There was still an hour and twenty minutes to wait.

The newcomer rustled. He glimpsed thin, transparently white hands scrabbling in a black cotton tote bag ornamented with scraps of mirror. As far as he could tell there was nothing in it except a repellent whiff of cheap fags, mingled with too-sweet perfume. A young girl then. He glimpsed the scrabbling hands again. Black nail varnish. He shuddered.

The scrabbling stopped. She coughed but when he carried on staring resolutely into the wall of fog, she tweaked his sleeve as intimately as if they were old friends, sending alarm jolting through his body as if Death itself had touched him. 'Ever so sorry to bother you but have you got a light?' Her voice was tired, wheedling.

'Sorry,' he said insincerely, still avoiding looking at her.

'Tried and tried to give it up,' she said. 'But I've always been weak-willed. Still, I don't need to eat much any more. I save ever such a lot of money that way.'

He knew then that he had no choice but to endure this encounter, play his part. He turned to face her and saw how pale she was, the hollows under her cheekbones, the exhausted, dazzled smile; felt his stomach lurch and knew he had been warding off exactly this moment. She saw him register the red and black medal worn over her thin black clothes, and touched it herself with disturbing tenderness.

'Going to a concert,' she said. 'They're in Bristol tomorrow night. I'll go anywhere to see them. I've been to Birmingham, Leicester, Norwich. Why don't you come with me? You're young. You're so unhappy now. I can see how lost you are. Don't be angry with me for saying it.' She put her head pleadingly on one side. 'Anyone can see it, just by looking at you. I only want to help you. You could live in Paradise like the rest of us if you're willing to let them change your life like they changed mine.'

She smoothed her skimpy blouse and he fought off a panic-stricken vision of himself drifting like her from town to town, concert to concert, blotted out like her from head to foot in hideous funereal rags, a human zero, shivering and not even knowing he was cold.

'Why don't you need to eat much any more?' he said roughly. He couldn't help himself. He had thought he was washed-up, finished, mad even but this truly mad girl had shocked him back to life. She was the real thing.

She smiled that elusive blinded smile. 'I can't tell you until you're one of us,' she said, 'and then you'll know. But we get everything we need from them, you see. All the rest of you –' she gestured at the still-smouldering litter bin, the old man coughing under his polythene, the raw orange street lights filtered through fog, that made each passer-by look ill or deformed. 'You live in Hell. That's what this is if only you'd see it. That's what this planet is: Hell. But we love them you see and so they give us all we need. The more we can let go –' she checked herself then and went on hastily, smiling over the slip, 'They're going to give us everything we could ever dream of. When we're ready. When it's time.'

'The Hoarsemen?' said Joss incredulously.

'Oh no,' she said exhaustedly. 'Not them. It doesn't come from them. It sort of comes *through* – But I shouldn't be telling. Oh why don't you come with me – what's your name?'

'Joss,' he said, despite himself. He had just seen her feet which were bare inside torn black plimsolls; they were blue-white with cold.

'Where do you come from then, Joss?' Again that intimate tone as if they had known each other all their lives.

Against his will he told her. He told her too much probably. He was hypnotised with horror for her. It was like watching a rabbit paralysed in the path of a runaway juggernaut, dazed by the blinding headlights, the blaring horn. He wanted to drag her to safety, tear off those graveyard garments, scream, 'Get out! Before it's too late.'

Instead he took her for a cup of tea and bought her a box of matches. He bought two curling bacon sandwiches too but she wouldn't eat. Even so she seemed obscurely happy, sitting with him in a seedy bus station café in Hell, telling him her life story.

Her name was Tarot. 'I had a hippy mother, you see, till I ended up in care that is. Not that I take it personally or anything. There were four of us. I was the last one. Last straw probably,' she laughed and Joss again felt his stomach turn, sensing how many times she had told this tale in the same words, punctuated in the same places with the same pleading laughter. 'I kept the name even if people think it's freaky because she told me it would bring me luck. I used to think I needed all the luck I could get but now I can have it all, everything I dreamed of and so can you, oh, come with me to Bristol, Joss, why don't you, and find out for yourself? You seem such a nice boy. It's going to be so beautiful. I wish you knew how beautiful life could be, how beautiful it's going to be when we –' her voice petered out.

There were tears standing in her eyes, spilling out over her lower lashes, streaking her thin ghastly cheeks.

'When what?' he prompted her.

The kids were storming up and down the ramps of the multi-storey car park beside the bus station, howling abuse at another kid who screamed insults back. The air was jagged with their anger. The guy in the ticket office was picking up the phone.

Tarot lifted her spectral face to him, her khol-rimmed eyes blazing with longing.

'When we go home,' she said. "When we go home at last.'

Cradling her arms round her bony knees, gently rocking, she hummed a threadbare tune that probably sounded better with quadruple tracking, with the full complement of harmonies, guitars, synthesisers, then quaveringly she broke into the words of her off-key lament: ' "Going home, going back home, let the sound draw you back to the place you lost so long ago, back home, your own green home." '

The police car came while he was in the phone box dialling Fran's number. They dispatched the kids without fuss, stood talking to them for a minute or two, then piled them in the back and drove away. He scarcely registered it because Martha had just answered his voice with an earsplitting shriek, ' – Joss! I knew it was you. I knew it was you ringing!'

'I want to speak to Mum,' he said exhausted,' before my money runs out.'

'You can't – there's only me. She's gone out looking for you. So's Mike and Luke and everyone. She's nearly out of her head. But I knew where you'd run away to. I knew what you'd do. Don't go, Joss. Don't go back to him. I'm not supposed to tell you but I heard her say it ages and ages ago and if I don't tell you you'll go on hoping and hurting yourself forever and ever – '

She was crying on the end of the phone.

'Don't burble, Marth. Don't get worked up. I'm just going to Dad's, maybe just for a day or two. I'm in a bit of a mess and I want to sort it out by myself.'

'You *mustn't*, Joss, honestly you mustn't, because he's not, he's not – oh Joss, don't hate me for telling you but she should have told you, she really *should* have.' Martha's voice rose higher and higher with hysteria.

'What – what are you saying?' He was trembling already from the feet and ankles upward, a steady deadly vibration as if an electric current was passing through him. When it hit his stomach he was afraid he'd be sick right there in the phone box. He was doubled up before she said it.

'Richard's not your dad, Joss. Not your real dad. Oh, Joss come home. Come back. Tell me where you are and Fran will come and get you.'

'No,' he said, his voice echoing flatly in his own ears, letting the receiver slide back on to the rest, cutting them off. The bus for Bristol lumbered in. After a brief regretful wave, Tarot got on and was borne away.

'I'll get myself home,' he said aloud.

It was already snowing when his bus came in. He found a space by a window and crouched in the furthest corner of the seat, taking up as little space as he could, his face averted from the other passengers. Someone had drawn a pyramid symbol in the dirt on the glass but by the time they reached Leicester

119

he couldn't see a thing. Just blinding white chaos.

That was the night Bethany Blessed came back. It was Aunt Izzy who went to the door, peered suspiciously over the guard chain, (no one called at Wintergrove this late at night) then yelled like a maniac for Maddy and Asha who came running; Maddy wielding a hideous vase like a club.

'Oh, Asha,' said Bethany, half-fainting into their arms. 'I know I shouldn't have come. I tried to manage. But I didn't have anyone – '

'Oh my dear girl,' said Aunt Maddy, snatching off her glasses as though she couldn't bear to see what she had seen all too clearly from the first moment. 'My poor dear girl.'

'So she *was* pregnant,' said Tamar. It was the first day back. They were in a huddle by the radiator in the school music room where they were less likely to be overheard.

'You knew, didn't you?' Asha forced Tamar to look at her. 'How did you know?'

Tamar was all in red today, ruby nose-jewel, skinny red leggings and a shapeless red tee shirt slipping off her skinny shoulders heedless of the snow banking up the windows and the biting easterly wind that had raged around the whole country for days now.

'Don't you ever know things, Asha? Just know without knowing how? Don't you get pictures in your head and know they're true?'

'Yes,' said Asha slowly, 'I do. But it isn't natural, I sort of – learnt. Recently,' she added uncertainly.

Tamar stared back at her. 'You're deep, Asha McGillveray. I always knew you were. What's been happening to you, eh? You and Joss – ?'

'Not me and Joss,' said Asha. 'That's over but it still feels like something sharp – here,' she placed her hands against her solar plexus where the pain was. 'It's just me now. And I want to know how you knew about Bethany.'

'I know too much for my own good, my mum says,' said Tamar mocking herself. 'Like, why I have to keep the little kids out of the way when the latest uncle comes round.'

'Uncle,' said Asha looking prim. 'That isn't very original.'

'She isn't,' said Tamar. 'She never learns, either. But she's a duck all the same.'

Her expression shifted from Mata Hari to plain Tamar Tetley. 'Oh, Asha I just knew. I saw it all happen in my head and I couldn't bear it. I can't bear what I know sometimes. How could Bethany ever go back to the flaming *Shores of Galilee* after what she'd done?'

'She's been living on the streets,' said Asha. 'As far as we can make out. I don't know how she survived. I don't want to know.'

'I know something else,' said Tamar. 'Want to hear it?' She was tracing a weblike pattern in the palm of her hand, then extended her palm into the air as if she was blowing a kiss, as if she was setting it free to do what it would.

Asha watched her uneasily. 'That's not one of theirs is it?'

'You're joking. Think I want a free lobotomy? Have you seen Ghoul yet, today? I mean, close up? Well he hasn't exactly been overdoing the turkey and mince-pies, Asha. And if his skin gets any more transparent looking you'll be able to read graffiti through him. No, this is a pattern of destiny, my little one. You're in it. I'm in it. Maybe Bethany is in it. And those sick vultures are in it.'

'The Hoarsemen,' said Asha. 'I know. I think I've always known.'

Tamar stood up. Asha thought for a moment she was going to leave and felt a surprising pang of loss. Instead she said almost shyly, 'Teach me to play a tune. Go on. Something dead pretty. Something that will really impress some gorgeous bloke one day and make him think I've got hidden depths.'

'A tune? Can you read music?' Asha couldn't help herself. She knew she sounded catty and superior but how could Tamar even imagine she could learn to play the piano just like that?

'Not a note,' said Tamar irrepressibly. 'Don't intend to learn either. I'll pick it up from watching you. I'm quick. I've got a good ear. I've got instinct. Go on – try me.'

Asha sighed. It was no use. All her wintery walls had come tumbling down and Terrifying Tamar Tetley had well and truly sneaked herself inside them. She might as well accept it with good grace. If the goddesses had stuck around they would have seen the funny side. The Ice Maiden and the Bad Girl, hand in glove. She could almost feel their ghostly blue-green shimmer, egging her on. After all, where had trying to be perfect ever got Asha? Why shouldn't she teach Tamar the piano for the sheer daft fun of it?

'All right,' she said. 'I disapprove utterly you know but I'll do it on one condition.'

'Like what?' Tamar crouching in her whirling dervish pose, started shooting out arms and legs in at least seven directions at once, before she wound up with a warrior yelp, facing Asha, grinning the famous Tetley grin.

'You teach me how to do some of that whatever you call it, akido or karate or whatever it is and come back with me for tea to help cheer Bethany up.'

'That's two conditions, Ms McGillveray,' said Tamar, going back to her ominous crouch.

'Don't quibble,' said Asha.

13 *Tuning in*

To no-one's surprise Joss was ill after his attempt to run back to his old home. But today he was a little better and Fran actually had an official Sunday at home. One by one the cats found their way upstairs to sleep off their share of the chicken; Evie nestling behind his knees on the bed, Beano perched behind Fran's shoulder, his eyes contented slits of amber. Ludwig glowering from the middle of the carpet, unpleasantly short of fur where the vet had lanced the latest abscess.

It took her a while to get started but she managed it at last.

'I thought you'd hate me,' she said, looking at her knees. She always looked about ten when she was upset.

'I don't know why you kept it from me, I don't know how you could. I feel so stupid, not knowing. You and Martha knowing and me –'

122

'Martha only knows because she was born with ears like radar scanners,' said Fran grimly. 'She heard a quarrel she was never meant to hear. I made her swear not to tell you.'

'So who –'

'Does it matter who?' she said, digging her nails into her palms. He could see blue crescents in her flesh.

'Of course it bloody does. It matters to me.'

'He's dead –'

'But I'm not,' he said furious with her, wondering if even now she was lying. All those years of living with the one woman who could have talked Scheherazade to death, to find she had somehow never told him the one thing he really needed to know. 'Your mother is such an open person,' people said, enviously. Open? Fran was virtually inside out! But it had been a blind, a trade-off, all that warm open communication of hers, a ploy to evade the truth. 'Don't I count?' he said savagely.

'I thought you were,' she said. 'I thought you were dead, that night. I thought I'd never see you again.'

'You've got to tell me, Fran. You've got to.'

'God, Joss you don't care how much you hurt me, do you?'

'I hurt too,' he yelled. 'How can I bear it if you know who he was and I don't!'

Her expression changed. When she spoke her voice was sad but straightforward. She didn't try to romanticise it or make it sound better than it was.

'He was just ordinary,' she said. 'I can see that, looking back. But I was young for my age, bloody immature, frankly, and no-one ever looked at me like that before or talked to me the way he did. I thought he looked like a film star. I know it's corny, Joss, but what isn't? There are no new stories under the sun, did you know that? You have his hands, actually. Fine lovely hands. And his hair. But the rest is you, all your own . . .'

Joss wouldn't look away, wouldn't let her off the hook no matter how her voice pleaded.

She sighed, went on. 'His name was Paul. He was going to Canada. He felt suffocated here in the Midlands. He said he'd always been a misfit. That appealed to me somehow. Made him seem more interesting. I'd never got on with my family either. It was as though we were cut from the same cloth. Two misfits against the world. Said he'd take me away with him if only he had the money – the last week he was here we went up to the –'

Don't say it, don't say it, he willed silently, remembering Martha ask him if someone was walking on his grave.

' – Earthworks. It was a scorching day. There was a lark so high it was like the sky singing. There was no-one else around. He was so gentle, Joss, at first, so sweet. Then he said I was cruel and cold, that I was hurting him. I was so naïve. I began to believe I really had done something terribly wrong. He said at least he had the courage to say he loved me. He said why had I gone there with him if I wasn't going to – to let him. He said I must have gone to torment him. He knew other girls were like that but he'd thought I was different. And if I really loved him –'

Joss knew exactly what the bastard had said and didn't need to hear it from Fran.

'Didn't you write and tell him?' he interrupted. 'About me? When you knew?'

'Yes, but I couldn't trace him for months and when I did I didn't get a reply. He never wrote a word. I thought I'd go out of my mind, Joss. My aunt looked after me. My parents didn't want anything more to do with me. There was still a terrible stigma about being pregnant and single then. A few months after you were born I met Richard. He was the perfect answer. He wanted to be a rescuer and, oh, I really wanted to be rescued.' She tried to grin but her tears spilled over and she scrubbed at them angrily.

'He wanted to look after us, make a family with us, but he said it would be much harder if you thought of him as a step-parent. You were only a tiny baby. To you he was your father. And when I heard Paul had died in a forestry accident, when I realised he was never going to – I told myself I was luckier than I might have been. Everything was going to be all right. It was only later –'

'Tell me the rest,' he said harshly, already knowing it, but having to hear every word, it was like tearing himself free of something fibre by rotting fibre. Old ropes that bound him. Ropes he hadn't known were there.

'It was lovely at first,' she said simply. 'And then, after we were married it wasn't.' Again the wavering grin: she blinked the tears away this time.

'Once we were married he hardly took any notice of you, Joss. And in the end he only noticed me if I was – I don't know – stepping out of line. As if he never trusted me deep down. As if he thought I might just run off one day and – '. She was examining her hands again, blinking hard. 'Do you want a cup of tea?'

'No,' he said. 'Keep going. But you stayed? Why, if he was so . . . ?'

'I thought if we had a baby together we'd be a proper family at last, he'd get that first feeling back, be sweet to you the way he was to begin with.' Her eyes filled again. 'I'm not really upset any more, Joss. It's just thinking what an idiot I was hanging on to my *Woman's Own* fantasy of happy ever after. Remembering how I tried not to let myself see that having poor Marth hadn't solved anything. I mean how can a little helpless baby *solve* something?'

'I still don't understand why you didn't leave him. Why did you stay so long?'

It was like looking down the tube of a kaleidoscope, seeing the familiar pattern explode. All Fran's new beginnings, her timid-fierce rebellions. His stepfather's scorn for them. Why hadn't Joss *seen*? But he had known, deep down, he thought. Underneath he had always felt obscurely guilty, always tried desperately hard to make Richard approve of him. And always known he'd fail.

'Because first there was you and then there was Martha – and I didn't have any qualifications. Oh, all right – I suppose I didn't have any courage either. I didn't have a terribly good opinion of myself by this time, Joss. It took me years to find it. But I found it bit by bit. Like scraping at rock with my fingernails. Year by year. But . . .'

'But what?'

'You *loved* him so much, Joss. All you wanted was to please him. You wore yourself out trying to please him but nothing

125

you ever did – Oh sod it, I hate crying like this, give me a tissue – '

She blew her nose loudly and thoroughly, was defiant again by the time she had finished, gave him a watery grin.

'Are you planning to get it together with MIDLANDS LIGHT AND POWER then?' he asked. He didn't feel particularly angry at the thought any more, just curious.

Fran sat bolt upright, amazed.

'Mike? Did you seriously think – Oh, Joss, good grief, all I want is time to get myself straightened out. I don't need another man. Mike's a friend. He's been divorced. He knows what it's like. He's just a friend.'

'Does Mike know that?' He twitched his eyebrows at her, Groucho Marx style.

He didn't know why he was clowning suddenly. Perhaps it was a relief to know the worst. Perhaps that was why it was suddenly easier to breathe. As if a vampire bat had lumbered off the roof and gone flapping heavily away, shrieking with thwarted ill intent.

'Yes Mike does,' said Fran laughing despite herself. 'Oh, for Heavens sake, Joss, hug me. This might be hard for you to believe but however bloody it's been sometimes, I wouldn't have missed having you and Martha for all the world. Try to forgive me for messing everything up, if you ever can.'

He couldn't speak. But when she saw his face she went teary all over again, grabbed his shoulders and hugged him so hard she almost broke his bones.

As though the departure of the vampire was the signal for good things to happen in Joss's life, the amps arrived the day afterwards.

As it happened he had been listening to music that morning, not blues this time but contemporary African stuff he'd taped off the radio months ago. Somehow, he had ended up looking at the guitar, had actually nervously, very very slowly unwrapped it. Nothing happened. No demon guitarists. No bad vibes. Not even a tiny supernatural tingle. Just his own burning need to know if he could play this beautiful instrument the way it deserved to be played.

126

And then the familiar rusting white Sherpa rolled up outside the door. That engine sounded sicker every day, Joss thought.

'Just brought them in case the acne comes back,' said Mike, coolly, dumping down boxes. 'Need any help setting them up?'

'I can't pay you,' said Joss, not able to believe he could have what he longed for, shaking with the physical need to tear off at once with the screwdriver, to know at once if the guitar could ever in his lifetime be coaxed to produce a sound remotely like the burning blue-turquoise music of his dreams.

'That's where you're wrong,' said Mike still dead-pan. 'You will pay me through the nose, as a matter of fact, Joss Emerson. Weekends, school holidays, evenings when you haven't got homework or you're not playing this flashy object with your mates. I need an extra pair of hands but I'm a mean bastard and I hate to pay anyone much. Putting you under an unfair obligation is absolutely up my street. And I'll still expect you to do exactly what you're told.'

'But I've never – I'm useless at that kind of thing – ' He began to sweat, hearing Richard's tired voice, 'For God's sake *leave* it, Joss. It's quicker to do it myself.'

'Time we made a real man of you then,' said Mike grinning his chauvinist grin. 'We'll start with the tap in your mum's bathroom.' He lobbed him a spanner. 'Get to it.'

He waited until they were out before he risked it, before he dared to pluck a single string, then he jumped at the sheer resonating power of it and the room turned dim gold around him while the last sunlit tremor ebbed away.

The first chords were tentative, and he botched almost every one. His errors came screaming back from the walls like soundtrack from a Hitchcock film. His fingers were wet with fear, remembering. The day he'd died in front of Otis and his mates. How you should never mix up life and dreams if you were not one of the chosen ones, the golden ones.

Then for some reason he thought of Asha, and the Box. Once she had tried to explain that if you wanted to do something that seemed impossible, all you had to do was 'tune in' to the others who had successfully done it before you, and ask them to help. He thought it sounded a bloody daft idea, though not quite as wild as some of her others. But suddenly it made sense. He wasn't planning to plug into anyone major, Eric Clapton or anyone. Just other kids who had longed to play music as fiercely as Joss and beaten their own paralysing terror of fatally screwing it up.

Ask them, Joss. Ask them to help you. They can't help if you don't ask.

'So help me,' he murmured to the blue guitar as if through it he really could speak to all those kindred spirits. 'Please help me. Show me how it feels to play without being scared to death of failing. Or scared to death of succeeding. Show me how you did it.'

Then it came. First the gentle stirring of his hair on the crown of his head, then the feeling, the amazing calm feeling, like coming home to himself. And the music began to flow down his hands, out through the strings of the guitar into the room; sweet sweet music.

It was not fire, not the raging turquoise fire of his dreams; this was water, water and sunlight on water, healing water washing away the past, carrying away everything that was not now, was not Joss, was not the music . . .

'Another chance?' said Otis uncomfortably.

'Not the way we did it before. I want you to hear me play at my house first. I want you to hear what I can do when I'm not out of my skull with stage-fright. Look, all you'll lose is an hour. I expect Fran will make us some supper if you turn on your charm. If I'm lousy like last time you can have a good supper and a good giggle and then go home. What harm can it do?'

'None,' said Otis. 'So long as you don't want me to say you're any good if you stink.' He pinched his nose and grinned.

'I won't stink,' said Joss confidently. 'But if I do you have my full permission to tell me so.'

'You'll have to wait for me. I've got basketball till four-thirty. Mind you, I'll be out earlier if we can't get enough fit people to play. Two kids had to be taken home last week, just flaked out as soon as they tried to run. Lee was always a weed anyway, but Stuart used to play cricket for the county. Had muscles like ginormous bags of groceries. Can't even run for the bus now. This Omega mob –'

'I don't mind waiting,' Joss said, interrupting, not wanting to hear any more.

It was while he was waiting that he saw her. Not that he hadn't seen her before of course. And right from the start, even though it was excruciating, by silent common consent they hadn't ignored each other or treated each other like poison the way some people did when they'd broken up. Just this dreadful space between them which no words were big enough to string across. They had almost been lovers and here they were, deadly polite strangers again in no time at all. He knew he'd made a mess of it but how could anyone ever put such a huge disaster right? Cleaning up an oil-slick was nothing beside it.

She was with Tamar Tetley in the empty classroom next to the gym. Dressed in baggy blue sweat trousers, her hair pulled up high in a pony tail that made her look about nine, she was standing in that strange loose-kneed stance people use in martial arts, her arms slightly forward, fists closed, as if they were resting on air. The ferocious concentration on her face touched him to the core. There was a large bruise on her forehead that had reached the green and yellow stage.

Asha McGillveray, who are you now? he thought. He had seen Asha as his perfect princess, his to rescue or imprison, and here she was, out in the world getting herself knocked down and banged about, grimly picking herself up again; saving herself through her own efforts. Through the open door he heard them murmuring.

'Push your heels out,' said Tamar, walking round Asha critically. 'That's better. Now step back with your weight on the right foot. Your feet should form a T square. Right – the arm movement in two stages, remember, a really fast sweep overhead, yes, like a scythe, perfect, Asha, then slowly, as if you're pulling an invisible bow. No, no – too soft, too passive, this should be warrior-like – yes! This kata is all about holding power, first you build it up, then contain it – then you let it all out. At the end you should be absolutely empty. I'll show you the next bit – '

Tamar assumed an identical expression of remote concentration, apparently connecting herself to some inner power supply. She repeated the first sequence, and it was like a dance, when Tamar did it, Joss thought, a dance, a prayer and a challenge all in one. Then like a rogue catherine wheel her skinny limbs began shooting out in all directions as if she had dozens more than the usual number of arms and legs.

'I do love it when you do that, Tamar,' said Asha impressed. 'You look like an exploding Swiss Army knife.'

'Thanks a lot. I actually preferred it when you said I looked like the Indian goddess with all the arms. It's only because it's done at different speeds,' said Tamar, not even out of breath. 'Now your turn, Ms McGillveray.'

'Tamar and Asha – what a combination,' said Otis, appearing through the changing-room doors and peering surreptitiously through the window. 'What are those two up to?'

Joss shook his head. 'I can't begin to imagine,' he said. 'But they're not dressed in black yet. Come on.'

'Well,' said Joss later, 'are you staying for supper?' Otis had been so quiet, Joss wondered if he'd somehow offended him. He knew how he'd played. He couldn't not know. The guitar told him. The power poured down his hands like liquid gold and he and the guitar spoke to each other and the conversation was getting better every time.

Otis shook his head and then correcting himself hastily, said, 'Oh, I'd like to stay to eat all right. It smells fantastic – whatever your mum's cooking downstairs. But I just don't know what to say. How could you play that badly before, I mean, no offence, Joss, but you were rubbish, you know you were and now – I mean, it's like, Eric Clapton, eat your heart out. What's going on? Were you having us on, or something?'

He thinks I was trying to make a fool of them, Joss realised. 'Why would I do that, you nerd? I just played badly that's all. I've been practising a lot since then.'

Otis shook his head again. 'That – how you played for me

just now – that isn't just to do with practise. Before, you played like some kind of loser. As if you were just waiting to get it wrong and for us to despise your guts. But now, when you play it's as if the music is the only thing in the world, and what anyone else thinks about it just isn't the point. There's not even you any more. There's just the music.'

Otis's words came back to Joss when he was trying to sleep that night. Fran used to have a silly record from her own childhood. *Sparky and the Magic Piano*. Sparky was an obnoxious American child who could play Daniel Barenboim into the ground just so long as he was playing on the magic piano. Joss still had vague recollections of a nightmare finale in which smug old Sparky sat down to play in front of his huge expectant audience and the piano heartstoppingly refused to oblige. (At that point a young Joss always had to hide behind the sofa.)

So why didn't Joss feel as if he was cheating when he played the blue guitar? He thought Otis had answered this. The guitar didn't just help him cut out his fear of other people's disapproval, it cut out his need to impress them too. When he took the blue guitar into his hands something happened to Joss that had never happened to him before in his life. A kind of completeness. A kind of love. It was what he had been looking for with Asha. And he had hated her, punished her sometimes because she couldn't give it to him.

But in a way she had given it to him, he thought. She had booted him down the hillside to sort himself out and he had been to Hell and back. And now he had found the music he had been searching for since he first lay awake all those years ago, hoping and wishing for the songs to come again.

14   Tribal Wave

'She isn't well again today,' said Aunt Izzy, anxiously. 'I wish she'd eat. She should see a doctor but if I suggest it she gets so hysterical I'm afraid she'll run off again.'

'We'll cheer her up,' comforted Asha. 'Tamar can play her new party piece.'

'Finish her off,' growled Tamar, 'more like.'

Until Bethany's arrival the spare room hadn't been used for years. It was stuffed with foreign artefacts; exotic, antique clothes and just plain junk that had overflowed from the rest of the house over decades. The aunts hated to throw things away.

Bethany was occupying the smallest possible area of the huge carved bed, staring into space, absently mutilating a corner of the quilt. Asha took her hand, uncurling it gently from the Indian cotton. 'I know it must seem like it, but it's not the end of the world,' she said.

'Isn't it?' Bethany's face was puffy from days of crying, her eyes lifeless blue stones, her hair uncombed. 'I wish it was. I wish I'd died in that storm, then it would all be over now.'

'You don't,' said Tamar, sitting on the other side of the bed. 'Or you wouldn't have dragged yourself here. You're just scared that's all. You're as tough as old boots, Bethany Blessed and you're going to have a brilliant life. You're going to have a fantastic little kid – '

Bethany buried her face in the pillow. 'How can I go through with it? How can I? I'm only sixteen. How can I look after it? I haven't got a family. I haven't got any money. I haven't even finished school – '

'You could always have it ad – ,' Tamar began but Bethany was upright in a flash, her face a blaze of white.

'Don't! Don't even say that to me. How can you *say* that?'

'Because she's trying to help you think sensibly about what you're going to do for a change,' said Asha, crossly.

They had been patient and understanding with Bethany for days. Perhaps it was time for a different approach.

'You can't wallow about for ever, you know, saying how wicked you are and how you deserve to suffer, condemning yourself to the everlasting whatsit. You might as well go back home if you're going to put yourself through all that sins of the fathers stuff,' said Asha. 'Getting pregnant doesn't make you a bad person, Bethie, just a *human* person. Look, we'll help you. The aunts will help you. We'll be your family if you like. But we can't do it without *you*. Besides you aren't a kid. In some countries you'd have been married years ago. You could have a string of babies. We keep people helpless longer here. You've got to face up to the – '

'But you don't know,' wept Bethany, clutching at Asha. 'He told me he loved me. You can't know how much I wanted to believe it. No-one said they loved me before. I knew he didn't mean it. I knew all the time. How could anyone love me? I'm no-one. I'm nothing. You don't know what it was like afterwards. How ashamed I was. How awful it is having no-one to – '

'No, I don't,' said Asha, waving away Bethany's hysterical outpourings as if they were so much static. 'I know I don't. I wouldn't have survived half of it. But you did and you did because you're tons tougher than you think and because deep down, however crazy it might be, you really want this baby and you already love it to bits so you'd better get off your bum and start making plans for the two of you.'

'Asha!' said Aunt Maddy shocked, coming in with a tea tray. 'Really! She's still very fragile, you know.'

'Rubbish,' said Asha brutally. 'Ornaments are fragile. Women are as tough as hell.'

Bethany spluttered into her tea, startled out of her weepy apathy. 'Asha – you really have changed, what's happened to you?' she said. 'You used to be all piano lessons and lacy collars.'

'That was just her cunning disguise,' said Tamar, trying on an Edwardian hat with ostrich feathers. 'I'm thinking of adopting one too. Asha thinks I'd be even more dangerous if I wore pink angora and looked sweet.' She summoned an angelic simper, holding it until her eyes crossed.

'You'll be playing Chopin next, Tamar,' said Bethany. It was the first time they had seen her smile since she arrived at Wintergrove. It wasn't a fully fledged smile but it was a good stab at one. She was sitting up properly between them now, not clinging or cringing, her hand resting gently on her stomach, her expression clearer and more open than it had been, since Asha had known her.

'Not Chopin, *exactly*,' said Asha.

'Chopsticks perhaps?' Tamar suggested.

'Do you think I could have a sandwich or something?' asked Bethany. 'I'm really starving.'

'I think the aunts could do better than a sandwich,' said Asha. 'They've been filling the cupboards with little delicacies for days in the hope they could tempt you to eat.'

They picnicked on the spare room carpet, girls, aunts, the monkey-faced kitten and all. Aunt Izzy made one of her curries and Bethany, who had miraculously let go of her need to suffer, insisted the fumes would not keep her awake later. It was an oddly assorted but entirely cheerful gathering Asha thought, fending off the marauding kitten (who had discovered that one of the dishes contained prawns).

How she could ever have panicked at the notion of sharing her birthday celebration with these people? She had been a different person, she thought. So different she could scarcely remember that old Asha. For a moment she felt Valli close to her, could feel her approval, breathed in her odours of cinnamon and sandalwood.

'This room,' sighed Aunt Maddy. 'We must do something about it. It's so stiff with the past in here one can hardly breathe. Why do we hang on to everything so, Isobel?'

Isobel helped Bethany to a second mound of yellow rice. 'Maybe we were afraid of moving forward,' she said. 'Maybe we thought it would be dangerous to do things differently.'

'New lamps for old,' said Asha softly, thinking that the aunts had already changed beyond recognition. They had accepted Bethany and her unborn baby into their household with far less fuss than they'd made when Asha brought the kitten home. And here they were, mopping up their gravy with home-made chapatis, perched on the floor like hippies, positively relishing eccentricity. What would Grandfather have said?

'Hey, this is good,' said Tamar. Having stuffed herself in blissful silence and given up teasing the kitten with the ostrich feathers, she was now rootling impertinently in a tea-chest. 'I know what this is, it's a thumb piano. It's African, isn't it?' She tinkered with the little instrument producing a satisfying melodic sound like water running gently over large pebbles. 'Bet you don't need to read music to play this.'

Asha never knew how it happened or why they gradually drifted downstairs, with bits and pieces of musical instruments from the spare room, how they wound up singing snatches of songs and giggling round the piano, Tamar, still wearing her ostrich feathers, flourishing some sort of tambourine around her head. Unless the Box was still exerting a mysterious influence from its old hiding place in her chest of drawers.

The extraordinary part was when Bethany stood up, and added her voice to their ragged rendering of *Amazing Grace*. Not in a girl's wobbly soprano, nor a bland Eurovision cutesy quaver, but a woman's voice using its full range, deep throated, husky; strong enough to fill a cathedral, wall to wall.

Their voices faded down uncertainly under the sheer swelling power of Bethany's. Finally everyone else shut up in simple disbelief. Asha's hands stumbled and stopped. But without faltering Bethany carried on unaccompanied, as if now she had begun she would sing forever.

When the last note died Tamar unfroze, cast off her moulting ostrich plumes, rushed to Bethany and seized her in a strangling embrace, crying and laughing all at once. 'How did you learn to sing like that? However did you learn? Bethany Blessed, you dark dark horse, don't you ever give that up for anything or anyone. Don't you *ever*.'

'MIDLANDS LIGHT AND POWER,' said Joss, as well as he could through a mouthful of nails. 'Why *do* you have that on your van? I keep meaning to ask.'

They were working late on the extension Mike was building to *Pinocchio's*. Joss still regarded himself as congenitally ham-fisted but he was coming to enjoy the times he helped Mike out. Mike was undemanding company, taking everyone as he found them. Joss liked the way he never set himself up as having the answers. In fact Mike was brutally frank about his own shortcomings, admitting how much he missed his own small son, now growing up on the other side of the world with his mother and stepfather in New Zealand.

'My old Sherpa?' said Mike, tickled. 'I bought it in an auction. Off a maverick electrician with big ideas who went bankrupt. You still haven't put that one in straight. You don't have to be so flaming timid with that hammer, it won't bite. Anyway I thought it was a lucky name so I kept it. How's the group going these days?'

He followed Joss's progress with genuine interest though he swore he was tone-deaf himself. He certainly sang as though he was.

'Better,' said Joss, hammering intently. 'They were so scared of being mediocre they'd backed themselves into a really exclusive little ghetto. So clever no-one could understand what the hell they were doing. We're developing our own style now. Still special, still real music, but the kind of stuff ordinary people might almost want to dance to.'

'You're not one of this sackcloth and ashes brigade, then? You know, the bunch of kids that trails around in undertaker's gear with their brains in neutral.'

'You're kidding,' said Joss. 'It's sick. Tyke says it's vulture music.'

'I'm relieved to hear you say so,' said Mike. 'One of their songs came on the van radio the other day, what was it called *Going Home*? It made me feel like putting my fist through someone's head, if I knew who to blame for letting this all get so out of hand. I decided I'd start with the smarmy D.J.s actually, and work my way systematically through the parents and the teachers. What are they thinking of? Allowing these poor kids . . . Joss, that song was morbid, sick with longing for some place that never existed anywhere except inside us. As if there was ever anyone but us, or anywhere else but here,'

Mike sighed. 'These kids have got it all inside them, everything they could ever need but they are trading it for a worthless dream. Maybe even a dangerous dream. Perhaps I'm not one to talk. I know I haven't always been the reliable pillar of the community you see before you today. But you see, what's happened, Joss, I think, is the planet's *shrunk*. Once people who were fed up with themselves and their lives could sail off to America or Australia and make a new start. But all those old escape routes have been cut off. So in our times we've got no choice but to stay put and sort ourselves and our poor suffering planet out. We've got to face the music this time, that's what I think – but some people just can't handle it – what are you grinning at, boy, this is free philosophy you're getting here, as well as valuable work experience and all the PG Tips you can swig down your gullet.'

' "Face the music," ' said Joss apologetically.

'Ha bloody ha.'

But after a bit Joss looked up from his work to find Mike grinning quietly to himself.

'I've started writing songs, you know,' Joss said super-casually.

'Yeh? Are they any good?'

'The latest one is,' said Joss smiling. 'The latest one is magic.'

'Ah, the latest one is always the best,' said Mike. 'Hey – careful with that chisel!'

He was too late. Joss was already clutching his wrist, the smile wiped from his face. 'It slipped,' he said, greenish with shock. He hated blood, especially his own, in such large quantities.

'Here,' said Mike. 'Let me – '

He seized Joss's hand in his two stubby-fingered hands, holding it firmly and without fuss.

'What are you doing? Is it an artery? Shouldn't I go to Casualty?'

'It's just a nasty gash. Don't panic.'

'It's getting awfully hot,' said Joss uncomfortably. He felt sick, having visions of his life's blood welling up unstoppably, great crimson geysers of it with every pulse of his heart.

'It will do,' agreed Mike calmly. 'Another few minutes should do it.'

Actually the pain was ebbing away quite quickly now. Perhaps he hadn't hurt it as badly as he thought. He wriggled his hand free to look. Joss was neurotic about his body. A born hypochondriac, Fran said.

'What did you do?' he demanded in disbelief. 'Did you do that?'

It had been bleeding, he was sure it had or where had all the mess come from, on his tee shirt, on the floor? But there was scarcely a mark, just the faintest inflammation that might turn into a bruise in an hour or two. Seconds before he was bleeding like a pig from a jagged opening in his flesh and now his hand was whole.

Mike sighed. 'Now you'll have a bruise,' he said disappointedly. 'If you'd only kept still like I asked. Still, at least you can finish off tonight's job now.' And he grinned his overseer's grin.

It was Martha Joss told, while they were washing up some nights later. Asha was the only person who would really understand but he couldn't tell her and if he didn't tell someone he would burst. Joss's whole world had turned upside down and inside out; sucked down some galactic hole into the unknown. When he had been going out with Asha, her blasted Box, the avenging Furies, even the Paradise Peep-show had seemed like fantastic hallucinations he could never shape to fit his own reality. He just could not put Asha's magical world and his rational scientific one together but lived with them uneasily side by side. But Mike Zamirski! He'd been a self-confessed yob, a tearaway in his twenties. 'Lived on beer and aspirin for years,' he'd told Joss. 'I like to think I mellowed in later life.'

'That must be why he offered to look at my eye that day,' he said to Martha. 'We just thought he was a bit batty, like those blokes that wander into hospitals and do brain operations and then amble out again!'

When he glanced up from the sink Martha was looking not

just impressed, but awed, her eyes enormous with the implications of his story.

'Joss,' she squeaked. 'Just think – a carpenter who does healing!'

'Don't be daft,' said Joss crossly. 'Anyway he's not a carpenter, he's a small-time plumber who dabbles a bit. Mike's the most ordinary bloke in the world. He tells awful jokes. He has hairs in his ears – he's divorced for heaven's sake. He's got a little boy in New Zealand. His wife left him because he was such a chauvinist she couldn't stand him.'

But Martha, though she allowed her holy rapture to fade, remained stubborn: 'Camouflage,' she said. 'A camouflage of ordinariness, that's all. You're taken in by what people look like, whether they impress you or not – so you don't see what they really are.'

'And you do,' Joss jeered, running hot water into the sink, hoping he could get away with leaving the casserole dish to soak. 'Female intuition. I should have known.'

'No, I don't always know,' said Martha. 'But sometimes I do, Joss. And he is a special man. You can be quiet with him and it isn't horrible silence. He sees the true inside of things. He isn't taken in by camouflage. If you leave that for Mum to do she'll be really mad,' she added smugly. She banged pans around in cupboards and then said, 'Are you having band practice tonight?'

'Yep.'

'Can I come and listen?'

'No, it'll finish too late.'

'Can I come one time, though?'

'Yes,' he said, softening. It wasn't often he could impress Martha but she was fascinated by the whole idea of him playing in a rock group. At first he had thought it would make a difference, knowing that he and Martha had different fathers. As if he was no longer entitled to have her as his sister at all. Once he would have cheered at the very idea. But when it came right down to it, he found he minded surprisingly badly that Martha might think differently of him. But Martha set him right, bossily as usual. 'After all, I've known for ages and I still thought of you as my brother. What else could you be? A space alien? And what does it matter anyway who *planted* you? Fran brought us both up. And Richard wasn't any madder about me than he was about you.'

It was true, he thought. The secret had only had any power over him whilst it was a secret. Now it meant very little to any of them. And Fran had changed too, he thought. The anxiety he had never even seen was there had stopped haunting her eyes. And funnily enough, she didn't talk nearly so much.

'I promise you can come to rehearsals one day,' Joss said. 'But you'll need to put loads of warm things on. It's really cold there. And it smells a bit from Tom. Actually, it smells a lot.'

Otis had told him months ago that the group had a perfect place to practise. Perfect was perhaps not quite the right word for St Barnabas, a semi-derelict church no longer used for services, turned over to the community for various activities a few years ago but scarcely used even for those any more. Tom, the down and out who dossed in the crypt, kept a glittering eye on things so the early vandalism had more or less died down.

If you kept away from Tom's end of the church the smell wasn't too bad and the mobiles of silver stars, a legacy from the playgroup, blended in with the remnants of sacred decor; the battered plaster angels, the splintered saints of crimson, emerald, sapphire. Large areas of the roof had been plundered for lead. Some of the windows were partly intact but the wind whistled through the gaps viciously on cold nights.

One Arctic evening Otis turned up in a flying helmet worn over a Peruvian woollen hat, worn over a balaclava and kept all three on just for the hell of it, though once they'd been playing for an hour or so they were soaked with sweat no matter how cold the church was.

The last session was the best. Joss felt part of the group, not just a Johnny-come-lately, finally realising no-one but himself was actually waiting for him to screw it up any longer.

Taking courage he played the riff of *Tribal Wave*, his new song.

Something had woken him one night, and as he lay there, his dreams hovering just within reach, he remembered he had been involved in a vast dream jam-session with a bunch of musicians of all kinds, all nationalities. As they played, more and more kids came to join in, and some of them, he knew with one of those flashes of dream recognition were those who had answered his call for help when he played his first chords on the blue guitar. It was as if they had been having this musical conversation ever since, as if they could go on having it for ever, if he wanted to.

He had to get up and scrawl it down, shivering, wrapped in his duvet; his vision of those kindred spirits, like minds, all coming together to make music for the largest tribal gathering there had ever been; the tribe of the future.

Otis and the others had picked it up tentatively on sax, drums, bass guitar until the music gathered them up, took wing, flew them to wild places, wild, wilder, wildest; all the time Joss's guitar sounding a steady golden core at its heart, the magnetic north that would call them all home if they roamed too far.

Otis had taken off first, eyes closed, face shining, shifting back and forth apparently effortlessly between four or five different tribal rhythms. The derelict church was incandescent. The plaster angels leaning down; the stained-glass saints jumping. Joss was in another dimension by now and wasn't even surprised to find the four of them were no longer alone. Not just Tom, gently waving his bottle of Southern Comfort, eyes closing with pleasure and alcohol fumes, but the others crowding in, on the edges of the visible; some of them younger than Martha, with pan pipes, bamboo flutes, fiddles, squeeze boxes, pans hammered out of old oil drums or just the rhythmic beat of their human hands and feet; their voices joining in the tidal wash of the words, different words, different tongues but the same song, the same human song rising up, circling the stratosphere.

> Wake up,
> there's going to be a tribal wave,
> washing away the old walls and the old ways
> making space for the new world to grow . . .

At the end they could hardly speak. Joss didn't know what

141

the others had seen or sensed. It didn't matter. They had travelled to that tribal gathering place and his song had taken them.

Otis was ticking something off on his fingers.

'What?' said Joss.

'Bulgarian Wedding music, tabla, Hi-life, Amerindian, Indonesian – I didn't even know I knew all those! But they were perfect – weren't they perfect? I think we had a bit of help tonight!' He blew a kiss to the plaster angels.

Joss nodded, not even amazed that Otis understood, seeing now that if it had been possible to go back to his old home, he would never have been part of this. Just what exactly he was a part of he couldn't express. Only that it was something bigger than any of them knew.

Christy, the sax player, a public school drop-out, had wrapped himself in an old army blanket and looked like a tribal elder himself with his aquiline nose, long turquoise earring brushing his collar. Tyke was prostrated on the filthy floor on his back, arms outstretched, eyes closed, a large battered hat half over his face. Joss hadn't noticed the hat before, properly. When Tyke sat up, his face one huge intoxicated smile, the hat fell off and he threw it to Joss who caught it neatly more through luck than skill.

'Oh God,' Tyke said fervently. 'I am drunker than Tom from sheer bloody happiness. Will there be Rock bands in heaven, you guys? If not I'm never never going to die! Keep the hat, Joss. You deserve a truly charismatic hat after giving us a session like that. Anyway, it suits your arty farty image much better than mine. I'm more your simple working class hero.' He twanged his scarlet braces insultingly.

Joss shifted the hat from hand to hand. He recognised it now, the battered hat of his visions, his dreams of the blue guitar. He wanted to talk to Asha. He wanted to talk to her so much he hurt all over, but he wouldn't blame her if she didn't want to listen to him ever again. He faced facts. This was what he had. This ache, this hat, this guitar; his friends, the new songs growing inside him. It would have to be enough.

There is never anyone else but us. Never anywhere else but here.

15 *The Last Days*

He was watching TV with Martha, waiting for Fran to finish her shift before he could go out and meet the others when the phone rang.

Martha turned the sound down but went on braving a film about the near-extinction of whales. Doggedly, night after night, she watched the planet's woes unfold, the way other people watched films of operations; then woke Fran in the night sobbing.

'Oh, Joss, sorry, I wanted to talk to your mum,' said Asha's voice at the other end.

'That's okay,' said Joss. 'Fran won't be long. She's at work. Can I give her a message?'

He was amazed to hear the words coming out in the right order, possibly even making sense, while his body floated out of range, bobbing about under the ceiling, nothing but a ghostly sheet wrapped round air; all he had to anchor him was the cool sound of her voice inside his head.

'Not really. I'll phone back later.' Her voice sounded so far away. It had a tidal ebb and flow to it, as if it was crossing oceans to reach him. He thought she was going to hang up then and had no idea how to prevent her but then miraculously she was saying, 'Are you okay, Joss? Is everything okay?'

'Yes,' he said, his heart stopping. 'Yes, I'm fine. I'm playing a lot of music nowadays. With Otis and the others.'

'Yes?' She sounded surprised but cautious.

'I've even written some songs.'

'Oh, Joss.' There was a long pause during which he heard her swallow before she said, 'That's lovely. Are you pleased with them?'

'You could come over one day,' he said, 'you could come over to St Barnabas and see what you think. See if you approve.'

'One day,' she said guardedly. 'Maybe one day I will.'

'I did what you said,' he gabbled. 'Remember – about tuning into people? I wanted to play the guitar and I was terrified and I did what you said. And it worked. Sometimes I think it's the guitar, not me at all. Other times I think the guitar is changing me and I'm changing it, at the same time, perhaps – '

Perhaps she wasn't listening. Why should she listen? How could he blame her, after the way he had behaved? But she didn't hang up; she was answering.

'The Box finished changing that day,' she was saying. 'After you went. I fell asleep. And the Box changed. But since then the go – they haven't spoken to me. I don't think they've deserted me exactly. Just that I've got to do it on my own now. Only the trouble is I don't know what I'm supposed to do.'

They were talking properly to each other again. He couldn't believe it. Not just sending the thin smoke of words coiling into space; really talking. But there was so much he wanted to tell her that the gears of his brain jammed with sheer shock and delight and he couldn't say another coherent word, just stalled and stuttered like a nitwit and finally, in humiliation, gave up.

'I'll ring back later, then,' Asha said into that desperate silence. 'See you around, Joss.'

'Bye,' said Joss numbly. That was it. Over and out.

When he went back into the room Martha had switched channels. There had been another earthquake with massive death tolls somewhere, there was a prison riot somewhere else. There was yet another food scientists said was unsafe to eat. The Middle East was in turmoil. Joss could have written the stuff himself. He was remembering the birds of light streaming from Asha's hands, wondering if he dared to write a song for her. *Asha's Song* . . . A line of melody began to form in his head. There should be a faint sitar effect, yes, sitar and tabla then it should shift to an almost Celtic air, poignant, lonely, but with the tabla keeping the tension underneath. If only they had a synthesiser to get that atmospheric misty sound. He'd have to talk to Christy who always knew someone who knew someone.

Then his attention was hijacked despite himself. Someone was talking about the music business. There was a film clip of a rock concert. The camera zoomed in on a girl in the crowd. Joss froze. Blinded spectral face turned towards some dazzling ineffable source, thin arms waving like underwater weed against a heaving ocean of black; it was Tarot – he'd swear to it. He was shaken. Tarot was mixed up with his memories of the worst day of his life. If he had thought of her at all since then, it was as he might remember a bad dream that refused to leave him when he awoke.

The clip petered out. They'd been trailing next week's in-depth report on a Midlands rock group whose sales were smashing all previous known records, not just in Britain, but worldwide. What was the the secret of their extraordinary appeal? There would be an exclusive interview later that week. The Hoarsemen had never given a televised interview.

Suddenly Joss felt genuinely afraid. He had seen something and he couldn't unsee it.

The Hoarsemen were not going to go away.

They were going to grow like a creeping algae which thrives on dry summers and industrial pollution and they were not going to stop growing until they'd done what it was they had come to do. He felt a chill around his heart imagining what that might be.

Angels of death, that's what the Hoarsemen were. Angels of despair. Asha had seen it straightaway. So had Otis and Fran. Mike saw it, too. But Joss had blinded himself to their true significance, the way he had blinded himself to the truth about his father. He had been struggling too hard and too long with his own despair to see the danger for what it was until now.

'I don't want to see that programme,' said Martha, clicking the remote control, wiping the final still of those incandescent faces from the screen. 'I don't want to see them.' She shuddered. He remembered she had said she liked them that day, coming down in the car.

'Why not?' he said casually.

'Because they make people see things and feel things.

145

Because they make people want to give up,' she said, worldly Martha who knew more about what was going on around her than Joss ever would. 'I'm going to *unplug* the TV the day that's on, so they can't send their horrible Omega music down it and get me too.'

Omega music. Music of the Last Days, thought Joss.

He had thought it a sick joke, this small-town, small-time band, calling themselves the Hoarsemen, cashing in on the doom and gloom of the century's last decade. But now he understood what he had seen that day at the Earthworks as he stumbled away and he had a shattering glimpse of what they meant to do.

Asha was alone for the first time for weeks. Suddenly she was thirsty for her old solitude, yearning for the days when she used to shut herself away with the Box and its eccentric guardians.

She had felt very practical and matter of fact ringing Fran. After all, Bethany needed medical care. Fran would know what to do. But talking to Joss had made her churn with distress. She had thought she was over all that, had made a new separate life with real friends. Was there always going to be this ache of loss like a pulled tooth, whenever she met him, spoke to him. She didn't hate him. She had never hated him. Her heart had leapt when he said he was writing songs, playing the guitar again. 'You see,' it babbled happily. 'He *is* changing. The goddesses said he would. You helped him after all.'

But she would rather stand under a tree in a thunderstorm than allow herself to love anyone ever again.

She opened her drawer, gently uncovering the crystal octagon. It hummed at her touch for old time's sake, she thought sadly, as a cat obliges with a purr when all it really wants is to be left to sleep. But that was all she could coax from it.

'Hello, Box,' she said softly. 'Old friend. Old mystery. The aunts said they used to tell their troubles to the bees so why shouldn't I talk to you? Something is going to happen, isn't it? Something big? You know everything, you really do know everything but you can't tell me. When you came you knew every terrible thing that had ever happened in the world. Remember when you had nightmares? Remember how I sang to you? Now I've changed and you've changed and we're both waiting for something and I get terrified just imagining what it might be. Won't you talk to me? You could send me pictures like you did before? Won't you help me?'

The Box glimmered at her silently, so lovely in its latest starry manifestation she wanted to weep. They had come so far together but why? For what?

Desperately she sent out her mind then, seeking the goddesses, reaching beyond the house, beyond the street, the town, soaring further and further, imploring them, '*Speak* to me. Help me!'

Her face was wet.

Then, when she had given up hope, the faintest tremor of response, a blue-green wraith of a whisper, across vast distances

. . . *the Last Days* . . .

'I don't understand,' said Asha trembling, hoping she had misunderstood, wishing she had left well alone, wondering if there was some witch's curse laid on her that she always had to know the truth however bad it was. 'What do you mean, last days of what?'

But the whisper was already filling her head, filling her room, spiralling like the sudden wind through trees before an electrical storm; her curtains blowing, the door banging on its hinges; the words no longer a thready far-off whisper but a thunderous command:

Prepare for the Last Days.

16   The Return of the Goddess

'Well I'd like to go and watch them rehearse,' said Tamar. 'There's nothing else to do and I fancy that Tyke like anything. Ever seen him, Asha?'

It was March and Tamar was buzzing with sympathetic spring fever.

Asha shook her head. The Box seemed as troubled as she was since that baffling communication from the goddesses. It hadn't resumed its full-scale night terrors, but Asha and the Box slept badly nowadays. Once again shadows moving and clotting on her wall when she woke at night; confused shapes, only vaguely perceived but somehow all the more threatening for that.

She was tired to death all the time, longing to creep away by herself but Bethany got depressed if left to her own devices for too long. But Asha was a wreck herself. Couldn't work. Couldn't even play the piano, usually her last refuge. She could scarcely even think coherently. It was as if she and the Box were gathering their combined energies for some terrifying leap forward. But into what? Lately she had come close to telling Tamar and Bethany about the Box. She had to do it some time, why not now?

'Bethany would like to come, wouldn't you, Bethie?' wheedled Tamar. 'She's been stuck in for weeks. She's getting prison pallor. Fran said she should get out more.'

Bethany nodded shyly. She was still confused about how she should behave. But if Tamar thought it was all right to be pregnant and have a good time, maybe it was. 'I'd like to go. But what if anyone sees me?'

'We'll disguise you,' said Tamar who always brightened up at the thought of intrigue. 'We'll smuggle you there.'

'I don't know,' said Asha. Hanny, sensing her unhappiness, scrambled up from her lap and peered into her face with his round golden eyes, so that she found herself laughing and comforting him. She couldn't imagine life without her sleek little monkey-cat. 'Oh, I suppose so. Maybe.'

Perhaps she needed something to take her mind off the morgue-like atmosphere at school. People she'd known for years, become used to even if she hadn't liked them, flesh and blood teenagers at least, raucously barging into each other in the corridor, now scarcely more substantial than the shadows on her wall; their faces blinded, blissful, yet thinner, paler, more ethereal with every passing day.

Some of them had stopped attending school, hanging around the town instead, as if they were expecting some kind of summons. If the teachers noticed they didn't say. Preoccupied with their own troubles they preferred small silent classes to large rioting ones any day.

It made Asha sick to see Ghoul dragging himself up the stairs, his breath rasping, his forehead clammy; Gunny, more skull-like than ever, his cheekbones caves of shadow, swaying in his seat to the Omega Sound in his head; Zoë and Gita doodling pyramid symbols in margins, smiling secretively at each other, with the completion of each scrawl. What were the symbols *for*? Asha was even beginning to dream about them herself which horrified her as if she too was snared in the dark sticky web being stretched across the planet to catch and harness who knew what?

Once Asha heard Zoe whisper 'Soon!' and Gita squeezed her hand, her doe eyes bloodshot with tears. Not tears of sorrow, Asha thought. Tears of joy.

What did they *know*? What were they waiting for? What did they understand that the others, the outsiders, Asha and the rest of them did not? She had been sure Bethany would know, the only one of the three who had been to the concert at the Apocalypse Café. But Bethany had never reached it, it turned out. Carl Lieberman never had tickets, and only told her so to get her to come out with him. Tamar told Asha it was no use asking the Followers themselves.

'It isn't that they won't tell you, Asha. It's that they can't. They can only talk in riddles. The Hoarsemen have programmed them and the Omega Sound is what keeps them programmed. It acts like a drug. When it wears off they realise how weak and hungry they are. Each time they surface the world seems even stranger and more terrible to them than it did before. So they plug themselves back into The Sound and they feel back on course, part of something again.'

The Followers themselves were calling it The Sound, these days, as if there was only one significant sound to speak of. That scared Asha too, imagining a hideous discordant cosmic vibration drowning out all small sounds of human effort, laughter, squabbles, lawnmowing. Passing a busker playing wild improvised flights on his saxophone in the town centre that morning she thought ridiculously: You're on our side. You won't let them turn everyone into sleepwalkers.

'What about the pyramid patterns?' she asked, but Tamar said she had no idea.

'It's no use buying the records either,' Tamar said. 'The records don't work so powerfully unless you've been "in their actual presence," as Ghoul and Gunny say. I saw the Hoarsemen, the first time they were interviewed on TV and they were nice as pie. Swore they'd got no idea why the young were following them around the country in thousands but they thought it was because the kids hadn't got anyone left but rock musicians to believe in. "We care about the same issues that concern our fans. Famine, war, pollution, the destruction of their planet. They trust us not to sell them down the river like their parents have, like their teachers, like our politicians. When we perform our material for them at concerts we give them back their faith in a beautiful future."' Tamar's mimickry was chilling in its accuracy.

'Beautiful —'

'Yeh — a beautiful graveyard,' said Tamar. 'If it isn't stopped. But who's going to stop it, Asha? Have you heard anyone speak out? You've got to be kidding. It's the perfect way to keep us out of their hair. It's so perfect it could almost be an adult conspiracy. After all, they've messed up the planet, why not finish off the kids as well. That takes care of the problem of what will happen to us in the future when the ozone layer is shot to pieces and the petrol's run out and the Green-house Effect has turned America into a dust-bowl. We won't be here to see it. Have you seen Zoë lately?' she asked abruptly.

'She looks like a stick insect,' said Asha to Bethany. 'I can't stand to look at her. She can hardly drag herself about but she has this insane little smile hovering on her lips all the time. Tamar's right. No one cares. No one's going to do anything.'

Bethany had been growing increasingly agitated, her hand curved protectively around her growing bump. 'I can't believe the Hoarsemen really want people to die? What good could that possibly do them? That kind of thing only happens in *Superman*, not in real life.'

Tamar shook her head. 'I don't think that is what they want,' she said soberly. 'Oh someone's planning something but I don't think the Hoarsemen understand it any better than their fans. I remember them when they used to jam in someone's back yard with tacky instruments bought out of catalogues. They were angry and despairing all right and they had a certain sexy *something*, but I don't remember them being awfully bright, to tell you the truth. Just hooked on getting rich and famous like everyone else. Someone's using them. Someone or something.'

Bethany paled. 'That sounds spooky, Tamar,' she said. 'As if they've sold their soul to the devil. Don't.'

But Asha knew Tamar was speaking the truth, experiencing that satisfying inward click of things fitting invisibly together that she recognised from working with the goddesses. Almost absently she sent her mind out towards her friend, the way the Winged One had taught her. It was like learning to swim in the sea, timing waves. She'd forgotten how good it felt.

'You mean using them to make money out of the kids, don't you,' said Bethany pleadingly.

'No,' said Asha, catching her breath slightly. 'She doesn't. It's much much bigger than that but we can't do anything now. Come on – I'll give in to the mindless majority. Let's go to St Barnabas and watch them practise.'

She was being bossy to cover her shock. To her astonishment her mind had exploded into Tamar's in a lightning-bolt exchange and, meeting her eyes, Tamar nodded, her lips tight, her eyes brimming. She had not wanted Bethany to hear what she knew.

Something inhuman was fattening off the despair of the

Hoarsemen's teenage followers. And in return for unquestioning devotion, in return for the sacrifice of health, family, future, something had made them an extraordinary impossible promise.

To their dismay, Bethany suddenly burst into furious tears. 'Don't shut me out,' she sobbed. 'I'm in this too. You're the ones that keep saying I can live a normal life even if I am sixteen and pregnant. But you're treating me as if I'm handicapped or something. You needn't think you're so special. I've been able to hear you two thinking for ages now. I don't understand what's happening to the three of us but we're in this together and if we aren't honest, if we don't trust each other and share what we know – we're no better than the rest of them.'

Tamar, guilt-stricken, tried to put her arms around Bethany but the girl shook her off. 'It's not you,' she wept. 'It's Asha I'm angry with. Ask Asha why it feels so funny in her room all the time. Ask her what she keeps hidden away in there. Ask her where it came from and what it's for and why she doesn't trust us enough to tell us, when we're supposed to be her friends – Go on!'

Tamar turned to Asha, bewildered. 'Asha – ?'

'I'm sorry,' said Asha, when she could speak. The blood had drained from her face. 'I wanted to tell you – '

But that was not the truth and Tamar and Bethany, whose minds now ebbed and flowed so alarmingly in and out of her own, knew it as well as she did. Though the Box had terrified her, plagued her, worn her to a shred at times, it had not only brought immense joy. Finding it had given her the perfect explanation for her past loneliness, past sufferings, even for losing Joss.

Asha was special. So special she was entrusted with a heroic task. With the Box in her possession she could become wise and strong and heal the world.

She had not wanted to be true equals with Tamar or Bethany, but to inspire, lead and dazzle. Now she couldn't even hide her self-disgust for the Box had worked its maddening alchemy on her friends, too, and they knew her thoughts as soon as she knew them herself.

'Come upstairs,' she said. 'I'll show you. All right, I know I'm a toad. If it makes you feel any better, Bethie, I want to crawl away and die of shame.'

Tamar laughed. 'Don't be stupid,' she said, comfortably. 'You only feel so awful because you work so hard at being good. It takes time to trust people. You haven't had much practice.'

'Shut the door,' said Asha. 'I don't suppose we need to draw the curtains but I usually do.'

It was Bethany, still sniffling and hiccupping, who drew them.

Asha's hands shook as she took the bundle out of the drawer, placed it on the carpet, gently unwrapping it. Bethany gasped as the room filled up at once with blue and green starlight. That was new, thought Asha.

In the fizzing heart of the light the octagonal crystal star of the Box glimmered and glowed, even humming faintly as though she was still touching it. There was no doubting its power any longer. It's because there's more of us, she thought. It *wants* to be shared.

'Did it really feel different in my room, Bethie? I must have got used to it. Well here it is, this is the Box,' she said, feeling absurdly as if she was introducing it, as if she was responsible for it in some way.

Tamar sat still as a stone, her expression sphinx-like.

Bethany was on her knees, her eyes huge pools of wonder. She stretched her hands towards the starry box then withdrew them with a sharp intake of breath as if she was afraid its beauty would burn her.

'It felt like singing,' she said, hardly audible. 'Soundless singing. It filled the house at night so I couldn't sleep. Oh, Asha I'm sorry I was so horrible. It's such – a *holy* thing. Of course you had to keep it safe till it was ready to be seen. It's just – I thought it was because you really despised me you didn't tell me.'

Tamar lit the candle. Its earthly beam swam out into the celestial light of the Box itself, coalescing with it. Then the three girls joined hands, the Box between them.

'This room feels very full suddenly,' whispered Bethany.

'And awfully hot. Sorry my hands are sweaty.'

Asha, her heart in her mouth, knew it was the goddesses crowding in but there were not usually so many, she thought. With a stab of joy she recognised the Winged One, and Beauty in dull rose-coloured silk, a white blossom in her hair. The motherly goddess had grown young again and had a child at her breast. The pushy one was wearing a jade nose jewel, a fiery looking helmet and shield and a very indecent jade green leather mini skirt; for a joke, she thought.

But beyond these familiar figures were other forms, other faces, far too many to squeeze into her bedroom, yet still they came flocking: young, old, white, black and golden; wise, wild, fierce and tender; shining, visionary beings.

Then Asha understood. The goddesses had never been separate except in her mind. There was only one. Like different facets of a single jewel these beings had always been, were and always would be one and only one. In the blue-green starlight of Asha's room they swam together, all boundaries blurring, the many faces becoming one face until the room sang unbearably with Her power and joy.

Tamar hid her face, silently weeping. Bethany held out her arms like a child, her eyes closed, her face ecstatic. Asha was terrified, her teeth chattering, but she had to speak.

'Forgive me,' she whispered, her lips scarcely able to form words. 'Forgive me.' She did not understand her own behaviour, just realised that all her life she had struggled with the vague sense of being responsible for some forgotten wrong, so cruel and terrible she could never put it right on her own.

There was no answer, only surging wave upon wave of love like a warm wind gusting through a bluebell wood.

Tears rolled down Asha's face.

Then She was gone. The three girls blinked at Asha's bedroom walls wavering in the candle-light.

'An older wiser Mother that's been forgotten too long,' the woman had said.

And She had returned from her long exile.

They walked to St Barnabas in a silence closer than conversation. Asha's limbs felt unfamiliar; strong, somehow new-made, as if light not blood ran in her veins. Tamar took them carefully by the back ways and they saw no-one Bethany knew. There were no sounds of music coming from the church when they arrived, but someone had got there before them, squatting exhaustedly in the porch; a girl in tatters of gauzy black, her slicked-back hair stiff with dirt, a black cotton tote bag clutched in her arms. When she saw them she staggered to her feet.

'Someone told me Joss Emerson would be here,' she said, 'but the door's locked. Do you know where I can find him? I've got to tell someone. They're coming. They're coming here in the middle of the biggest open air concert there's ever been and They're going to take everyone away.' Then she began to shake all over.

17   *The Song of All Beginnings*

When Joss turned up he was with Tyke.

'I don't see the problem. Tin Ear is a brilliant name for a band,' Tyke was arguing as they came through the door. Their faces changed as they saw the girls.

'Tarot – ' said Joss. 'How did you – ?'

Then, catching sight of Bethany he did a double-take.

'Hallo,' she said nervously.

'Don't you dare apologise for yourself,' whispered Tamar fiercely.

'A man told us we could wait inside,' said Asha, her nostrils still twitching slightly. 'Tarot was tired. She hitched from Oxford to see you, Joss.'

'Do you want something to eat?' said Tyke. 'You must be half-dead.' Then he smote himself on the head. 'I didn't really say that,' he said to the plaster angels. 'Did I say that?'

The girl tried to smile but tears splashed down her face. 'No thanks,' she said. 'I don't eat much. I seem to have got out of the habit. I'd really like a cup of tea, though.'

'I'll have a word with Tom,' said Tyke. 'He has his uses if

you're not too fussy. I promise I'll wash the cups *very* thoroughly.'

Otis and Christy arrived as he vanished into the gloom and Joss introduced everyone.

'But you disappeared,' said Otis to Bethany, astonished. 'I didn't know you came back.'

'I'm keeping away from my family,' she said. 'Until the baby's born.'

Tamar squeezed Bethany's hand. 'Better, much better,' she whispered.

'Sorry,' said Otis. 'I didn't – I mean –'

'Don't worry,' said Bethany sunnily. 'I'm fine. I'm living with Asha now.'

'Tom says does the little girl want something stronger in it?' said Tyke returning with steaming mugs.

'Is there something stronger than Jeyes Fluid?' Christy asked, peering into the fierce black brew, his eyes watering.

'Why did you come all this way, Tarot?' Joss came to sit beside her. 'How did you find me?' She was even thinner than when he had first met her and the white transparency of her skin had a grimier pall. Her throat was bare where her medallion should have been.

'You told me where you lived, don't you remember? That night at the bus station. I always remember someone kind. A woman in a café told me you come here when you're not helping some Polish bloke.'

They waited for her to go on, but Tarot was staring into her tea. 'I don't know how to tell you,' she whispered. 'Now I'm here it doesn't seem as if it could be true. It feels safe here. It feels nice. I only knew I had to come. I didn't think about what I'd do when I got here.'

Silently Tamar came to sit next to her and Asha also moved instinctively closer.

'There's going to be a concert,' said Tarot. 'Not just any concert. A concert like there's never been anywhere, ever. An open air concert. They're holding it near here. I can't remember what it's called but it's one of those old stone kind of places, like Stonehenge.'

Joss was watching Asha. She's not in the least surprised, he thought. She said the Earthworks was a place of power. And those jokers know just what they're doing. I wish the hell I did.

'Thousands of Followers are coming,' Tarot was saying. 'It's going to be free. Because the Hoarsemen love their fans so much. And now they're such big stars they want to share their success with them. Thank them.' She gave a cynical little grin.

No one said anything. Tarot drew a shuddering breath. 'They've worked out the best day and everything. I don't understand it, but the moon's going to be full and we're supposed to prepare for it for days beforehand, right? But only the Followers know that part.'

'How?' Joss was fidgeting with his guitar strings. 'How has everybody got to prepare beforehand?'

'Listen to the Sound constantly,' said Tamar, interrupting. 'Draw a hell of a lot of symbols, am I right?'

'Yes,' said Tarot, surprised. 'How did you know?'

'It helps to bring Them closer,' explained Asha.

'What is this – some kind of seance?' objected Christy.

'You see not eating or sleeping changes our energy vibes,' said Tarot who was also looking baffled, 'and makes it easier for the Sound to flow through us. That's why we listen to it all the time, so we'll be in harmony with each other, all our minds working as one mind, so we'll be ready, so we can guide Them in, help Them land.'

'Help them land?' spluttered Tyke. 'Bloody Hell – what is this?'

'It'll hover over us,' said Tarot. 'And we'll just be drawn up into it effortlessly like rays of light.'

'Christ,' said Otis. 'Would it be too crude to ask about the heavier bits of your anatomy?'

'Left behind,' said Tarot. 'Like husks. I used to think it would be beautiful,' she began to cry. 'To leave the shell of my old self behind and be reborn as a child of light. It's why we wear black. To hide our true light until the time comes. Until They come. It was the best day of my life when I understood what They were telling us through the songs. I knew I wanted to be taken away to Their perfect world and be happy forever. I didn't want to go on living in Hell. I had hope when I was a Follower. I had a reason. They were going to give us

157

everything we'd dreamed of. If we would only love Them, love Them enough to leave everything behind.'

'But I don't understand why you're here,' said Joss gently. 'If you're a Follower and you *want* to leave everything behind – '

'Because I can't be a Follower any more – ' Tarot sobbed. 'Because I – ' She drew up her knees and bowed her head over them as though she was in terrible physical pain, rocking herself with misery. 'Because of what will happen to the *others* – '

'The others?' Joss didn't understand.

'The people who aren't Followers,' said Asha. 'The people who turn up out of curiosity or because they fancy a free pop concert. The Hell's Angels. The hippies who travel around all the concerts and festivals.'

'There you go again,' said Christy. 'I hate it when you do that. I didn't see Tarot's lips move once.'

'It's bigger even than that,' said Tamar, just as if Christy hadn't spoken. Her eyes were closed. She seemed to be listening hard. 'It's a generation we're talking about. A whole generation.' She opened her eyes then and shook her head to clear it. 'No, how could that be possible?' she muttered as though to comfort herself. But her eyes remained clouded and her words went on hanging in the air, chilling them all.

'They say it would take too long to prepare *everyone* you see,' said Tarot. 'But They need as many people as possible to come to the concert. There still aren't quite enough Followers to guide Them in. It's like *thought* energy. The Sound tunes us to Their thoughts more perfectly and because of the place they've chosen – there's something under the ground, some funny kind of lines, they made it sound like electricity cables – '

'Leylines,' said Joss tensely.

'And the – I don't know, the position of the stars and stuff, on that particular day the Sound will be the most powerful ever. By the end of the concert even the kids that aren't real Followers will be properly tuned to Them. They won't be able to help themselves. But – but they won't be prepared, like the rest of us.'

'So – I can't really believe in this Close Encounters stuff,' said Tyke, scratching his head, 'but what are you trying to say – won't they just be effortlessly sucked up like the rest of you and hitch a free ride to the Happy Ever After?'

Tarot's face was a mask of grief. 'I was hanging around after a concert, oh I knew I'd never get to meet one of the Hoarsemen, the security's too tight now they've become so big, but I thought I might meet someone who knew them, you know. I expect it sounds stupid to you,' she said to Asha.

Asha shook her head silently.

'And I heard some of them talking about what might happen to the others. They sounded quite – scientific about it. Some of them would probably die outright. They'd be the lucky ones, they said. Because the others, the more sensitive ones, would be *almost* ready, they'd feel the longing – they'd see the beautiful vision – of how it's going to be in Their world – '

'But they won't be able to come with you, will they?' said Tamar simply. 'Because they haven't been tuning their energy fields to the Sound for months, and slowly letting go of all their connections to this world, day by day. They haven't been starving themselves or tuning their minds to Their thoughts coming through the Sound – '

'And they'll go mad,' said Tarot. She clutched her mouth as if she was going to be sick and stared around at them all, her eyes dark holes of terror. 'They said they'll probably go mad. They sounded quite sorry. But it couldn't be helped. We were the chosen ones and they weren't.'

There was a long silence.

'I couldn't be a Follower after that,' said Tarot. 'And that was the best thing I had in my whole life, following the Hoarsemen. Learning to love Them.' She rocked herself silently for a few moments. Tamar impulsively reached out a hand then checked herself and pulled viciously at a piece of her own hair instead, her eyes brimming. Tarot had withdrawn herself to a place utterly beyond human comfort.

They could hardly hear Tarot's next words. 'A Follower died, when I was sleeping rough down in Oxford. Jenny. She had a weak heart. The Sound was too much for it, along with hardly eating, sleeping out in the cold, though I tried to make sure she always slept near the fire. The others said Jenny'd only gone on ahead and she'd meet us there.'

'What do you think?' asked Joss, putting his head close to hers, trying to catch her words.

'I think she's dead. I wish I was her.' She was tracing a pattern in the dust on the floor then, catching herself, scrubbed it out despairingly. 'I can't seem to stop doing that.' Her hands shook.

There was another long silence broken by the bizarre trundling sound of Tom wheeling an old pram down the aisle.

'Well you're very solemn, aren't you?' he called, as he headed for the door. 'Is there to be no singing today? Come on – I always like to hear you boys sing.'

'We're not really in the mood,' said Joss. 'Not today. It doesn't feel very appropriate, Tom.'

Asha stood up. 'You're wrong,' she said. 'Play your guitar for Tarot, now, Joss. Sing the song you wrote. Sing it for her.'

'Oh, leave it out,' said Joss uncomfortably. 'After what she's told us. After what she's been through.'

'It's why she came,' said Tamar.

Bethany nodded. 'Even if she doesn't know it.'

'God, you girls are like something out of Macbeth,' said Christy, shaking his head. 'Still – suppose we get on with what we came here for. I passed up a hot date to come and play with you guys.'

He picked up his sax, blowing an experimental warble.

Tamar grinned. 'What a poser,' she whispered to Bethany.

Otis was on the drums already, tapping a loose light beat.

Tarot was still rocking, hunched into herself, emptied of whatever it was that had kept her going until now. She'd mustered enough energy to drag herself here, to tell her macabre impossible story, in the pathetic belief Joss could help, because he'd once bought her a box of matches in a bus station in Hell. By some superhuman effort she'd torn herself out of the sticky web of the Hoarsemen. The trouble was she'd torn her entire world to pieces with it. Now she was ready to lie down and die.

God, why him? How the hell could Joss help anyone? And

how could he sing in the face of such pain, such despair as Tarot's?

Tyke doodled chords on the bass guitar, waiting. Everyone, Joss saw, was waiting.

'Oh shit,' said Joss. 'I hate being outnumbered.' He got to his feet feeling sick.

'After you, Emerson,' said Christy, nodding. '*Tribal Wave* is it? One, two, one two three four – '

Please, said Joss silently, his hands paralysed on the strings. Help me like you did before. Help me reach her, help me bring her back. Have you ever done this, any of you others out there? Have any of you ever had to fetch a girl back from the dead?

A warm breeze was blowing from somewhere, stirring the hairs on his crown. The guitar quickened under his hands. His fingers groped for the chord. He felt the shift, the fusion as he made the familiar connection with the incandescent musician who had once so terrified him. The splintered saints were watching. The church dimmed to gold. The sunlit sound flowed through his guitar filling the air.

But it was not the same as the first time they played *Tribal Wave*. From the first, the sound of the band was ragged, thin. There was no angelic intervention this time, no throng of invisible musicians. Just four kids singing and playing rock music with more enthusiasm than skill in a derelict church.

Tarot's expression didn't change. She didn't open her eyes once. She never saw Joss ferociously willing her back, hauling her back to the world of the living with the fragile thread of his song. And when it was finished Tarot went on crouching and rocking in her tatty graveyard garments, like a ghoul, like a bottomless bloody well there could never be enough love or hope to fill.

Then an enormous tear slid down her face followed by another. She opened her eyes then but she still didn't look at Joss. It was Tamar she clutched, mascara tracking down her face.

'I want to get rid of these,' she said, twitching her skirt away from her body, wincing as if it hurt her. 'Have you got anything you could lend me?'

And when Tamar said she could come home with her right away, she could have a bath and wash her hair too if she wanted, Tarot picked up that tatty black bag of hers and walked off to wait by the door, her face stony. As if, he thought, she was angry with Joss for some reason.

'We'd better go, too,' said Asha. 'Next time I'll bring the Box.'

'What's going to happen, Asha?' he said, desperately. 'What are we part of?'

But she only touched his hand briefly, gazing levelly at him with her wide grey eyes, told him to wait and trust, and left. But she had said next time, he remembered. He would try. He would try to wait, trusting that it made sense, that it was all leading somewhere, step by step.

Before Asha came to the next band practice Joss tried his best to explain about the Box to Otis and the others. But they watched with considerable cynicism as she fished it from her bag and placed it at their feet, fizzing gently blue-green like a Roman Candle.

'It's been changing,' said Joss, trying to help Asha. 'It was lead to begin with, then wood and now –' he gestured feeling his words scatter into so much static in the face of their incredulity.

'And now,' said Christy sweetly. 'It's going to change into a butterfly.'

'Is that your jewellery box?' said Tyke. 'My sister's got one with a little ballet dancer on the top.' Then he jumped as an extra swirl of light zipped in his direction, skimming his nose before it burst into stars and his expression changed. 'Nice trick,' he said nervously.

'Is it safe to have it in here?' asked Otis. 'It seems rather *active.*'

'It won't blow up, if that's what you mean,' said Asha. 'I think it likes being shared. Tarot couldn't come. She isn't well. Bethany's looking after her.'

'Asha's house has turned into a commune,' said Tamar. 'Anyone else want to move in? Well, aren't you going to play for us?'

Tyke kept glancing nervously across at the Box as the band

warmed up. Joss gave up trying to explain to them just as Asha had given up with him. Perhaps it didn't matter what they believed the Box to be, he thought. They would have to experience it for themselves.

But it was Joss who was taken aback by what happened next. As he struck the first chords on the blue guitar the Box began to stream with light; the full spectrum, this time, wreathing rainbows of it, swirling in and out of brilliant blinding white.

'Well isn't that pretty now?' called Tom, trundling his pram past, loaded with the day's finds. 'Don't they say every group has to have a gimmick? Have you got a name for yourselves yet, boys, by the way?'

'No,' yelled Joss, looking defiantly at Tyke. 'We can't agree on one.'

Asha came to the church the next night and the next. Sometimes Bethany and Tamar came along too but Tarot still avoided Joss. That hurt him quite a lot. With the help of the blue guitar he had probably saved her life. So why did she hate him so?

After a while Otis and the others got used to the Box, choosing to see it rather as Tom did, a harmless light show, a pretty conjuring trick. Joss supposed the goddesses would say they weren't ready.

But Joss knew the power of the Box grew stronger each time it heard the blue guitar. Joss had the oddest feeling that his guitar and the Box were old friends joyously re-entering a longstanding conversation, almost a love affair, he thought. The Box fed its ecstatic light into the guitar and the renewed power of his guitar fed into the Box; together they were generating something strange and new. He didn't have the faintest idea what. He was trying to do what she said. He was waiting, trusting. Waiting.

One night Bethany sang. Once they'd got over their astonishment at this dumpy schoolgirl with her visibly swelling belly, belting out raw rock and roll as if she'd done it all her life, Otis and the others were delighted.

And Tyke said smugly, 'The Hoarsemen have only got Omega Sound but Bethany's got Alpha Sound.'

When Otis looked blank Christy said, 'Dear me, don't you know your Greek? Tell him, Bethany.'

'Alpha and Omega,' said Bethany. 'The beginning and the ending.' She patted her stomach, beaming. 'It's in the Bible. Book of Revelations.'

Tyke's quip sent Joss home brooding and for days he fretted at its implications. If Omega Sound turned people into victims, plugging them into the cosmic wavelength of despair, destroying their will to live, if Omega Sound was the Sound of *unmaking*; mightn't there also be a Sound of creation?

In the Beginning was the Word, he thought. How about: In the beginning was the Sound. Alpha Sound. Mightn't Alpha Music be the antidote to the paralysis of the Sound and if so, what the hell would it sound *like*?

His first attempts at producing it almost made him heave, reminding him of singing 'Jesus wants you for a Sunbeam' when he was five. The thing about the Sound, Joss realised, was that it touched people in the innermost core of themselves. The sadder and darker it sounded, the more pain a person felt inside when he heard it, the truer it seemed to him to be. Hadn't Joss himself always loved the blues?

Then one morning he woke feeling thirsty, trudged downstairs for a glass of water and ended up wandering into the little back garden just as the sun was coming up.

As he stood watching the oldest show on earth, the birds shrieking astonishment from tree to tree, (as if they'd been convinced night was a permanent state of affairs, Joss thought,) the first intimations of a song slid into his head, complete with melody. *The Song of All Beginnings*.

He was cold. He felt downright stupid in the garden in his pyjamas but the song went on doggedly unfolding in his head, line by line, and so he stayed, watching the sun fill the sky, until both the sun and the song had finished with him.

He played it for the others a few nights later.

'It should have a lot of other instruments in it to sound the way it sounded in my head,' he said. 'You sing with me, Bethany or it's going to sound excruciatingly thin.'

But the Box had its own ideas. From the first chord, it began to emit a deep, startling but richly satisfying hum. Tyke whipped round nervously as if he thought the church had filled with choristers while he had his back turned. But it did sound incredibly like the chanting of invisible presences. After a while, the resonant humming sprouted chiming bell-like overtones, harmonising with itself and with the melody of Joss's song. The sound was so dense they could almost touch it; it was fibrous, earthy, spiralling like young vines; enveloping them as fertile healing heat, soaking into their pores, the roots of their hair, their cells, ('even my bone marrow,' Bethany said afterwards), swelling to the rotting rafters until it died away with the last chords of the song, leaving them stunned, invigorated, glowing.

The silence was broken by Bethany. 'Look,' she cried. 'Look at Asha!'

'What?' said Asha alarmed. 'What about me?'

'In your hair – don't move, you'll frighten it.'

A large butterfly of vibrant peacock hues had fluttered from the rafters and was settling on Asha's hair like a flower, its wings gently opening and closing.

'Perfect,' said Christy beaming. 'A Yes vote for Alpha Sound from the Butterfly lobby.'

'Oh, it's not fair,' complained Asha. 'I'm the only one of you who can't see it.'

'A message from the Cosmic Aunties,' said Joss enchanted. 'I wish I'd got my camera. It suits you, you know. From now on you should always wear a butterfly in your hair.'

'It's all right for you,' she grumbled, but for a second she let his eyes meet hers, laughing, before she looked away.

It was after midnight when he climbed the last yards of the steep hill before the turning into Chilkwell Street. An old Morris, painted with clouds and rainbows, its rear doors tied together with string, drove past, revving noisily. The long-haired driver grinned and nodded at Joss. A girl drowsed in the passenger seat. Another sprawled in the back with a small child. Joss wondered mildly where they were heading. A camper van lumbered in its wake, its windscreen filled with the dense greenery of several house-plants. A rusty 2 CV chugged inches behind.

It wasn't usually so busy on the road this late at night. Then he glanced back down the hill and understood. Behind the Citroën was a steadily crawling procession of vans, battered Fords, motor bikes, even a horse and cart. Word of the free concert had got around the hippy underground. The trek to the Earthworks had begun.

While Joss was wasting time in a derelict church, singing songs, admiring butterflies, the Hoarsemen were organising their last performance on earth. And one way and another they meant to take their audience with them.

18 *Exodus*

The drone of sick engines flogging themselves past the end of Chilkwell Street kept Joss awake until the small hours. He half surfaced at five to hear police cars whooping past, blue lights flashing, then fell back into uneasy sleep.

Next day the regional news reported landowners furious to find hippies camping in the vicinity of the Earthworks. By evening the invasion had made the national news. A spokesman for the Hoarsemen apologised to farmers and assured local environmentalists that fans would not be allowed to damage the ancient site.

At school there was no sign of Gunny, Ghoul or the others.

'I wish they *would* come,' said Joss, looking round an eerily empty cafeteria. 'We could try to – '

Then before Tamar could shrivel him totally with her stare, he said hastily: 'All right, I know it's gone too far for that. But I'm not like you and Asha – I still seem to be trying to live in two worlds at once. The normal one where this just couldn't be happening and – '

'I think you'll have to get used to living in one world,' said Tamar. 'There isn't any "normal" any more, Joss. But that doesn't mean it's not real.'

'It's not knowing how we're meant to – '

'I know,' Asha sympathised. 'It's terrifying.'

'You could let me finish my sentences though, couldn't you?' he said gruffly. 'You could at least pretend you don't know what I'm going to say. I mean what are we supposed to do? Stage a rival concert at St Barnabas or something?'

'Not a *rival* concert,' said Asha. 'And not at St Barnabas.'

His jaw dropped. 'You are kidding, aren't you? You aren't – you mean –'

'The same concert,' agreed Asha. 'Of course. I thought it was obvious. What did you think we'd all been preparing for all this time?'

Joss would have thought it hysterically funny if he hadn't felt so sick. All her talk about taking each step as it came and 'trust'. Jesus! She'd been leading him by the nose like a lamb to the slaughterhouse all the time.

'If it had been "obvious",' he said, getting to his feet, 'all you'd have seen of me is two bloody great vapour trails coming out of my heels. Forget it, Asha. I don't care if we've got the – the Box of Delights and – an entire Caribbean Steel Band, that still wouldn't be enough to –'

He stopped himself this time. Both girls were regarding him with silent pity. As though it didn't matter *what* he said, he thought, raging.

'I can't do it,' he said. 'It's insane.'

Asha stood up. 'Do you know the source of Their power, Joss?'

'Look, just leave it alone, will you. Don't even try to trick or shame me into changing my mind. *I can't do it*. Public suicide doesn't turn me on, all right? See you around.'

'You could at least answer her question before you storm out in a huff,' Tamar pointed out.

'*You're* the ones who read minds,' he said. 'So you know as well as I do that I haven't the faintest idea who or what They are, where They are from or even if *They* exist at all.'

'We'll give you a clue,' said Tamar, singsong. 'The smaller we get, the larger They grow.'

'What is this – riddles now? You two are from another age. Why don't you do your Female Oracle routine around some other sucker?'

He didn't bother to go back to the classroom, just headed

for home; his head exploding with rage. Followers were already trudging away from the bus station, carrying rucksacks, sleeping rolls. To get home Joss had to dodge in and out of dozens of them. He wasn't so fit himself, but it was pathetically easy to overtake them. They toiled along at a painful pace, their faces blinded, blissful and utterly vacant. Some of them were singing softly, droning the same sounds over and over. One of them stopped and chalked the now familiar symbol on a wall while his friends waited, breathing hard.

He quickened his stride, soon he was running through the dark droning throng. It was all he could do not to shove his fingers in his ears. He'd go back to school later to meet Martha, he thought. He couldn't let her face those zombies on her own.

At the corner of Chilkwell Street three of them waited for a girl who had slumped on a doorstep, her head between her knees.

'Are you okay?' he said. 'Shall I get you some water or something?'

The others closed in. 'She's fine,' said a girl protectively. 'She doesn't need anything. She'll be fine once we get there. Won't you, Karen?'

'Have you any idea how long it takes to walk to the Earthworks?' demanded Joss.

Karen got shakily to her feet. 'I'm ready now,' she said. 'I'm just too happy – it was too much for me.' She laughed apologetically, her small emaciated face blazing with excitement and away she tottered up the hill, her friends supporting her.

After supper Mike rang to say the van was playing up again, so Joss had his first evening at home for weeks. Fran and Martha were out. He sat by himself in front of the television, switching from channel to channel, catching the news broadcasts, watching the same shots of Followers trudging through Midland countryside with rucksacks and sleeping-rolls.

This was the shadow to Joss's exuberant tribal wave, sweeping in, washing away the old, making space for the new.

This was a dark tribe, a lost tribe, in search of the Promised Land.

Interspersed with this pathetic exodus were other images from Joss's troubled planet; an earthquake in Eastern Europe. Oil spillage off the coast of Devon. Forests dying in Germany. Scientists were investigating a mystery virus.

He thought of Asha shining with hope in the park. New lamps for old. Perhaps she was right. The old myths were worn out and the planet was dying with them. The Followers, overwhelmed by the terror of their times, wanted only to escape, to be borne away to a better place; desperately wanting to believe themselves a race of chosen children, rewarded at last for patient sufferings.

The smaller we get, the larger They grow. The smaller we get –

At quarter to five next morning he gave up on sleep and crept out, taking his bike. It was drizzling. Mist clung to hedges and telephone wires. What did he think he was doing? Why was Joss pedalling miserably up a long hill in the rain when he could have been home, warm in bed?

A sodden sheep gawped morosely at him through the bars of a gate. It was a stupid-looking sheep; but the sight made him want to bawl his eyes out.

The smaller we get, the larger –

They'd have security men and dogs at obvious entrance points. It seemed safer to risk an irate farmer than the Hoarsemen's hangers on. He hid his bike in a ditch, dived into a field of something green and rotten-smelling that he suspected was brussel sprouts, clambered over barbed wire, zigzagged downhill through bracken and squelched his way through a marshy little spinney until he could get close enough to take a proper look.

Skeletal towers loomed through the mist.

Scaffolding, he thought, puzzled. Then he realised; of course they'd have to build a stage, fix up spotlighting, sound equipment. Didn't these jokers ever do anything on a small scale? Giant reels of cable everywhere: and for some reason a massive cinema screen.

That was when it dawned on him. It was ludicrously

obvious but he hadn't given it a thought. The elaborate light and sound system was not just for the benefit of devoted Followers who came to the concert.

The concert had never been intended to be a purely local event.

The Hoarsemen's last performance would be global, beamed around the world via satellite. A whole generation, Tamar had said but no-one, including Tamar had wanted to believe it. A generation wiped from the face of the earth. The unmaking of the future on a scale that numbed his imagination. Not through war, plague or famine, but because no-one cared enough to stop it. *No-one cared.* His mind reeled. His vision blurred. He was shaking.

He got back to the road somehow. A decrepit camper van was parked on the verge. Inside a child cried irritably. A man with a beard sat on a folding chair, drinking from a steaming mug, watching the sun struggle to emerge through the drizzle. He smiled at Joss as he hurtled by. 'The rain will stop in an hour or two,' he said. 'They'll have clear skies for tonight.'

An innocent remark but in Joss's state of mind everything only added to the appalling unreality.

All the way home Tamar's words pounding in his head; *the smaller we get . . .*

It was still only six-thirty when he got home but he couldn't wait longer to phone.

Asha answered at the second ring.

'What kept you?' he said.

'Joss?'

'Television equipment,' gabbled Joss. 'I went up this morning to take a look round. There's sound and lighting gear everywhere. They're going to beam the bloody concert round the world by satellite. It really is going to be the Greatest Show on Earth. Also the last.

'And the answer to Tamar's riddle, should you still be talking to me, is "We are." Okay Asha? The source of Their power is *us*. If the Followers believed in their own power, in their own future, instead of handing it over to a mob of faceless extra-terrestrials, they'd have nothing to feed on.'

'Yes,' she said. She waited.

'And I always knew that we'd have to do this and at the same time I didn't let myself know it, can you understand? All the time I was trying to teach myself to write and play Alpha Sound but I never let myself think about why or how it would have to be used. I never let myself see how *big* this was. All along I knew we'd have to be at this concert and why. But I couldn't bear to believe it. Do you see?'

'Yes,' she said, barely audibly.

'So what do I do? What do we do? Don't tell me to wait and trust.'

'Wait and trust,' she said. 'And ask Mike what he's doing tonight.'

'Mike?'

'We'll need a van. Or were you planning to carry everything on your back through the countryside?'

'I hope you're just pretending to be calm and collected for my benefit,' said Joss. 'Because I've got the worst diarrhoea I've ever had in my life.'

'I'm pretending for your benefit.'

He heard the tremor in the last word.

'Then it's almost possible to like you again,' he said fervently.

He phoned Mike next.

'Bloody Hell,' said Mike when he realised who it was. 'You're keen.'

'There isn't an easy way to explain this,' said Joss, 'but we're going to need your van tonight.'

He solved what to do with the morning by sleeping through it by mistake. He only meant to sit down to glance through the paper. He was woken by someone hammering on the front door.

He opened it to find Luke in a panic, the baby in his arms.

'Is Fran in?'

'No, not for hours.'

'Well could you do me a favour – look after Orchid while I take Liana to Casualty. She fell down the step and cut herself badly. She'll need stitches. Naomi's in London.'

'Well – I don't – it's not really very –'

'I've brought her bottle,' said Luke. 'And I've just changed her.' He looked pretty terrible himself. Perhaps he couldn't stand blood either.

'Okay,' said Joss helplessly. 'But I warn you I've never –'

He held out his arms reluctantly. The baby's lip trembled. She gave a little wail of fear.

'Oh don't cry,' he begged. 'Please don't cry.'

'She'll be fine once I've gone, honestly,' Luke promised. 'I'll be back as soon as I can. But I'm afraid they usually take a while.'

Joss carried the howling baby into the sitting-room in a mild state of shock. Babysitting Orchid was not the ideal strategy he would have chosen to prepare himself for tonight's ordeal. Why was his life always so – He caught sight of himself in the mirror. A boy with a shrieking baby apparently trying to throw itself out of his arms, looked back with a trapped expression.

Trapped! Joss felt absolutely confounded. Here he was trying to behave like a hero and what happened?

And suppose Luke didn't come back in time? Joss would be stuck with Orchid. He'd have to ask someone to hold her while he played his guitar. That wouldn't do much for his charisma.

That was when he started to laugh. He couldn't help himself. He hooted. He roared. The baby peered into his face, amazed, and forgot to cry.

'I know who you are,' he said sternly. 'You don't fool me. You're just a pawn in the pay of the Cosmic Aunties, that's who you are. You've come to test me out, am I right?'

The baby hiccupped.

'Are you thirsty?'

Orchid waved away the bottle imperiously with tiny mottled hands.

'Can you sit up properly yet or are you just a little old jelly baby?'

He propped her against a cushion. She stayed more or less upright, staring around her with round expectant eyes.

'You have got vertebrae inside that all-in-one thingummy, then. Well how would I know? You could be a droid, for all I

172

know. You're an unknown species to me.'

He crouched down in front of her. She chortled.

'Isn't it weird being brought up by your dad? Wouldn't you rather have a nice normal dad like mine who didn't know one end of a nappy from the other and only talks to you when you get a bad school report? You could grow up really warped, you know.' His throat ached. Had Richard ever sat on the floor with him when he was a baby and talked nonsense to him? He remembered that Richard had made a toy garage for his birthday once. There had been tiny petrol pumps which broke off bewilderingly in Joss's hands, one by one. Joss had wanted to see if there was real petrol inside them. There had been a terrible row and the spoiled garage was dumped outside in the rain for the dustbin men to take away. 'Yes, you're a freak, Orchid. I don't know why you're smiling. You're going to grow up thinking fathers are human.'

She crowed and beat upon the air in a flurry of fists.

'You are so damn pleased with yourself aren't you? Is this semaphore or something? Do you like music? You might as well get out of my house now if you don't like music. I'll sing you some blues. Do you like the blues?'

He took hold of the boneless little hands, gently beating time. 'Woke up this morning, Orchid was on my mind. Woke up this morning, that ole jelly baby Orchid was on my mind – '

Luke let himself in the back door a couple of hours later and forewarned by the deafening silence, tiptoed through the doorway to the sitting-room. Joss was lying on a sofa, the baby against his chest, its head drooping over his shoulder, snoring faintly.

'For God's sake don't wake her,' hissed Joss, not moving a muscle. 'She's just gone to sleep. I'll bring her back later.'

'Was she any trouble?'

'She was bloody exhausting. How do you stick it?'

'Thanks a million, Joss. If I can return the favour – '

'What are you doing tonight?' said Joss swiftly.

They drove over to Wintergrove first, Joss, Mike and Luke from next door. Tarot just pushed past Joss without speaking, curling herself up in the smallest possible space at the back.

She'd put on a little weight and looked so ordinary in her jeans he would never have known her. She'd even let her hair grow out. It was mousy. Ordinary. He was surprised at his disappointment.

'Bethany should go in the front,' said Asha.

'I don't think she should go at all,' Joss objected. 'It's completely crazy.'

'She's supposed to come,' said Asha.

Joss lifted his eyes to heaven.

'If you try to stop me, Joss –'

'She can hold the Box,' said Asha. 'It might get damaged in the back.'

Bethany plonked it on her lap where it glimmered starrily.

'It's very warm,' she said, surprised. 'Actually it's quite hot.'

'It has been all day,' said Asha. 'And it's been humming.'

'Did they forecast blizzards or something?' asked Joss. 'You've all got your winter coats on.'

'Better safe than sorry,' Tamar said. 'It's going to be a long night. We can always sit on them.'

'Is there anything I should know about that thing?' asked Mike, calmly putting the van into gear.

'What would you believe?' Asha tucked her coat around her more closely.

'After what Joss has been telling me about the Hoarsemen, and what I've sensed myself in this town these last few days, – practically anything,' he gestured towards the Box. 'It makes me feel – well the closest I can come to it in a very small way, is how I feel inside when I've done a bit of healing for someone. Isn't it very old?'

'It's been here since the beginning of our world, we think,' said Tamar. 'But it's probably older than that. And it's probably changed a few times since then.'

'What's inside it?'

'We don't know yet.'

A sweet high chiming burst from the Box, startling them all.

'Otis lives up here,' said Joss, swallowing.

Tyke and Christy were already waiting for them. Otis had tried to fill them in as well as he could.

'What happens to the Followers who can't make it to the concert?' asked Luke, as Mike's old Sherpa jounced through the dark countryside with an uncomfortably full load.

'You mean, do they still get spirited away to the Promised Planet?' asked Tamar.

'We don't – ' Joss began.

'Oh there'll be other ships,' said Tarot. 'It'll be simultaneous. All over the world. Followers will know where to gather. Hear Them speaking to them in their own language.'

'Who are *They*, Tarot?' asked Christy. 'Green men or what?'

She shook her head, angrily. 'Advanced beings,' she said. 'Everything we aren't – '

Then Joss realised why Tarot was angry. He'd hauled her back out of the dark by the hair, given her back her life and she didn't want it. As a Follower she had belonged to something larger than herself. Nothing in Tarot's ordinary human life could compensate her for that loss. *Advanced beings*, he thought, despairingly. What kind of advanced beings were willing to destroy a whole generation, the entire future of our world? He supposed Tamar was right. The more Tarot shrunk her own life down, the less hopes and dreams she had for herself, the more wonderful They appeared to her. The thought appalled him. All over the world Followers letting Them take their energy, then pathetically hero-worshipping Them in all that stolen power and glory. But They couldn't take it, if we didn't give it, he thought. We're free. We're only victims if we choose to be.

'If I park here, can you carry everything you need?' asked Mike suddenly. 'There's a lot of activity up ahead.'

'What do we do now?' asked Otis. 'Are we just going to mill casually around the auditorium or what?'

'Wait and trust,' said Joss and Asha simultaneously.

The Earthworks supplied a perfect natural auditorium but no seats. Hundreds of people were already sitting on the ground, waiting. Others passed silently back and forth. Joss recognised people from school.

The man was right, thought Joss. It was a perfect night. Mild but clear. A full moon was climbing the heavens looking close enough to touch; its craters appearing like ruddy stains against the deep almost amber yellow. A hot weather moon, he thought, not a spring moon at all. He remembered Tarot saying the full moon had been part of Their calculations. A number of Followers were already yearning at the stars and he too peered apprehensively upwards but was relieved to find the sky empty of flying objects. Not so much as an aeroplane.

Whatever rites the Earthworks had seen in its time, this had to be the most bizarre, Joss thought as muted figures continued to drift into this ancient arena of earth and rock and seat themselves under the ominous blood-orange moon.

'What is this?' whispered Tyke, clearly unnerved. 'A massive bloody funeral? They're so quiet. This must be the quietest audience that's ever waited for a rock concert to get going.'

The hippy families chatted softly amongst themselves but they too seemed subdued by this atmosphere of almost breathless foreboding. A couple of bikers unbuckled leather saddle bags and dug out some cans of beer. They looked as if they'd had quite a few already. Joss wondered how they'd respond if he tried to tell them a space-craft the size of the Town Hall was going to descend and hoover up the chosen few.

'They've got the St John's Ambulance Brigade here,' hissed Christy. 'Don't you think they might be a bit out of their depth?'

Asha had the Box stowed under her winter coat out of sight. She was not cold now so the coat was a trial to her. In fact she was perspiring. Both the Box and the evening seemed to be growing warmer with each passing moment.

'I hope it doesn't start humming while everything's still so quiet,' she whispered to Joss.

'I expect its timing will be impeccable,' he said, surprising them both. 'Better hope I don't throw up on my shoes. That's much more likely.'

The stage was a long way off. Tiny figures appeared and disappeared, towing snaking cables, adjusting lights, testing microphones. Men with huge headphones trundled cameras around.

'The bastards are going to be practically invisible from here,' said Joss. 'They could shove any crappy old foursome with guitars up there at this range and no-one would know the difference.'

'That's why they've got the big screen,' murmured Otis. 'So everyone can see them in divine close-up. Shouldn't we get nearer the front?'

Asha shook her head. 'Not yet.'

There was a buzz of excitement. Someone had run on to doublecheck the amps. Someone else swarmed up the scaffolding, tinkered with a spotlight and bounded off again.

'Where do you think the Hoarsemen are hiding themselves until the big moment?' murmured Luke.

'They've probably got caravans back of the stage. They won't come on till everyone's really hungry,' said Otis, a veteran of rock concerts. 'This is where they usually have some talentless prat winding them up, getting the teenies begging and screaming. At least we're spared that. The Hoarsemen aren't just top of the bill. They're all of the bill . . .'

'Listen,' Tyke was wincing. 'What's that?'

The vibration was barely audible at first.

'Where's it coming from?' Christy was craning his neck.

'All around,' said Tamar. 'It's the Followers.'

It was rising like a desolate wind sweeping around the auditorium; the droning that had panicked Joss the day before, but amplified intolerably by numbers and the acoustics of the Earthworks to a throbbing sea of discord.

'The lights have come on,' said Bethany. 'Look at the screen!'

At first just the swirling and rippling of wave-like patterns, next exploding cells or stars, galaxies forming, coalescing and dispersing; all rhythmically coming and going like a human heartbeat.

Otis was tapping his fingers on his knee, his face impassive. 'Reminds me of when my brother had his mobile Disco,' he said. 'Only his was more cosmic.'

Suddenly the stage blazed with light. The heartbeat went into overdrive. A few yards off a girl fainted away with a small whimper.

'Where's Mike?' said Luke suddenly. 'And Tarot?'

At the same time Tamar said, 'When did Asha go? She was here a second ago.'

But at that moment there was a surge of joy from the auditorium as four wild long-haired figures, bare-chested, wearing baggy silk trousers in electric scarlet, emerald, gold and sapphire exploded on to the stage.

And then the sky caught fire.

19 Dancing with the Dark

Asha found her by the stream, near the rowan tree where she had seen the snake. She had not known she was going to leave the others until she found herself running through the night, the chant of the Followers fading behind her, her feet finding the path without faltering, to the place where the small girl, her skirt kilted above her knees, paddled by herself in the living moonlit water.

The Box was unbearably hot.

'I can't hold it any longer,' Asha said. 'It's burning me. Why did you call? The others need me.'

The child scuffed the water with her bare toes, drops scattering back into the stream, as she balanced like a stork on one leg, with obvious pride; a skinny little girl of about six, with glossy dark hair, a soft radiance surrounding her like a cloud.

'Look at your Ugly Box,' she said. 'Look what you have done to it, Asha.'

Asha took the Box from under her coat and almost dropped it with horror.

An infinitesimal crack had appeared, running around the whole circumference of the Box dividing it into two. Through a space no thicker than a hair Asha glimpsed blinding spiralling whorls of – it had to be light but light utterly unlike any seen on earth, light that was also myriad, seething but infinitely intelligent activity; compassionate light that pulled at her, called her, yearned for her like a lost self.

Now she knew for sure that the Box had been fashioned in some workshop of the gods. That to look inside it was to pry into the sacred workings of the universe. And as the Box began its ecstatic chiming she understood with awe that this sound was the joyous singing of the light.

'But I was so careful,' she cried. 'I honestly didn't –'

'I think you have been guarding Her so well you had almost forgotten She was intended to be opened one day!' said the child. She grinned back and Asha could see where she had lost a milk tooth. 'But now She is awake Her light longs to stream into your world. The dark time is over. Give me your hands, Asha.'

'*Her* light? You called the Box "she"?'

'Of course, but in other terms it is the light itself which is She. The Box was just created to protect Her until the world –'

But with a horrific rending sound like an old curtain whose fabric had rotted, the night sky tore over their heads.

Asha screamed.

'I've got to go. There's no time. The others need –'

Where there had been calm, star-sprinkled skies there yawned a boiling hole, a chasm churning with a molten tumult unbearable to behold.

'Give me your hands, Asha. Displays of power don't matter. Time doesn't matter. There is only truth. Only now.'

Weeping with terror but unable to disobey, Asha stretched out her blistered hands. The tough little hands that clasped hers were as cool as waterlilies.

Suddenly Asha knew the child whose form the goddess had assumed, knew intimately each bitten nail, remembered even the scar upon her wrist, but before she could cry out, extraordinary colours began to flow between their hands and she was incapable of speech.

'Welcome the light, Asha,' said the goddess softly, almost singing the words. 'Welcome the sacred light and power of all that is female, all that is needed to heal and renew. Not the power of women and girl children only but the female power that lies feared and forgotten within men.'

She was flickering in and out of forms: now she was Valli, now the woman in the junk shop under the Dark Arches.

'Do you know the true meaning of her name? The other one, the one they say let loose the causes of darkness into your word? *'Giver of all gifts'*. Take your gift Asha. For now light and dark shall dance together again as it was meant they should.'

'But is the world really ending?' cried Asha unable to take in a word of this. 'Are They coming? Because if They land there won't be any –'

But the goddess had gone. Only the Box remained.

She picked it up, its heat no longer bothered her; and started back to the others beneath the burning sky. She wondered if the goddess has also touched her eyes. For all around, as far as she could see, the gridwork of ancient power lines formed a radiant web against the darkness.

'It has to be some kind of mass hallucination,' said Joss. 'But how could they make us believe it was happening, if it wasn't?'

'The Hoarsemen couldn't,' said Tamar. 'But They could.'

The Hoarsemen had not even glanced up when the sky began raining fire, just hurled themselves fanatically into their first number like demented prophets, dancing like dervishes, sliding across the stage on their knees.

The stage pulsed with their sheer primitive life-force. Their sweaty torsos reflecting the flaming sky looked daubed with fire. When their faces appeared in close-up on the screen, they were the faces of maddened saints, dark eyes glittering with the pain of the world.

'God gave Noah a rainbow sign.

Not the flood the fire next time,

The fire next time, the fire next time –' they roared.

Secretly Joss had hoped they wouldn't be any good when it came to it. But they had raw husky amazing voices, and sang in weird, unexpected harmonies that pulled at your gut, he thought, and went jolting up your spine to crackle around in your skull like forked lightning. The bastards were masters of sound. They were *witch doctors* of sound. The Hoarsemen weren't just hyped-up small town rockers. They were the real thing. They were stars.

They had stolen the fire refrain from an old spiritual, Joss recognised. But the *way* they used it, weaving it into their message of death and destruction, making it their own.

The massive screen showed a city blasted into poisoned dust. The shadow of a young tree had burned itself into a wall at the moment of the atomic explosion, like a bizarre snapshot that would remain until the wall itself crumbled to dust.

What terrible things we do to each other, Joss thought, aching. The destruction of his century was so vast it was impossible to take in, let alone begin to put it right. How could human beings ever forget the crimes their kind had committed, what tender new shoot of the future could grow out of those carrion-millions of lost, wounded, betrayed? Yes, he found himself thinking. The Hoarsemen sing for the wounded. They sing for us.

Tamar was pinching his arm, hissing at him.

'Now – we've got to go now.'

'We can't – Asha's not here.'

'She'll be there to meet us.'

'How can you be sure?'

'She just told us,' said Bethany.

But Joss was feeling extremely ill. Briefly his vision blurred as if to readjust. For he had begun to see not in normal colour but in leached-out, over-exposed monochrome as if he too had been caught in the middle of some catastrophic explosion. Where had he been? What was he doing here, with these people?

Slowly the colours returned. The moment of unreality passed. Tyke and Christy were shaking themselves, he saw, as if they had water in their ears.

'You locked into the Sound,' said Tamar quietly. 'Be more careful.' She and Bethany had been gripping each other's hands, he remembered, as if that helped them.

For some reason Luke seemed fine, still calmly, soundlessly

181

moving his lips, cross-legged on the grass, as serene as if he was in his own sitting room. Of course, Luke was the kind of bloke who'd be bound to have a mantra when he needed one, Joss thought. Otis too seemed blithely untroubled.

He poked Otis. 'Why didn't the Sound get you?'

'What?' Otis pulled plugs of cotton wool out of his ears.

'We're *going*.'

It was ridiculously easy to slip between the rows unnoticed. The fans were oblivious to anything but the figures on the stage.

'You must be melting,' said Tyke. 'Why don't you girls take your coats off?'

'Not yet,' said Tamar sweetly. 'We'll only lose them. You know what girls are.'

The Hoarsemen had launched into the next number.

'That's a hell of a low plane,' said Otis, tweaking his cotton wool again, frowning.

'Don't stop,' said Tamar. 'Keep going till you get to the front. Look, there she is.'

The Hoarsemen were singing *Wounded World*. On the screen a camera panned a diseased forest, cut back to the betrayed expression in the eyes of a small child. Power stations belted out toxic clouds. The same child gazed blankly out of a top floor window at a treeless street, choked with traffic.

'*Earth's your poisoned burial ground –*'

'It's not a plane,' said Tyke his voice cracking with terror. 'Oh, will you look at the size of –'

'Keep going. Just keep going.'

Effluent gushed into streams and rivers. Someone filled a glass of water from a tap, handing it to the child. She shook her head and turned away, a tear seeping down her face.

Over their heads the sky was slowly blotted out.

'Tell me this isn't happening,' said Christy.

Asha was waiting for them.

'I have to go first,' she said.

'What about us?' hissed Joss. 'This is not a safe place to be, Asha. Their music gets right inside your – cells. It seems like the only truth there is when you're listening to them.

182

And I don't know if this is another one of Their conjuring tricks but er –' he desperately indicated the sky. But she scarcely glanced up.

'They can't do it unless everyone lets Them, remember,' she said. 'If you keep Them out of your mind, They can't get close enough to do anything. The only power They have is the power we give Them.'

The audience was in a moaning ferment by this time. The atmosphere had gone beyond fever-pitch even before the incredible appearance of the huge object slowly silently filling the blazing heavens above the Earthworks. Now the Followers were openly sobbing, desperately scribbling pyramids in the air, imploring Them to reach down and take them away.

Tyke had turned as white as a sheet and was breathing too fast. After a moment Tamar and Bethany moved to stand on either side of him, linking their arms through his without a word.

'What do you think he makes of that?' asked Christy, pointing to a horrified cameraman almost toppling from his scaffolding but still valiantly filming.

After *Wounded World* there was a pause during which the Hoarsemen, apparently oblivious of extra-terrestrials hovering several thousand feet over their stage, mopped their sweat with towels rushed on by drones in overalls, just as if nothing out of the ordinary was going on. In fact now Joss was close enough to see the Hoarsemen's faces he saw with a pang of shock that they were utterly blank. Surely this was the Hoarsemen's shining hour. What they had planned and worked for. But there was no blinded bliss in their eyes. No yearning for Them. They didn't even grin at each other or strut and clown around like other musicians Joss had seen. It was as though when the Hoarsemen were not performing they scarcely seemed to know where they were, or even *who* they were, he thought.

The black guitarist swigged from a bottle of mineral water. He swilled the water round his mouth, then set the bottle down. At that moment Joss looked right into his face. And for a chilling moment the Hoarseman looked back and Joss saw that the glittering eyes were no longer human but simply windows for Them to look through.

Then the four Hoarsemen went crashing into *Omega Sound,* seemingly inexhaustible once more.

This was Their hymn, Their anthem, thought Joss. And They would use not just the energy of the Followers but the ancient powerlines of the Earthworks to intensify the power of Their thoughts, amplifying the Sound like a cosmic amplifier, guiding Them in, magnetising Them to our wounded planet. Like to like. Darkness to darkness. Despair to despair. Could They see the Earthworks blazing the message across space like a gigantic beacon?

Save us. Help us. Heal us.

'Now,' said Asha.

Without fuss, she slid off her coat climbed on to the stage keeping in the shadows.

Omega Sound was getting everyone so frantic no-one noticed her. Even the security-men had eyes for no-one but the increasingly frenzied Hoarsemen. But Joss was trembling. What the hell was Asha up to? Suddenly, senselessly he badly needed to look at the screen again. What out-take from his worst nightmares would be up there this time? Poisoned seas? Whales dying in gouts of blood? The twentieth century must have generated enough dying and despair to keep the Hoarsemen in videos forever.

He closed his eyes and caught his breath.

A half-naked child about as old as Liana, darted between enormous bulldozers, foraging for scrap in a stinking waste tip about the size of a small town.

But when his eyes flew open to escape the horror of it, the same appalling image flickered on the screen in front of him. Wasteland.

They've got into my bloodstream like a virus he thought. I'm done for.

But Bethany slid her hand into his, shocking him back.

'Look,' she whispered. 'Look at Asha.'

A murmur of bewilderment rippled through the crowd.

As though the Hoarsemen simply were not there, Asha calmly confidently walked to centre stage. To Joss's surprise she was wearing a simple lavender dress, a dancer's dress, thought Joss. Under the lights her swept back hair shone like water. And she was holding the Box.

For some reason the Hoarsemen went on grinding out their song, as if nothing had happened. Perhaps they were expecting someone to rush on from the wings and bundle Asha off. No-one else seemed to know what to do either. The henchmen weren't used to spontaneous incidents at concerts. The Followers had to be the most docile fans in the history of rock music. Or perhaps everyone, including the hangers-on, was so hypnotised by the Sound they accepted Asha's appearance with the Box passively as part of the show; another dramatic illusion like the burning sky. But Asha went on calmly standing there as if it was the Hoarsemen and Their hideous hovering spaceship that were the illusions, and she was just waiting for everyone to see it.

And suddenly Joss understood.

Asha had been through this already.

Night after night, on her own with the Box. The world's nightmares flickering on her wall; guilt, despair. All of it. But she'd gone through it. Instead of being overwhelmed by the darkness, with the help of the goddesses she had found the strength to go through and beyond it and now it had no power over her. It was Asha who had the power now. The power to choose what was real and what was not, the power to act and change. And the truth was, Joss had that power too if he dared to take it.

'Start singing,' he said suddenly. 'You can do it in a whisper if you want to, but start singing.'

'What? What?'

'Anything, anything you like.'

Barely audibly, and very baffled, the others began gabbling obediently to themselves. Otis took out his ear plugs and struck up *When the Saints Come Marching in* and Tyke sang along with him. Bethany sang *Stormy Weather*. Luke hummed something classical. No-one could possibly hear them through the surging anguished drone of the Sound. But that was not the point.

The atmosphere of electric yearning which had filled the

auditorium since their arrival, shifted and began to sink tangibly.

'Keep singing,' ordered Joss. 'They can only get us if we're passive. When you act, They can't get into your head. If you're creating something, They can't destroy you. Because you can't breathe out and breathe in at the same time.'

Joyful with his discovery he broke into full-throated song.

'When a woman gets the blues she goes to her room and hides,

When a man gets the blues, he catches a freight train and rides –'

The Hoarsemen were still going through their hectic manoeuvres but with an increasingly mechanical air. There was an atmosphere of imminent chaos. The drunken bikers, coming out of their trance, sensed impending disruption and began to boo.

Suddenly the ancient darkness of the Earthworks sprang alive with myriad dancing filaments of light, like an extraordinary living web.

'Who switched on the Christmas trees?' shouted Christy amazed.

'You did,' said Bethany. 'We did. This is our home. Our planet. The light's always been there, just waiting for us to remember who we are.'

'And who are we?' asked Joss.

Asha held up the Box.

Slowly, imperceptibly, like a rose unfurling, the lid began to open.

An unbearable beauty streamed forth.

The Hoarsemen faltered.

'Omega Sound. Omega sound,' they sang, trying to dance around Asha and the Box since she made no attempt to move.

'Keep singing,' yelled Joss. 'Just keep on singing.'

'When a knight won his spurs,' sang Christy. 'He was gallant and bold.'

'These boots were made for walking,' warbled Luke.

And They let go.

Like underwater swimmers brought too quickly back to the surface, most of the Followers doubled up in pain.

The great blot of the spacecraft juddered and grated overhead in obvious difficulties. Now the Sound was no longer being channelled into the Followers, all that accumulated vibration violently returning to its source seemed to be shaking Their own vehicle to pieces. Suddenly at tremendous speed, the spacecraft veered away at a right-angle.

Something was wrong with the sound system. Painfully drawn-out earsplitting yowling sounds were followed by the roaring of static. Then it packed up altogether.

The despairing images on the screen blurred, darkened, died away.

One by one the lights went out until the only illuminations were the dancing changing radiance of the earth's own web of light and the starlight streaming from the Box.

In the shattering silence Followers struggled to their feet, blinking, rubbing their eyes, baffled, betrayed. The Hoarsemen had vanished. The spaceship was a dwindling shadow against the amber moon.

Remembering Tarot Joss knew this was where it could go terribly wrong. Deprived so brutally of Them, Followers could go mad, riot or even just lie down and die of despair.

But Asha was calling him wordlessly and of course he could see what exquisite sense it made, that here they were, pushing their way to the front, leaping up on the stage as naturally and simply as if they did this every day.

Then the lights came on again. Not singly but all at once. The Box had a perfect grasp of stagecraft, Joss thought. Feedback howled painfully from the sound system. The sound must be back too. Joss plugged in his guitar, amazed to find there was not even a tremor in his hands.

Bethany was wearing a glorious dress, he noticed with astonishment; as blue as his guitar, a dazzling iridescent blue that made him think of dragonflies. For some reason, being pregnant only made her look more fantastic. Tamar was glittering in a dress of beaded jade that almost covered her thighs for once. Seeing his astonished face, Asha grinned back.

They had planned this female metamorphosis all along, he

thought, remembering the subterfuge of the coats. And suddenly he wished Tarot was with them. A transformed Tarot in a dress of many colours.

But Tamar was hissing, 'The hat, Joss. The hat.' And from somewhere, incredibly, she produced Tyke's battered hat and Joss caught it and shoved it to the back of his head. To Joss's own surprise he had already started talking smoothly into the microphone.

'Well, what an incredible evening and there are still plenty of surprises because we're here to finish the show for you with a new sound, a sound you'll be hearing more of, a sound that's going to get you all dancing in the dark – '

Tamar was pulling faces at him, miming he'd forgotten something.

'What?' he hissed, feeling that he was doing spectacularly well in the circumstances. Hundreds of lost spectral faces gazed vacantly back at him from behind the lights.

'The name of the group,' she hissed back. 'Tell them what we're called, bozo.'

'You know we haven't got a bloody – ' he began, when he heard it, the familiar sick sound of a rusting white Sherpa tanking across the bumpy terrain towards them.

And then he had it. The perfect name. It was all he could do not to laugh like a maniac.

'Allow me to introduce – The Midlands Light and Power Company! Better make for the high places, there's a Tribal Wave coming . . .'

Otis, crouching over the best drum kit he'd ever seen in his life, got stuck blissfully into the elaborate tribal beat. But Joss waited.

Not yet.

To his vague surprise, Fran and Martha were getting out of the van.

Almost. He wanted the tension just right.

Yes. The inner click.

He nodded at Bethany. And the music came scorching down the blue guitar.

It was not like the night in the church. Compared with this performance that was a dull shadow. He didn't have to pray for help this time. It came in bucketsful. The tribes were gathering all right. He felt them, saw them all around. He only glanced across the lights once and saw one of the hippies pulling her boyfriend to his feet, and the two of them begin irresistibly moving their bodies to the music. Others followed. Luke had found a tambourine and was rattling it harmlessly from time to time, beaming all over his face, tapping his huge green shoes. Tamar was performing incredibly indecent gyrations. The midriff of her dress was not solid, he realised now, but transparent. Behind the jade gauze her navel flashed jauntily diamanté, catching the lights.

But the Followers stayed numbly fixed in their places as if there was no reason for them ever to move again.

Dance, he willed them through the blue guitar. Dance yourselves alive again. Dance yourselves back into the tribe. *Dance* your future alive.

When the song finished there was a scattering of applause and even a few cheers. But before Joss could give the signal for the next number, he saw Asha glance at Bethany who strolled to a microphone and spoke into it in her strong husky voice.

'Before we sing our next song for you, there's someone out in the audience who should really be up here with us. Where are you, Tarot?'

Joss was so appalled his heart almost stopped.

What was she up to?

People shuffled, looking around uncomfortably but no-one answered. Bethany had been to too many evangelical meetings when she was growing up at *The Shores of Galilee*, Joss decided. She was going to ruin everything.

Then, to his horror, Tamar joined in. 'Please, Tarot. We can't do it without you.'

More silence. And yet more silence. Enough time to die several times over. More silence.

Then a metallic scrambling sound.

Heads turned to watch the small figure clambering out of Mike's van, a figure dressed from head to foot in tattered black.

Tarot had gone home to change *back* into her Follower's gear.

Joss wanted to kill her.

'Tarot,' said Asha. 'Come up here with us.'

Tarot moved towards the stage like a sleepwalker. It took forever for her to reach it. Not knowing what else to do, Joss found himself leaning down unwillingly to swing her up beside them.

Immediately Tamar gripped her friend tearfully by the hand.

'Thought we'd lost you,' she whispered. But Tarot didn't respond, only stood stupefied as if she scarcely knew where she was, clutching her large black bag.

The audience shuffled. The atmosphere was sinking like a hot-air balloon losing height. Low. Lower. Lowest. Now Joss knew for sure that he would never understand women. Why on earth did they have to sabotage it? Everything had been cooking so perfectly. The gorgeous dresses, the Midlands Light and Power Company, the joyful music, dancing the future alive. Why drag this girl in her graveyard gear whining and whimpering into the future with them?

There she stood blinking in the lights, twisting her transparent hands on the handles of that horrible dark sack of hers. She never even had anything *in* it, he thought. And the audience looking back in frozen silence.

'Now we're complete,' said Asha softly then.

Walking up to Tarot, she kissed her gently, taking the black bag away from her.

Then Asha placed the Box deliberately into Tarot's hands.

And as if it had only been waiting for this moment the lid of the Box flew up like some incredible celestial seed pod and out flooded Her earthly singing light.

Afterwards Joss supposed they must have played it pretty bloody well, his *Song of all Beginnings*, Bethany's powerful voice filling the night, the thrilling harmonic chiming of the Box as She poured out Her vision of peace and plenty not on to screens and spools of magnetic tape but into the living earth, the living air of their own planet. And the awakening light of the Earth itself leaping exuberantly to meet Her and join with Her creation.

And Joss's song of making, amplified by the light beyond

his wildest dreams, ringing out far beyond the Earthworks to mend, heal, renew.

All repairs, he remembered, and wondered what shape the old man was wearing now. Was he out there in the audience somewhere, grinning back at Joss, disguised as a dancing hippy, Hell's Angel or cameraman, or just an ordinary bloke, doing his human best like Mike Zamirski?

At one point the amphitheatre became an orchard, (the whole world for all he knew) twining creepers blossoming overhead like an exotic canopy, spilling grapes, figs, glowing peaches into the astonished audience.

> '*Step outside the moment,*
> *through the door*
> *to all beginnings,*' sang Joss and Bethany.
> '*Find yourself*
> *standing at the source*
> *of all beginnings –* '

But the thing he would always remember was Tarot, standing stock still, incredulous in her tatty black dress, with all that beauty pouring out of her hands. And the scarcely believing, slowly changing expression on her face.

And he understood that the Alpha Box was big enough to hold it all, that it was necessary to hold it all, male and female; all the endings as well as all the beginnings, ugliness and despair as well as hope and beauty. The secret was to keep faith, to go on holding them side by side in perfect balance; the darkness and the light. What else had the blue guitar been trying to tell him all along.

Play things as they are.

And at the end the Box itself dissolved into light, and after a time people began stirring themselves, wanting to get back to their lives. The technicians were packing up, having to stop occasionally to prise persistent tendrils of vines and honeysuckle from around their gear.

Joss was mildly surprised to see the aunts. Aunt Izzy had a red rose in her hair. No one spoke much. Except Fran and that was to scold Bethany. 'Promise to go straight home and rest now for the baby's sake.'

Everyone piled into the van only of course it wouldn't start. Mike was comically dismayed. 'But I had it fixed yesterday. I can't understand it.'

So they piled out again, locked their belongings inside, and set off home on foot, confident that sooner or later someone would offer them a lift. Luke was kidding Joss, telling Bethany he could recommend a wonderful babysitter.

Then he asked which Bethany wanted, a girl or a boy, but before she answered Joss realised Asha was way ahead, almost out of sight and it was suddenly so blindingly obvious what he must do that he couldn't wait until she was in earshot but went racing after her through the crowd, ducking under the laden branches, calling her name over and over. She heard him at last and stood waiting where a random tumbling of ancient stone had become a small vineyard, a faint smile hovering on her lips.

'I just thought – we don't have to go back yet, do we?' he said breathlessly. 'We could stay, watch the sun come up. I'd like to get it right this time.'

She hesitated so long he thought he must be wrong, that nothing had changed between them, that he would have to live with his crass errors slung round his neck for ever like some massive medal for male stupidity. The sins of fathers and sons.

Wait and trust, he said to himself without real hope. *Wait and trust*.

And then she grinned, taking his hand.

'But just remember I can do karate now,' she pointed out unkindly.

And Joss and Asha made their way back through the vines to watch the oldest show on earth.